The Valley
of
Dry Bones

James Berry

Acknowledgment

To Judith, our Jewish matriarch whose
legacy was her Messianic faith.

CONTENTS

The Lord set me in the middle of a valley...and I saw a great many bones. He asked me, "Son of man, can these bones live?...O my people, I am going to open your graves and bring you up...and I will settle you in your own land...and David my servant will be their prince forever." (Ezek. 37:1, 2, 3, 12 NIV)

Prologue

The early sunrise was casting its orange luster across the horizon when a vehicle with darkened windows pulled onto the tarmac of a private terminal at the Munich airport. The driver moved the vehicle close to a waiting chartered plane with engines running, jumped out, opened the rear door for two passengers, and took from the boot two pieces of luggage. With a case in each hand, the driver followed his passengers toward the waiting aircraft, each carrying a briefcase. At the top of the stairs, the senior pilot greeted the man leading the way.

"Good morning, Mr. Pencovich, welcome aboard for the flight to Constanta. My company welcomes your patronage, and it appears you've contracted a number of charter flights with us. That being the case, we'll be seeing a lot of each other."

"That'll not be the case, Sir. The person you'll see a lot of is the gentleman behind me—Mr. Albescu."

"Well, it'll be a pleasure working with you, Mr. Albescu," responded the pilot. "My company is here to please, and we'll do our best to meet your high expectations. Let's get you settled in so we can be on our way."

Both men were led to first-class seats just outside the cockpit. While the driver stored the luggage overhead, the

1

two men went back and welcomed a professional team of engineers, architects, contractors, and project managers already onboard the plane. This was a maiden flight that would begin the construction of a five-star, upscale resort on the coastal, white sands of the Black Sea near the ancient city of Constanta, Romania. The staff had been carefully selected and vetted by Michael Pencovich, the man who carried the title of Overseas Coordinator at Katharina Enterprises. The two-hour charter flight would take them to a country they'd never been and would experience firsthand the economic devastation visited upon a people living under a corrupt government with a centralized planning system.

The driver waited until the two men returned to their seats in front of the plane, then asked the one in charge, "Did we get everything, Sir?"

"I believe we did, Luis. You know my return flight schedule, so I'll see you then."

"Yes, I have a copy of it, Sir."

"If there's a change, I'll let you know."

Only in the hearing of the public did the driver use formality in addressing his special passenger, Mr. Pencovich, otherwise, they were on a first-name basis. Strict formality was protocol for all drivers. The man he drove about was always a challenge; some might even say an anomaly. It was common knowledge that he was part of the inner circle of a giant corporation, someone who always went out of his way to build relationships with employees, and it included his drivers.

The driver pulled away from the parked aircraft knowing Michael Pencovich was on a special mission, a mission that required him to go to a country in disguise with his natural blond hair and heavy beard showing a dark color. People thought him to be gifted in special ways—always one step ahead of everyone else and was considered strange and mysterious in a positive way. Rumor had it that he gained widespread notoriety in the resistance movement in Eastern Europe during the war, and was the person who won the heart of the beautiful lady who ran the company that employed the driver, a lady of wealth who was never interested in a man until the stranger from nowhere showed up. The driver parked and waited for the plane to lift off.

Once settled in, Mr. Pencovich went to work on the files he brought with him in his briefcase. He scanned a series of architectural drawings showing the stages of development of a proposed five-star resort on the beautiful coastal sands of the Black Sea. Nearby would be docks and recreational fishing boats. It would be an enterprising business for vacationing Europeans and used as a cover to smuggle Jews out to sea at night to be picked up by passing freighters. Today was an inaugural flight to a groundbreaking event to formalize its beginning.

The country they'd be making a sizable investment in was communist and a member of the Soviet Block. However, they welcomed certain foreign Western investment, and tourism was at the top of the list. It was a country known for its cruel suppression by secret police and a corrupt autocratic ruler. Those approved for this project had been through classes on how to conduct themselves inside the country.

Pencovich and Albescu sat side-by-side in their first-class seats. Though born and reared in Romania, they had little in common beyond the mission they considered a calling. Both were Jews differing in physical features: one was tall—carried a ruggedness that spoke of natural raw talent; the other, smaller in stature, gave the appearance of an accountant going over tax records with small-rimmed glasses covering his narrow-set eyes. Each had survived the Holocaust—one by using the laws of survival in the wild—the other by being perceived as a goy, even a member of the community church. Though dissimilar in backgrounds, they carried a common burden: guilt. For Pencovich, guilt came from what he did to avenge the deaths of family members; Albescu's guilt was from inaction. He was the son of a Jewish mother who saw the pain and suffering of her people, yet failed to intervene.

Guilt was the voice of the soul inside the human psyche—always accusatory and heard only by the victims who bore the evidence of a conscience. Though it was a voice demanding correction, it allowed the victim the freedom to be the final arbiter in finding the pathway for resolution. Those without a conscience were left to their own bleak despair of denial and ruin.

Guilt never practiced favoritism. The volume of its voice was determined by the strength of the conscience. Albescu carried a heavy conscience and was now on a journey of silencing the voice of guilt by joining forces with others for the noble cause of moving Jews to their homeland.

The constant hum of the aircraft pushing itself through the thin atmosphere of thirty-five thousand feet quieted Albescu's spirit and gave rise to reflections on events that changed his life.

He had been hired by an unknown party to do research on a family that perished in the Holocaust and was required to deliver the results in person to one who turned out to be the chairman of Katharina Enterprises. Unknown to him, the chairman had researched his life and was privy of his recent actions of helping Jews get out of the country of Romania. It was a daunting and fearful day when he came face-to-face with the man who could destroy him.

"Mr. Albescu, your late father was Romanian and your mother was Jewish. You were four-years-old when she died in the Spanish flu epidemic in 1918, and I happen to know that you have secretly helped Jews in your position at the West German Embassy in Bucharest."

"You have undressed me, Mr. Isler. I detect from your words that your inquisition carries either honor or blackmail."

"It is intended to be the former," the chairman said. "Money will buy almost anything except loyalty. Loyalty can never be bought. One can pay money for an act that may appear to be loyalty, and one may reward loyalty with the payment of money, but money alone will never motivate loyalty.

"Mr. Albescu, how loyal are you to your Jewish heritage? To what extent would loyalty to your Jewish legacy motivate you to help Romanian Jews get to Israel?"

He couldn't believe what he was hearing. The man behind the desk knew more about him than his children. Only his wife knew his mother was Jewish, and until that day, he thought he alone knew anything about his helping certain Jews get out of the country. He felt like a Moses being discovered after killing and burying the Egyptian.

Swirling confusion rushed through his mind. The chairman was leading him down a path that had danger lurking in the shadows. He had already put himself and his family in jeopardy by helping Jews leave the country through his connections at the embassy in Bucharest.

"Mr. Isler, people in my position have limitations on the extent of their loyalty. I have a wife, a son, and a college-age daughter."

"What would your loyalties be if you had no concerns over your wife and children?"

"That would put me in a different position altogether."

"And what would be the conditions that would guarantee security for your family?"

Long silence followed. The chairman saw his face register uncomfortable reluctance in his reply.

"My children and wife would have to remain outside the country with funds available to be with them every other week."

"Presently, you work for the West German Embassy and seem to handle the German language very well. If you made me your silent partner in a business that required frequent travel to Europe, you could live as a family here and operate the business in your country as cover."

"And may I ask what my portfolio would be in these clandestine operations?"

"The overview would be the creation of an upscale resort on the beautiful coastal sands of the Black Sea with recreational deep-sea fishing and daily sightseeing open-boat cruises. Your patrons would be Europeans. Along with this would be your responsibility of creating a network through which information would be passed to key operatives. The business would act as a front to smuggle Jews to waiting freighters and would have to be successful with a strong bottom line so as to avoid suspicion by the government."

This was his first meeting with the young chairman who offered him a broader road to redeeming himself of the guilt in neglecting his mother's people during the Holocaust. Three months later he was at the chairman's office being led to a conference room by a secretary; a knock on the closed door brought an immediate response. It swung open, and standing in the doorway was the chairman himself, a man known to be one of the wealthiest men in Europe. The secretary was first to speak.

"Dr. Hans, this is Mr. Albescu."

"We have already met, and it's a pleasure to see you again, Mr. Albescu. Freda, please have the coffee shop send up some sandwiches and drinks."

"Mr. Albescu, I'd like you to meet Sonje Shuster, our vice chairlady, and Mr. Pencovich, the company's overseas coordinator."

Both were seated at the conference table. They stood, shook hands without speaking. The chairman took charge of opening the session. "Everyone be seated, please."

He remembered being nervous that day. He hoped his eyes didn't show it. The people in the room were of power and money. The lady across from him was tall, lissome, and beautiful. She and the chairman looked too young to be in such responsible positions. The third member of the group resembled the young chairman, and experience was written all over him. Ms. Shuster, the vice chairlady, took charge.

"Mr. Albescu, the chairman has given me and Mr. Pencovich the responsibility of overseeing this project. I will handle the business end of it, and he will supervise the engineers and consultants in the physical development. He will also be your contact person when the smuggling operation begins.

"All matters that are personal, such things as finances, travel, lodging, and college tuition for your children will be arranged and handled by the chairman. The first action to be taken is that you will meet with professionals who will survey and evaluate potential tourism sites. You will be the figurehead in the country to answer their questions and work with them in obtaining a suitable investment site. It is important that when offers are made on viable properties that they see you as the investor and not a European company. As the chairman informed you in your first meeting, you will take out a sizeable loan making yourself a partner with a legal dummy corporation in Europe. This will hide from the Romanian government and the public who the real financial sponsors are. Our lawyers will start on this right away, and it will be up to you to determine when and how you leave your employment with the West German Embassy."

Those were his early beginnings of the new world he'd entered. After laying all the groundwork with the government in the land purchase of suitable ocean-side property, today would be the groundbreaking ceremony of a business promoted as an entertainment paradise—all as a cover to move Abraham's posterity back to Israel.

Albescu's musings were interrupted by the stewardess taking a breakfast order from the man seated next to him.

"Mr. Pencovich, we are serving ham, scrambled eggs, and hash browns on this flight. Or if you'd rather have cold cereal, we can provide that."

The passenger addressed as Mr. Pencovich remembered his days of living in the mountains during the Holocaust war years when he made use of wild hogs as one of his basic staples. Survival in the wild overruled his Jewish kosher diet. That was the time when his religious upbringing was lost to the energy of avenging the deaths of his family. Today, he would have ham in remembrance of those years when the wild, forbidden species contributed to his survival.

"I'll celebrate the day with ham and eggs with coffee."

"What would you like to be served, Mr. Albuscu?"

"I'll have what Mr. Pencovich has ordered."

"I'll be right back, Sirs."

The team of people on the plane knew the gentleman who enlisted them for the project in Romania was an important person by his arrival with a personal driver and the deference given him by the pilots and stewardesses. What they didn't know was that he had further connections with an international parent company that acted as the holding agency for the company hiring them.

When the plane touched down in Constanta and moved to the charter terminal, one large van and car were waiting to take everyone to their hotel. Two government officials arrived to inspect passports and visas as they exited the plane. Standing at the doorway, the pilots saw everyone board the van except Pencovich. He made his way to the large sedan parked behind the van, opened the door and sat alongside the driver. The vehicle pulled out slowly and drove from the airport in the opposite direction of the departing van.

Pencovich knew this land like the back of his hand. He had entered the country incognito, and the man driving him was a member of a secret underground fraternity of Zionists with the mission of laying the groundwork for one of the biggest operations since Israel became a state.

"Do you know your assignment for the day?" asked the passenger.

"Yes, Sir."

"Good," replied the man who sat across from the driver. "It's a six-hour drive from here and you can let me out at the edge of town and wait until I return."

The passenger leaned over close to the driver and whispered, "Is your car clean?"

"Yes, Sir, this vehicle is kept in a secured, locked garage…no listening devices in this car!"

"My name is Michael; only address me in a formal manner when the public is around. What name do you go by?"

"Joseph is the name assigned to me."

The driver's passenger dropped off to sleep leaving him to ponder the uniqueness of the man he'd picked up. It seemed strange that he wanted to go to the insignificant village of Ediniti.

Chapter 1

The Book

An old man living in the rural countryside outside his village left his modest home for his afternoon, daily walk over rolling, heavy-forested hillsides. Today, he chose a path few people trekked or knew anything about. When he reached the midway point of his walk, he stopped and sat on an old fallen log. It was his resting spot before continuing his journey under nature's pristine, high-towering trees, a paradise where he took in the fragrance of wildflowers and listened to the whistling breezes that rustled leaves overhead, all punctuated by chirping, singing birds. He was a man bonded to nature, had studied and lived in the thick of it all his life. *He had many trails he walked over, but this one was his favorite—it passed through a wide-open glen that carried deep-seated memories of personal history.*

The robust, aging man stood to his feet with renewed vigor to continue his walk. This was the point on the trail when memory caused a surge of excitement: it led to a place that always connected him to a bittersweet time of his life. With renewed energy, he picked up his gait, increased his stride, and shortly came to a stop. In front of him lay the ruins of what was once a large thriving lumber mill but now showing nature's attempt to cover-up the piles of crumbled remains. Few remembered its place in history when it boosted the local economy employing scores of men in producing a product for the housing industry, and he was the one who supervised its successful operation. But that was before the war—before the Nazis came to power and joined forces with the invading Germans, the time when roving SS squads went through village-after-village massacring entire Jewish populations. Ediniti, his nearby village, was one of those marked for genocide.

A photo showing the mill as it once stood in its heyday was taken from the old man's pocket. What made the picture special was that it showed him standing alongside his Jewish friend, the late owner of the mill, and who today shared the mass grave with others outside the city, a grave no one talked about, and to do so would bring unwanted attention from the government, a denier of what happened in this land.

Deep scars that bore the history of pain always surfaced when the old gentleman visited these ruins. Placing the photo back in his pocket, he moved in closer and gave a sudden stop to his steps. He saw what appeared to be the tall figure of the backside of a man standing in the shadow of a large tree jutting out over a section of debris.

The old man wondered who would be interested in visiting this site of rubble, a place where nature competed with wildlife to reclaim the failure of man? He moved forward toward the figure, and when he reached speaking distance, he stopped.

"Good morning, Sir, what brings you to this old site?"

The stranger didn't turn around, nor did he reply.

"Are you a stranger around here?" the old man asked, raising his voice.

Again, the stranger standing in front of the old man with his back facing him said nothing.

Like a statue frozen in time, the stranger continued his silence as his world turned inside. He knew the voice talking to him. It was the voice of the harbinger who brought him horrifying news that all his family had been killed by Nazi Iron Guard and German SS soldiers. That was the day when he morphed into an avenger. It was like yesterday.

It all happened on that fateful day when he and his two life-long friends had been cleaning up the campsite high up in the mountains after completing their assignment of counting and marking trees for harvest. It was a remote area and difficult to reach, and when they heard the sound of a bike breaking the atmosphere, they became concerned. People never went to that region of the forest—it was too remote, dense, and secluded. Each team member found his rifle and waited for the man on the bike to arrive.

All his life he and his friends had learned to survive by sticking together in a community of anti-Semites. When in a mixed crowd of peers, it was always safer to move about as a group, and because he looked Aryan with blond hair and blue eyes, looks of aspersions from the goyim rarely occurred. Their reactions that day to the sound of the motorbike came having lived among anti-Semites.

He was relieved when he saw the man on the bike was the foreman of his father's mill but knew something was wrong by the foreboding look on his face. That was the day when the world as he knew it was gone—lost forever. He was a messenger of doom, the bearer of ill-fated news that all his family members had been massacred by German and Romanian Nazi soldiers, aided by locals who seized property. It was the time when something inside him died, a day when another kind of life formed from what was dead, and the man now speaking to him was the giver of that new life in the form of a book with names of those guilty of plunder, rape, and murder. It became his roadmap for justice.

When the flash memory faded from the stranger standing in the shadows, the old man behind him heard a response that carried feeling.

"Sir...I'm no stranger to this place. I have a lot of history here and have come today to pay respect to those memories."

The old man's world stopped when the stranger spoke. Events in one's history had a way of leaving indelible marks on the human psyche. He grappled with what was tumbling around inside, struggled to steady himself on his feet. He was in senescent decline but had not lost his mental faculties or his acute hearing. *He knew the voice of this stranger but how could it be? Memory brushed aside the doubts...he knew this man, knew him as a child growing up, even attended his Bar Mitzvah at the age of twelve. The person standing in front of him was Michael, the son of the late owner of this lumber mill that now lies in a heap of ruins.* The flood of the Holocaust years swept over the old man. He remembered seeing streets of his own village filled with the dead from the mass slaughter. That dark day of evil made him the emissary of unthinkable, horrifying news. He still had nightmares from telling young Michael what happened to his family. Even to this day, the sounds of his eerie screams and agonizing moans still haunted his memory as if it were yesterday.

He remembered before leaving Michael that day that he left a small logbook with him, saying, "I have taken time to gather all the information I could about those who participated in the killings, thefts, and rapes. Not being Jewish, people talked freely with me knowing they would never be held accountable for what they did. They were bragging like boastful idiots about what they'd done. Everything is written down in detail, and someday it will be used in a court of law as evidence. I must tell you that much of the information in this logbook is from people who witnessed firsthand what happened and were abhorred by the event. Someday, retribution will be made for this evil."

What he didn't tell Michael on that day, but included in the back of the little book he was leaving, were the names of four men who raped the girl he was to marry.

On that fateful day, he remembered Michael listening with riveted stares of hopelessness, numbed and shattered. He was a lifeless zombie succumbing to a private death spiral, helpless and withdrawn. When he handed Michael the book, their eyes met, and he saw eyes that didn't belong to the innocent young man he knew as a child. Even his face had changed into a cold, frozen image. What he'd been in life was being morphed into something yet to be realized, and he never forgot the words he spoke that day.

"Mr. Popescu, I assure you that as long as I have breath, there will be retribution, not in a court of law but in a court of my justice."

He remembered the words of that young man in the days, months, and years that followed, the times when mysterious deaths occurred among the names written down

15

in that book, and it was his legacy of not informing the authorities upon hearing news of their deaths.

The old man was about to take another step toward the stranger who had entered his life as a voice from his past when the stranger spoke again.

"How have you been all these years, Mr. Popescu?"

The old man's balance wavered. History rushed at him with swirling turbulence. He managed to keep his steadiness, took another step closer to the stranger.

"I have been fine, Michael, and how have you been all these years?"

The stranger in front of the old man turned around. Eyes showing painful memories stared at each other, each telling an unwritten, silent story. Memory and sight were speaking louder than words.

"I know your voice, Michael, but your face...I don't recognize it! Your beard...your hair....What happened to your blond hair? The old man extended his hands up and felt his face. "Michael, you're alive!"

Standing on a blanket of floral beauty rising from the forest floor under the veil of a cerulean sky, nature serenaded the old and young embracing, like father and son. Both had common histories here at this site. Though they were Jew and Gentile, each carried the horrors of the Holocaust, but today they celebrated the memories of the good times.

The trail that took the old man back to his home welcomed the companionship of two visitors from two different worlds: one carried the pain of the loss of his family in the Romanian Holocaust, the other, a loyal goyim family friend who abhorred the acts and gave assistance—a picture of a hopeful world to come.

At the end of nature's forest trail, everything opened up into a large valley showing small plots of land dotted with plain drab homes with small animal sheds. Though everything looked old and dowdy, the beautiful floral gardens that grew vegetables and fruits gave humble homes picturesque beauty in the midst of a people that had little. When reaching the home where the old man lived, the two stopped outside the picket fence that enclosed the dwelling.

"This is where I still live, Michael. Does it look the same as it did when you were a lad?"

The younger of the two paused, drew a deep breath. The man who asked him this question was now marked with age showing furrowed lines across his leathery face. He knew his guest when he was but a young lad.

"Your place looks exactly as it did when my father dropped me off to play with your sons."

The visitor saw tears pool in the old man's eyes, followed by the pain of memory with twitching, quivering lips. Michael was sensitive to pain in this land and knew the vacuous atmosphere that settled around them required silence…he waited for the broken old friend to speak.

"Yes, those were the beautiful, happy days…then came the war years, the Russian war, where we lost both of them, and not only did I lose them, the pain of loss cut short my wife's life: she died of sorrow."

The old man's friend knew the stroke of personal pain. Hurt coming from this kind of loss was universal—he lived those experiences every day, and there was no way to measure the depth of that kind of personal loss, whether experienced by his elderly friend, or himself, a Holocaust survivor.

"Yes, Michael, this is my humble home. I've lived here all my life, except for the six months I spent in prison."

"Prison! What do you mean—prison?"

"Let's go inside and I'll tell you all about it."

The man called Michael made note of the old gentleman's care of his home. He was a detail person, was a master artisan, and could do most anything. Added to this was his ability to organize and manage men, and with these qualities, he rose from being a worker at his father's mill to running the whole operation. His craftsmanship showed itself with everything inside his home, all the way from living room furniture to kitchen cabinets.

"Come, Michael, to the kitchen table, and I'll put us on some hot water for tea."

It didn't take long for Michael's host to get into the story of his life.

"Michael, I'll be honest with you. When I left you and your two friends in the mountains, I thought I'd never see you again. Many of your people who fled to the mountains from the Nazis didn't survive. Those were horrible years, years I still have nightmares over. By the way, how are Moshe and Bub...? I believe those were their names."

"Moshe and Bub are doing well."

"What are they doing nowadays?"

"They're working with me in my nephew's shipping company." Michael was on a special mission here in this country and answered his question without elaboration.

"Now, I'd like to hear about this prison matter you mentioned."

"Excuse me for a moment. You need to see something first."

Michael saw the old man go to another room and return with a logbook. It was identical to the one given him in the mountains years ago, the one he used as a roadmap to bring justice to those who killed his family.

"Michael, do you remember what I told you on that dreadful day when I gave you a book like this in the mountains? I told you that 'I made two copies, one for you, and one for me and that you would find names of people who did specific acts.'"

Michael's mind was swirling with flashback memory of what he became after being morphed into something from which he was now carrying guilt. *Perhaps he shouldn't have come here today. It was difficult enough dyeing his hair and beard for disguise in his mission to review a project for Katharina Enterprises but couldn't resist the temptation to visit the place where he was born and suffered the loss of his family.* Breaking into his thoughts were words from the old man.

"I want you to take time to look over what I wrote in my copy after leaving you on that rugged mountain site. After you've done this, I'll continue my story."

Again, Michael wished he were at the coastal resort where he was in charge of overseeing the development of a commercial business that would be used as a cover to smuggle Jews out of this country into Israel. That was his purpose of coming to this country. Now he was being forced to relive what he tried to forget. Memory was serving as a dark nemesis.

"Look over the book while I make our tea. Do you take sugar and cream?"

"Sugar and cream will be fine."

Michael had a photographic memory and could quote verbatim the list of names and their individual acts as originally recorded by the old man. But when he opened the book, he noted that Mr. Popescu had added his own commentary to each name. In the margin alongside each name, he had written a date with the word EXECUTED, all in upper case letters. Of the names listed, one stood out above others. Where Colonel Funar's name appeared, there was a date with the description of his present status—all in caps: ARRESTED IN WEST GERMANY FOR WAR CRIMES. The old man had kept his book current.

Michael was facing his history and was in the country where it all happened. The man who was his host could have him arrested by the authorities, but too much was going for him: those he executed were Nazi war criminals, and the despot now ruling this country was a communist. However, the greater weight in his favor was the man preparing his tea—a righteous Gentile who had risked his life hiding and helping Jews during those horrid years.

The old man placed a cup of hot tea on the table by Michael. "Michael, information in the book you hold in your hands comes from what I am and what I believe. I am a Christian who believes God made the Jewish people to be a repository of His truth, that the nation of Israel was a national womb that gave us His Son Jesus, and that He will return to Jerusalem to rule the world. My faith sustained me when I took measures to help Jews in hiding. Some were kept concealed in my home until a safer place was found for them. Our country is agriculturally rich and fertile, and it was easy to pick up supplies of grain from farms and go undetected in my deliveries to those in hiding. But then things changed!"

The old man saw his guest struggling with personal history, history with dark chambers that were avoided and that his story was forcing him to reenter those forbidden places.

"This may be hard for you, Michael, but bear with me. One has to understand what was going on after the Germans came into this country and took over intelligence operations, and you of all people know this better than anyone. In cooperation with indigenous Fascists, they planted spies throughout the land to monitor activities that might encourage internal partisan resistance. These spies blended in with local populations and attempted to go undetected. Unfortunately, locals yielded to bribery and did the spies' bidding, which made operations broad and effective.

"After the village massacre of the Jews, powerful people in the town, collaborators with the Nazis, seized your father's lumber industry and attempted to run it themselves for personal gain. However, some of the workers refused to be a part of it, including me. I started my own small business manufacturing furniture located at the edge of town with several workers from the mill. Having my own shop allowed me to create a schedule convenient for picking up and delivering grain and lentils to those in hiding. However, with the new SS operations in place, quislings who received bribery money to spy on their neighbors passed on their suspicions of me. It reached the central figurehead in charge of our region, whereupon he became involved, broke into my home when I was away and found this book that described atrocious crimes and murders bearing the names connected with the acts. The record itself wasn't of great interest to him. It was the inclusion of the term EXECUTED written in caps that gave cause for him to believe I was part of a conspiracy in aiding and abetting an internal partisan movement.

"That day when I came home there were local gendarmes waiting to arrest me. They took me to the police station where I was interrogated, then sent off to a prison where most of the inmates were political dissidents, all without a trial or a fair hearing. I would have been executed had it not been that Germany was beginning to lose the war. Romanians who were pro-Nazi were trying to walk a tightrope, knowing that if Germany lost the war it would not go well for them.

"The man in charge of Nazi intelligence would come to the prison every week to remind me that I would be let out if I informed on those I aided. His visits stopped two months before Russian forces entered this country."

The old man could see his story had opened the wounds of Michael's history in this land. His eyes showed a little of what he saw when he left him on the mountain where he morphed into an avenger.

"Michael, I'm sorry that my story has opened a lot of hurt. Being reminded of how things were in those days is an unpleasant path to go down."

"Mr. Popescu, there's plenty of hurt in my life, but it

22

serves to make me a better person because it reinforces and validates what I can do to help my people in this country."

"And what might that be?" asked the old man.

Michael knew his mission carried the danger of exposure, and today he almost stepped over the line and violated his discipline of secrecy of why he was in this land. But he knew at the right time this old gentleman would someday work in concert with him in moving Jews to the country of their ancestors.

"At the appropriate time, Mr. Popescu, you'll know." Michael moved quickly from the subject, asking, "How'd you retrieve the copy of your booklet the authorities took from you when you went to prison?"

"When they released me, they returned my personal effects, among which was the book. They went out of their way to ameliorate my situation to the extent of almost apologizing. The authorities saw the handwriting on the wall—Russia might win the war and serious repercussions could be in the making. What was thought possible was realized—we ended up with another repressive form of government living under communism with despotic and corrupt leaders.

The old man now showing memory pain of prison life, turned to his young friend, saying, "There's something I have yet to tell you that you should know. During those months in prison, I was interrogated from time-to-time with questions about my former acquaintances. The man assigned to investigate me was a member of the Romanian Nazi Iron Guard, an anti-Semitic militia committed to the dispossession of Jews with pledged genocidal loyalty.

"In one of those sessions, he brought several photos

taken randomly by an amateur street photographer. The occasion was at a military parade where the following day two soldiers were found executed. Most of the people in the photo were identified as locals, but one showing light hair and standing tall could not be identified and became a person of interest. I was informed that they used those photos to further investigate other similar cases and found witnesses who went on record that a person matching his description was seen in the area.

"The lead investigator even offered me money if I would confirm the photo was that of a Pencovich, and when I refused they threatened bodily harm. It was then I told the interrogator, 'If you want to know about that person, dig up his family's remains buried in the mass grave and ask them!' I was saved that day only because the news was breaking that Russian forces had routed German and Romanian armies on the war front. The winds had begun to blow another direction and everyone sought to save his skin by running from Nazism. Collaborators and quislings quickly converted and crawled into their lairs of silence and denial. Had not those events been history, I would not be standing here revealing my story. We learned in our struggle to live with what we were dealt in those days—the good, the bad, and the ugly as life would have it, and it was mostly bad and ugly—even to this day."

Michael saw the old man's experience being relived. It was written on his face, seen in his eyes, a time in his life when resolute character demanded action that was hinged to another dimension: he'd rather die with a clear conscience than stand someday before his Maker with one soiled and violated by the trappings of human weakness.

Brave men always swam against the tide, and the story being told was one of bravery.

Michael never knew about his friend's imprisonment. For the first time, overwhelming enlightenment came to him that someone beyond his own self-prowess contributed to his success and survival during those years as an avenger. He was alive today because of this man.

Michael looked at the face of the old man whose eyes were as bright as the day when he first came to his home as a lad. He had learned something on his undercover visit to this land: because of virulent anti-Semitism, his family lay buried in a mass grave, but there were a few beautiful flowers scattered about the landscape, and this old man was one of them. He knew old Popescu had no family and little money—perhaps many friends, but they were as destitute as he was. His material life hung on a thread in this repressive, third-world-like country.

"Mr. Popescu, if you could wish for something beyond your reach, something that's not within your power to provide, what would it be?"

"Michael, you want me to dream beyond my restricted, unreachable world? If you allow me to engage in fantasy, let me indulge myself. I would like to afford a new motorbike, have enough funds on hand to buy provisions in the market instead of having to grow a garden every year in my old age. But I'll not wish for that. What I wish for more than anything in the world is to plant my feet on the streets of the old city of Jerusalem where my Lord will return to rule the world in peace. I wish for this more than anything."

The old man's voice trailed off with a look of seeing something in another world. Michael restrained himself.

His mission in this country was building an infrastructure to smuggle Jews to the land of their ancestry, moving a people who were denied exit visas to a place of freedom, and the whole operation was highly secretive. *What an irony, he thought. The two were far apart—one Jewish, the other Gentile, yet, both had common goals—the welcoming of the King of all kings to the city of Jerusalem where He will rule in peace and justice.*

Michael had on his person a large supply of money to be used as keys to open closed doors. Graft and corruption in this country were a way of life, and bribery money would open almost any door. Today, he would use one of those keys to open a different kind of door: a man of noble character and friend to Israel would be granted a wish that was beyond his reach.

"Mr. Popescu, you have cast your bread upon the waters, and today it has returned. A man will come to your house this week and assist you in getting a passport and visa for a trip to Munich where I will meet you. From there you will fly on to Israel where you will walk the streets of Jerusalem."

A jaw-dropping look came over the face of the old gentleman, then felt Michael place a large roll of Deutsche Marks in his hand. "What you have in your hand is more than enough to purchase your new bike, and the man visiting you this week will see to it that your trip is fully funded for your travel to the land of your wish."

Michael's loyal friend lifted what was given him up close to his eyes, stared at it, saying, "Michael, you are in this country on a special mission, and it is not for me to know the reason."

"Mr. Popescu, you still have perceptive skills."

"And you, Michael, are just like your late father—generous and kind."

"My dear friend, those words alone have made my trip here a special event."

A calm smile spread across the old gentleman's leathery face. "My sunset years have brightened by what you have done, and I look forward to seeing you in Munich." With that said, Michael embraced his dear friend, walked to the edge of his property followed by his host.

"Mr. Popescu, I'll see you in Munich. Right now my driver is waiting in the village where I was born."

The old man watched his young friend fade into the distance with only his backside in view. The first and last scenes he had of this man today carried no face—only his backside. It spoke of the bigger picture of his life here in this land—a man without a face, not for the avengement of taking life but saving it by filling Jerusalem with Abraham's posterity from a country of oppression.

Chapter 2

Extortion

A beautiful wealthy woman in charge of running an international corporation listened to the music of her alarm as she lay in bed reflecting on her marriage of six months. For the first time, she had awakened without the warm comfort of his arms around her, accompanied by quiet, gentle whispers of affection. He was out of the country on a special mission, and his absence allowed her emotions to explore the biblical truth of two becoming one. She never understood what that meant until Michael came into her life. It was a portal of mystery she'd crossed—a mystery that had transcendent meaning. Deep hidden pain, hitherto denied and locked away in a dark inner chamber, had been opened by the power of love and acceptance of another. Before Michael, she needed material things to satisfy the demands of her survival instincts. This was achieved through her successful market investments and her rise to prominence in Katharina Enterprises. Now, she was willing to walk away from it all as long as Michael was at the center of her life. Even the painful memory of her abuse in the concentration camp had faded because of his acceptance of her as a complete, chaste woman. *Biblical truth overshadowed her thoughts: Jesus had healed her psyche by making her a complete person through His life, death, and resurrection.*

Her musings went undeterred. Though she lived in a luxurious, upscale home in a gated community before marriage, she chose to live in Michael's modest, high-walled compound with security guards staffing the compound around the clock.

She didn't look forward to the coming week. She and Michael would be separated for three days—he to Romania on a special assignment—she to a daily schedule of dealing with committees, board meetings, and issues around the world.

Max, the head of security for Katharina Enterprises, sat at his desk with his typical look of a large baldhead that matched his enormous size. It was customary for him to start the day with a starched shirt and wrinkle-free, pinstripe suit, but by the end of the day the starch was gone and the suit in need of a steam press. Those who saw him in the early morning thought him to be overdressed, and by the end of the day, others considered him a poor dresser. The extremes of appearances between early morning and late afternoon characterized his persona. The bold, crusty traits he carried on the outside that people saw didn't mirror his true nature. People called him the Enforcer, someone who ran security like it was an extension of the military with rigid protocols and formality. Unfortunately, it was the rumpled, late-afternoon-look that most people saw, and few were around early in the morning to see his better side.

Max had just settled in at his desk after greeting his secretary when his intercom light came on indicating a message from the secretary.

"Yes, what is it?"

"Max, there's a Mr. Biggs from the mailroom, and he wants to see you for a moment."

Max thought it unnecessary for someone from the mailroom to break into his schedule when he could call or leave a message.

The secretary opened the door and a small, thin, beady-eyed man entered Max's office holding something that looked like a large manila envelope. Intimidation was written on his countenance.

"How can I help to you, Mr. Biggs?" asked the big man seated at the desk. The mailroom was part of Max's security purview, and because of Katharina Enterprises' commitment to Israel, intensive efforts were made to inspect all incoming mail for hazardous materials.

"Max, I have here with me a packet addressed to the vice chairlady. It came registered, and I signed for it. It appears to be clean of any hazards; however, its country of origin fits the protocol that it be given special attention, so I'll leave it with you to be acted upon."

Max took the packet knowing that had this article been sent to anyone else other than the vice chairlady, the mail would've been delivered through regular channels.

"Thank you, Mr. Biggs—I'll see that she gets it."

The chief of security noticed there was no return address and that the addressee bore the name: Mrs. Sonje Shuster Pencovich. The large packet carried an official Romanian stamp showing Bucharest as its point of origin.

Max always displayed curious, incisive wit and perception in matters of security. This was his job. Sonje Shuster had a name change through marriage just six months earlier, and it was quite out of the ordinary for a party in Romania to be cognizant of this event. In fact, her husband was in that country on a special assignment. Max looked again at the posting date. It had taken three weeks to reach the mailroom.

No one was allowed to see the chairman and owner of Katharina Enterprises without an appointment, and this also applied to the vice chairlady who was in control of much of the major decision-making of the company. However, Max worked closely with the inner circle of the family-owned company, and being at the helm of security, it afforded him access to those at the top.

Sonje Pencovich was in her office when her secretary called.

"Sonje, Max, the chief of security, is here and wants to drop off a piece of mail that he says, 'fits the company's protocol for security.' Do you wish it to be delivered to your office or left with me?"

"What country is its origin?"

"It was sent from Bucharest."

"Send it in with Max."

Max walked behind a lady who had been with the company for several years and was more than just a secretary to the second-in-command, they were close personal friends though it didn't appear so in the workplace. It was a perfunctory drop-off. Max handed the package to the vice chairlady and left. Unknown to Sonje, her new world was about to be challenged by voices of the past.

Hans Isler, the wealthy chairman of Katharina Enterprises, had as his mission the moving of Jewish Diaspora back to Israel. The operation centered on the Black Sea and involved nighttime pickups on board his company's freighters. When Romania welcomed Western investment in the country, he seized the opportunity to establish a major covert operation. It involved heavy financial investment and strategic planning with key operatives. The project was highly secretive and any communication arriving in the mailroom from that country had to be reviewed by the vice chairlady or chairman. Two things made this packet an important delivery: it was posted in Bucharest and carried the vice chairlady's married name, Mrs. Sonje Shuster Pencovich.

With eyes fixed on her married name, a thousand thoughts tumbled inside Sonje as she carefully opened the packet and read its contents:

Dear Madam,

I have information and evidence that your husband, Michael Pencovich, is a perpetrator of the crimes of several killings in my country during the war years of 1943-1944.

You will find enclosed in this packet photographs of your husband that were taken on a public street near the site of one of your husband's victims.

I have researched your position of wealth and am demanding the payment of two million dollars in cash to guarantee my silence. Upon delivery of this sum of money in dollars, I will give you the evidence I have that gives credence to his guilt. You will receive a

subsequent letter giving directions on when and how
payment is to be made.

The letter was typewritten and left unsigned. Sonje read the letter again. Numbed by what she held in her hands, she forced the use of the left side of her brain. Extortion was as old as time, and demand payments would never end. On a judicial level, Michael's actions during the war in executing those who killed his family would stand the test of time. He was a lone voice of resistance in a modern world that had lost its way. His people had been hunted down like animals, slaughtered on a wholesale scale, forced to flee and hide from the terror of unbelievable horror. Sonje's suppressed memory surfaced an unforgettable scene of the time when she was in the concentration camp. It was the day when they were ordered to unload a German munitions truck, and because an older Jewish man didn't move faster when ordered to do so by the SS guard, he was shot. Memory served up its pain: she could still feel her share of the weight of his limp body when she and others were forced to remove him from the roadway. *People who fell under Michael's sword were SS types, and today this letter made her even more proud of his innocence of guilt. The extortion letter was disturbing, but it would serve to be therapeutic by forcing to the conscious level personal pain and horrors experienced during the war.*

Sonje was a person who dealt with absolutes, numbers, and facts, lived and worked in a field that required rational thought and insightful action. What she had in front of her carried the weight of emotion, but she would act on reason. She called her secretary.

"Freda, cancel all my meetings and appointments today. I don't want anyone in and around my office. For the rest of the day, I may or may not be in my office, but under no circumstances am I to receive calls."

Freda knew something was going on with her boss, and though they were close, she knew when to walk softly.

"You can depend on it, Sonje, and if there's anything I can do, I'm always here."

Sonje was a problem solver. That's what she did for a living ensconced in a position of power in a man's world. In the looming new age of women's advancement, she was used and written about as an icon of success in major financial newspapers, magazines, and reviews.

Sonje was on the phone immediately to the Israeli Embassy. Her company had the mission of giving vast amounts of its profits to assist Zionist causes through covert intermediaries, and because of this, they were sometimes called upon for help. The nature of the matter at hand required privacy and action by certain types of professionals. Within the hour, two men were at the security desk downstairs being cleared for a conference with the second most powerful figure in the company. Ten minutes later, they were in the vice chairlady's office with a mini forensic-collection kit. They would take everything sent to Sonje, put it through extensive forensic tests and wait for the forthcoming letter giving directions for the payment.

When the Israeli team left the vice chairlady's office, she was on the phone with her secretary.

"Freda, cancel my previous order. I'll be on schedule

for my agenda for the rest of the day."

Sonje was on the phone to Mr. Biggs, the clerk in charge of the central mailroom. When she introduced herself, he felt sudden trepidation. Why would the second-in-command of this international company be calling him?

"Mr. Biggs, this is Sonje Pencovich. Please be aware that I'm expecting a package from Romania, and I want you alone to deliver it to my office. If I happen to not be in, let my secretary know so she can contact me."

"Yes, Ma'am, I'll keep a watch on anything coming in and see that it reaches your office right away."

"Thank you, Mr. Biggs."

Tomorrow, she'd confer with Michael about the matter.

The large company vehicle carrying Sonje to the airport to pick up Michael stopped in front of the arriving flights terminal. It was pushing nine o'clock, and she had waited all day for this event. Marriage to Michael had changed her life. She had lived in an emotional survival state since her days of abuse and mistreatment in the concentration camp. Though German, she along with her father and mother were sent to a slave labor camp for hiding Jews on their premises. She never saw her parents again, was abused by guards, and suffered hardships along with Jews who were selected for labor instead of extermination. From the day of being freed by American forces until the moment of meeting Michael, she could not be moved to be interested in a man. It was forbidden, a place never visited. Prestigious suitors went out of their way to gain her attention, and the further up the corporate ladder she climbed, the louder the knocks on her door. Her success in the corporate and financial world gave her the power to build the walls she needed for self-preservation. Even her mode of fashionable dress was symbiotically entwined in the complex nature of that pain. But one day Michael stepped into her life and awakened what was dead. She would never forget that memorable event.

She had come to work early and found that the front office personnel had not arrived. Turning to go to her plush office down the hall, she heard the door open. Thinking it was the receptionist, she turned to greet her but saw a tall, rugged-looking man with dominant facial features standing and looking about the room, mesmerized by its affluence. She was first to speak.

"May I help you, Sir?"

The man gave no response to the one speaking but continued looking at the elegance of the office décor.

"Is Jacob in?" he asked.

"You must be in the wrong office, Sir."

He looked in her direction where she was standing— their eyes met. Neither said anything for a moment. Eyes were doing the talking. Without words, body language measured something common to both: the mystery of hidden pain. *Who was this man, she thought, who carried a look of purpose with energy that spoke of rustic valor and confidence?* Without speaking, a strange aura emanated itself between the two. Common experiences of two strangers were serving to awaken an uncommon world. Two cells had come together that morning giving life to both. On that day, Michael awakened in her what had been dead. For the first time since she left the camp, she felt the warmth of a fire being lit, and the man was the uncle of the owner and chairman of Katharina Enterprises.

The driver opened the door and waited for the vice chairlady to exit. Her thoughts about the man she'd married held her frozen to another time. He looked in at his passenger. "Are you all right, Mrs. Pencovich?"

"It's difficult to leave the house of memory when the memories are pleasant, Luis."

The lady of power and wealth stepped out of the vehicle showing an effervescent sparkle of excitement.

"Luis, you are to stay with the vehicle and Michael and I will meet you here."

"Yes Ma'am, I'll be here."

The driver paid special attention to his boss who was now entering the terminal building. Her exquisite dress carried the image for which she was known, and those who knew her well would affirm that her inner beauty and treatment of others were as beautiful as the fashions she wore. However, tonight she had pushed the elegance part up a notch for the man she was meeting.

On her walk to the gate where Michael would be arriving, she remembered how heightened her feelings were throughout the day. It was a struggle to focus on conference calls, committee meetings, and interviews, and though no one saw what she felt, she was sometimes embarrassed over her anxious giddiness. This was her new wonderful world. At forty-two, and showing the age of being ten years younger, her life and zest gave credence to her happiness. God had been good to her by sending a person into her life who brought healing to her emotions and calm to the soul.

Marriage for her had been a spiritual journey.

Sonje's giddiness returned when Michael emerged from the tunnel that opened into the waiting room. Expecting to be picked up by his driver, Michael saw the beautiful picture of Sonje running toward him like a schoolgirl, and leaping into his arms with feet dangling off the ground, said, "I don't want you to leave me again."

"In that case, I'll have to take you with me."

"I'll hold you to that, Mr. Overseas Coordinator!"

Sonje would wait until the next day to bring up the subject of the extortion letter.

———————————

Three days had lapsed and Michael was back at his office when Birdie, his secretary, buzzed him with the message that Mrs. Pencovich was on the line.

"Michael our friends of Israel will be here within the hour and will be bringing their forensic findings. Are you free to meet with them in my conference room?"

"Yes, I can manage that. I'll be right over."

"Give me five minutes to clear my schedule."

Sonje called Freda, her secretary, known as the gatekeeper and who ran a tight ship. "Freda, please rearrange my schedule for this morning so I'm free for the next hour. Two men will be brought to your desk by one of our security people, and you are to take them to my conference room when they arrive. I am not to be disturbed for any reason."

Freda had just hung up when Michael approached the gatekeeper.

"Good Morning, Freda. How's the gatekeeper

today?"

"Michael, the boss is waiting for you. Would you like me to send in some coffee or tea?"

"We would like that. Thank you! Have them deliver it to the conference room."

Chapter 3

Forensics

Two men in casual dress carrying briefcases walked behind Freda to a door over which was written: Conference Room. She held the door open for the guests, saying, "Please be seated. The other parties will join you in a few moments. There are coffee and tea on the table at the end of the room."

The men were forensic specialists who had as their job description the collection and examination of evidentiary materials. They were an invisible arm of the Israeli government on call ready to be mobilized at a moment's notice. Because this case involved extortion resulting from action taken against those in support of the Holocaust, the matter fell under their purview and was expedited because of the person requesting it.

They quickly laid everything out on the table, including their forensic findings, then indulged themselves with freshly brewed coffee. Both were seated when the vice chairlady entered the room with two men. They stood to their feet. The lady who had a previous session with the two forensic experts took control of the meeting.

"Today, we'll all be on a first-name basis. I met you gentlemen in our previous visit and your names are Ben and Josh. Mine is Sonje, and the men with me are Michael, our overseas coordinator, and our special guest, Hans Isler, the Chairman of Katharina Enterprises."

After introductions, Sonje continued. "Let's all be seated so we can ascertain where we go from here."

The first to speak was Ben. His physical features gave the image of a gentle, round-faced, pudgy doughboy. Heavy dark eyebrows just above the rims of his glasses accentuated his pale receding hairline. But when he spoke first impressions were lost.

"May I say before we get into our forensic findings, that it is because of people like you Israel can exist and function in a modern world. We have enemies near and far, some are known, and others lurk in shadows of darkness. This keeps us vigilant. Your company is a friend to Israel, and on behalf of our organization that works largely undercover, we say thank you to Dr. Isler and his team of people.

"Now, let us get on with the report. We had little to work with, only a letter with a couple of 5 by 8 photos along with the manila envelope they came in. I'll give you just a cursory overview and leave the technical and scientific stuff for you to read in the reports here on the table.

"When we met with the vice chairlady a few days ago, we took her fingerprints so we could differentiate between her prints and others that may be found on the articles taken to our lab. It turned out that her fingerprints represented about a one-to-four ratio to another set found on both sides of the letter, the photos, and the envelope. We were surprised that even on the envelope after all the handling that went on, we found several that matched those inside. Fingerprints are like footprints but invisible to the naked eye in most cases. If left undisturbed, fingerprints have been known to be found on objects up to twenty-five years. Of course, these prints we found on the letter and photos are very new.

"Now, to the second matter. The fiber used in the paper to write the extortion letter was not made from wood pulp but from cotton fiber. Most cotton fiber paper is made from old, discarded clothing. Romania being the poor country it is in the Soviet Bloc, its people lack the affluence for buying large volumes of clothing and the clothing they would discard is pieced together to make blankets and bed coverings. Also, paper mills in the Soviet Union depend largely on trees as the pulp source for paper production.

"The next item of interest is the hand-written address on the manila envelope. A rolling ballpoint pen was used to write the Address. That pen was not put on the market until 1966, and it contained an ink that was water based and mixed with a very identifiable chemical called formamide, which smelled like ammonia and served to retard the drying-out of the ballpoint."

Three busy minds around the conference table were swirling at what was implied. Ben had presented the report in a straightforward, professional manner without offering opinions or assumptions based on his findings. He left that for his colleague Josh. Ben sat down and his partner stood.

"I'm sure I cannot make any deductions from the report you've heard that you haven't already made. The common conclusion is that the party who wrote that letter most likely bought the paper and pen outside the country. Insufficient data do not allow us to go anywhere with this; however, something may be more telling when the next extortion demand comes in."

Michael was always one step ahead of others when action was required with limited information. But today there was a reason he was out front: Mr. Popescu, his prison time, the photos of a young blond man that were shown to him while in prison, and his book. The man that had those pictures worked for the government and could have survived the old regime purge when the communist took over. Michael was first to speak.

"The man who sent that letter is experienced in the psychology of securing information. There are two ways interrogators secure information: the use of torture and gentle persuasion. The first, the infliction of pain, only yields half-truths, whereas, gentle persuasion is the method of using time to alter how one thinks, a process of degrading the props that support a person's worldview. This latter process requires patience and time." *He remembered Popescu saying, "When in prison, the Nazi interrogator would come every week to interview him." They were using the gentle persuasion approach on him because they knew he was willing to die for a cause.*

Michael continued. "The man who wrote this letter is not a novice. A novice would have already sent us specific information on how and when to deliver the money. This man is using his professional experience and has chosen the gentle persuasion approach. He is trying to manipulate us into wanting to make payment so badly that when we reach that point, he'll have greater control in the transfer. He'll probably send another letter with additional incriminating evidence. My suggestion is that we wait him out. In view, that he has access to military and police archives, and that he obtained Sonje's married name and my picture from wedding announcements in newspapers and magazines in this country, it's likely the man has connections with the Romanian government in some form and may even be stationed in this country. After the war, I created another identity, and the name Pencovich became as silent as those of my family who lay in the mass grave outside the city where I was born. It's been the notoriety, the wide publicity of my marriage to Sonje that has awakened someone in my past."

Everyone around the table sat dumbfounded after Michael spoke. He had painted a graphic picture that carried emotional scars. Sonje struggled to be strong for Michael, holding back tears. The chairman, a Jew whose adoptive German mother had saved him out of the Holocaust and made him the sole heir of Katharina Enterprises, sat with eyes fastened on his hands folded together on top of the conference table. Even Ben and Josh, men trained to react only to lab-report findings, sat in hush. Ben was first to respond.

"You are very insightful, Michael. Two of us here may be scientists in our specialized fields, but what you are doesn't come from academic learning but from the laboratory of human experience coupled with a form of extra-sensory perception. In my work of forensic discovery, I rarely find people on your level, and it just may happen that I'll need your help someday."

Everyone knew Michael had more to say but wanted to keep his cards close to his chest. He seemed to know when to speak and when to remain silent. What lingered in Michael's mind were the words from Ben's report: *that fingerprints up to twenty-five years old had been found on objects. The book...that book taken from Mr. Popescu by the SS Nazi informer may still show some fingerprints even though it was over twenty years ago.*

Hans, the young doctor, and chairman of the board, considered Sonje his adopted sister. He paid careful attention to her after Michael made his statement: she was glowing with a smile and a look of admiration of the man who had changed her life.

Ben closed the session. "I hope what we've examined and presented to you today has been to your satisfaction—it's all science, and it may or may not be helpful. When your next extortion demand arrives, let us know and we'll go through it."

The three around the table stood, thanked the two for their work, and the same security officer who escorted the two forensic technicians to the vice chairlady's conference room led them back down to the first floor where they found their way out.

Sonje had invited Hans to the meeting, and Michael had no objections. It was the chairman's policy to never push himself into matters that he had delegated to others, and it carried over to Michael and Sonje. He had been instrumental in Michael's new life of faith and was thankful to God that the two of them were good for each other. What he would remember from this meeting in the days ahead was what Michael did before they broke up. He walked over where Sonje sat, put his arms around her, saying, "I want you to leave this matter to me. Vital information has come in recently, and I believe it has legs that will take us where we need to go. It will take some work to reach that point, and the sooner we get Popescu in this country, the sooner this matter will be settled."

Chapter 4

The Stranger

A vehicle carrying a passenger in the back seat pushed its way along the main, narrow, pedestrian-filled roadway. It was Saturday, and the rural population had come to town to do weekly shopping giving the town a colorful festive image of itself. To reach the city from the coastal town of Constanta, it had taken the driver six hours of hard driving. Having been here once before, he knew the challenge of navigating through the network of undisciplined motorbikes, old Soviet cars, draft animals pulling wagons and carts, and street vendors bartering everything from farm-raised vegetables to homemade quilts.

When the driver reached the other end of town, he drove a short distance on a side road and stopped, looked back at the passenger in the rear seat. "The gentleman you want to see lives about one-half mile up that trail. I would walk with you, but I've been told not to leave the car."

"It's wise you stay with the vehicle," said the man in the back seat. "I'm sure I'll find his house."

Marku Albescu, a front man for Katharina Enterprises was on an urgent mission of supervising the extraction of an old man from the country of his birth.

He stepped out of the vehicle, looked at the rough, well-traveled pathway set on a slight incline. People here who lived in the countryside didn't have automobiles. Anything motorized consisted of a two-wheel bike and sometimes accompanied with a sidecar. Small plots of land dotted the landscape like a checkerboard with little houses in the center. The stranger was Romanian, a city person, and this was his first experience of traveling to a remote part of the country. He had left the seaside resort construction project at Constanta in the hands of technical personnel brought in from the outside, and by using local skilled labor the project was moving forward and creating favorable public relations in the community.

In front of him lay soft, rolling hills covered with nature's floral greenery. It reminded him of Idyllic pictures found in children's fairytale books he'd read as a child. Nature's beauty always had a way of silencing unwanted noise. He stopped, turned, and looked back at the city with its gaiety, clatter, and blare. Then life's truism spoke like a voice from above: man created the city, but God made the country. Everything around him stood in contrast to the bustling, loud city they just drove through.

The trail of floral beauty the stranger was walking over pulled him back to the time when he was a boy living in the country with his father and stepmother. Being four-years-old when his mother died of the Spanish Flu, he didn't remember much about his birth mother, and when his father remarried, he stored everything that belonged to his mother in boxes, including all her saved letters from her family and the diary she wrote in from time-to-time. As a young child, he opened those boxes every few weeks, looked at her pictures and read everything over-and-over. Her diary writings were mostly about her love for him and her personal experience she had in life growing up being Jewish. She was proud of being Jewish. Though his mother was gone and little memory remained of her from childhood, he came to know who she was from the messages she left him in her diary. It was her writings that shaped what he became.

The stranger stopped. It was a moving experience to revisit his childhood memories. Had it not been for that diary his mother left him, he would not be where he was today. As a child, the book was his friend, a companion that went with him to special rural country sites to be read when lonely and in need of a friend. With the view of rolling green countryside hills and the fresh smell of nature, the stranger wished he had his mother's diary with him so he could sit on a nearby rock and relive a childhood experience.

Nature had served her purpose, and if he had flowers to lay at the roadside, he would honor the spot in memory of his mother, though dead, was still shaping who he was by the diary she left him.

The man took from his pocket a small map, looked at it carefully, walked a hundred feet farther, and came upon a home with a well-kept yard full of fruit trees and vegetables. He was about to open the gate when he saw the outline of a figure working in the garden. He didn't want to frighten the man, but from what he'd been told, this old man couldn't be frightened.

"Mr. Popescu, is that you in the garden?"

The stranger saw an elderly man raise himself. He looked over where he stood, saying nothing, laid his tools down and walked slowly up to the visitor, the fence separating the two. His countenance showed stress.

"Who sent you?" asked the old man.

"Michael sent me."

"Michael who?"

"Michael, the man who gave you money to buy a new motorbike."

The stranger saw a quick flash of softening in the face of Mr. Popescu.

"Well, why didn't you say so in the first place? That's the code word, you know! Come on in!"

The man opened the gate to his compound and when they reached the front porch, the stranger saw luggage packed and ready to go.

"I see you got Michael's message. Did you follow instructions written on the list?"

"Yes, I followed his instructions very thoroughly, and he'll be surprised at what I found for him. So plans have been changed?"

"Yes, something has come up, and I've been assigned to get you out of the country as soon as possible."

They moved on inside the house as the stranger continued talking. "Serious changes are in the making, and I can't tell you what they are because I'm not privy to them. At this point, I'm responsible for getting you out for your own safety. Something is going down and you could be collateral damage. After today, you will forget you ever saw me and you're not to know my name for your own good."

"I thought those days were over until I saw what Michael requested me to bring along. Nazism and anti-Semitism are like nuclear waste—they have a long half-life."

The stranger looked around the old man's house. He had everything arranged as if he'd be returning in a couple of days. He was instructed that neighbors and friends were to be told he'd be away visiting friends and relatives, that no one was to know he would be out of the country.

Mr. Popescu, showing a certain reservation about his sudden departure, said to the stranger, "You know, I wouldn't be doing this if it weren't for Michael. Some people die in order to live, while others live to die for a worthy cause, and there's just a shade of difference between the two, and I would like to think that I share a little of both."

This old man, thought the stranger, has the wits of a mongoose fighting a cobra. There are reasons he is highly esteemed in the Jewish community.

"You're going to be out of the country for a while. Who'll take care of your home and the beautiful garden?"

The old man sent a silent message to the stranger. Eyes roamed about the house. The walls and what hung on them had been part of him most of his life. Everything was what he was, and if he didn't have the hope of returning someday, his grief would be unbearable.

"My cousin, yes...my cousin will watch over my place. That's been arranged."

Memories pushed the old man back to his younger years, a time when the house he was leaving was used as a gathering site for Jews fleeing those seeking to ship them off to camps.

"Are you Jewish, Sir?" the old man asked the stranger.

"Mr. Popescu, you are not to know my name or anything about me. Those are the rules."

"Yeah…I forgot—does seem a little unfair."

"It's all for your own good. Let's be on our way."

Six hours later, the time approaching near midnight, the vehicle carrying the stranger and Mr. Popescu stopped in front of an inconspicuous home somewhere in a small coastal town on the Black Sea. Seen in the distance across the calm, coastal waters was the bright moonlight showing its reflection accompanied by the sounds of waves pounding ancient sand.

A light was on in the house, and by the time the driver pulled the luggage from the boot and the three of them approached the front porch, someone opened the door. Everyone moved inside where they saw a photographer with all his equipment set up.

"Mr. Popescu, we need a passport photograph, so why don't you sit while the man does his thing so he can be on his way!"

"There's a lot of drama in this operation," said the old man who was now showing weariness from his travel.

"Mr. Popescu, you are to stay inside this home for two days. Everything you need is here. Don't go outside. You are not to be seen by anyone, and at dusk, day-after-tomorrow, approximately forty-two hours from now, the driver and I will return to pick you up and take you to a plane for your flight to Munich. The flight is two hours, and you are to avoid as much as possible conversation with anyone on board the plane. Upon arrival, Michael will meet you. You'll need cash; do you have any cash with you?"

"That's the least of my worries; I have all the money

Michael gave me for the new bike."

"Good! There are prepared meals in the fridge you can warm-up as needed."

The stranger shook the old man's hand and drove off with the driver at the wheel.

It was approaching dusk with a beautiful deep red glow forming on the horizon, and an old man, restless and fit-to-be-tied, waited for someone to pick him up. Confined to the quiet quarters of this seaside home where the sounds of restless waves pounded on the ever-shifting sands, sleep came easy. It would be nice to see what one heard, but that was against the rules. He knew Michael had directed all this for a reason. That boy was smart, was always smart. But better than that, he was good, always been good. Then came the Holocaust. That was when he became bad in a good way.

Breaking into his thoughts was a loud knock at the front door. The sound carried a pleasing ring to it, and when it swung open, the stranger who was navigating him through waters he didn't understand, stood at the threshold. His driver was waiting in the car.

"Are you ready to go, Mr. Popescu?"

"I've been ready for two days."

"A lot of people would envy what you experienced here at the seaside, smelling that fresh salt air and listening to the tumbling waves breaking over the sand."

"I heard the breaking and tumbling waves but never smelled the salt air because there's no salt in the Black Sea."

The stranger closed the door, looked at four pieces of luggage on the floor. "It appears you're all packed and ready to go!"

"As I said, 'I've been ready to go for two days.'"

The old man saw the stranger reach into his pocket and pull out something. "Mr. Popescu, this is your Romanian passport, and it's stamped with a visa for your travel to Munich. When Michael is finished with your service, you'll be on your way to Israel. It took some doing to get this passport this quickly, but as you know, in this country a little money expedites things. Tonight, the government will have no record of you leaving the country, and Michael wants it that way."

The stranger saw the old man's eyes look off into space. "On this side of my mortality, I have been given the privilege of walking the streets Jesus will be walking on when he returns to rule the world. Sir, do you know who Jesus is? He was the promised Messiah, you know!"

A bombshell exploded inside the stranger—*the diary—his mother's diary. She talked about Jesus being the Messiah and that was the reason she'd married his father, even over her family's objections. His mother never stopped talking to him with that diary, and today it was a new message coming through an old man speaking like a prophet. He had accepted his mother's Jewish heritage and carried it with silent pride, but today an old man was forcing him to see another side of his sainted mother.*

"Mr. Popescu, your affirmation of faith is an invitation to an open door that I shall consider in time."

"Let's be on our way then," said the old man. By the time they reached the private terminal, darkness was settling in, and the crew working at the Constanta resort project was boarding the chartered plane for a week's rest at their homes in Munich. The old man waited in the vehicle with the stranger and his driver until the government people went through the formalities of checking documents. As soon as they left, the one in charge said, "Let's go!" The driver and Stranger each carried two pieces of luggage and were met by the pilot at the top of the stairs. The stewardess directed them to a seat in the front. He watched the two men store the baggage overhead. *This was a strange experience, thought the old man. He'd been through many intrigues in his lifetime but nothing like this. If it weren't for Michael being in charge of all this, he'd think he was being used for something nefarious.*

"We'll see you when you return, Mr. Popescu. Have a good flight."

The old man watched the stranger and his driver being escorted to the exit door by the pilot. He pushed his seat back and looked up at the closed overhead bin holding papers that Michael requested. His thoughts were interrupted: "Sir, you'll have to fasten your belt and bring your seat to an upright position."

This was Popescu's first air flight.

Chapter 5

Old Luggage

Michael's driver pulled up close to the private terminal where a chartered plane was seen taxiing toward the disembarking spot for passengers. It was filled with highly skilled professional people returning home for one week's rest. Michael's managers on the Constanta project had worked out a schedule where workers spent two weeks on the field and one-week home. Their schedules were staggered to eliminate slow-downs.

The driver waited until the passengers had disembarked the plane and boarded the waiting shuttle that would take them to a site where they would be cleared through customs. He drove close to the bottom of the stairs jutting down from the open door of the fuselage and stopped. The driver got out and opened the door for his passenger. Both walked up the stairs and entered the plane. Popescu was standing alongside one of the pilots, and when he saw Michael with his natural blond hair, he grabbed him with a bear hug. "Michael, my boy, you're a sight for sore eyes!"

"Let's get you home so you can get some rest—we have a big day tomorrow! Where's your baggage?"

"In the overhead storage bins."

Turning to his driver who stood nearby, Michael said, "Luis, help us with the luggage!"

The old man who bore calluses on his hands, walked empty-handed behind Michael and his driver, each carrying two pieces of luggage. Some might call him a peasant by his rough mannerisms and blunt way of speaking, but those who would write history would assign to him iconic nobility.

The old man seated alongside Michael had never been out of his country. Vehicles were bumper-to-bumper and there were so many lights—Munich looked like a Christmas tree, and when the driver pulled up in front of a walled compound with a large iron gate with a security person coming over to identify the driver, the old man was overwhelmed with the imposing scene.

"What is this, Michael?"

"It's where I live."

"It's like a prison."

"Some might think so, but the people in here are the good guys."

When the vehicle drove through the gate, it seemed like a thousand lights came on illuminating the entire inner compound. Awestruck, the visitor wondered what next big surprise would happen.

The old man saw Michael's ring hand, and knowing his tragic history, he was reluctant to ask—but did anyway: "I never asked you, Michael, but I see a ring on your finger! Are you married?"

"To the most wonderful lady in the world!"

"I'm glad for you. I know I'm full of questions, so forgive me. Is she Jewish, and where did you find her?"

"That's a good question. I found her on a self-imposed island and we each gave the other life. No, she isn't Jewish, but she suffered as did many Jews during the Holocaust."

The driver came to a stop in front of a guesthouse inside Michael's large compound. The old man saw Michael roll up the partition between the front and back seats. Privacy was needed for what the old man was about to hear.

"My family name in Romania died and was buried in the mass grave in Ediniti. Because of my blond hair and blue eyes, I created a new identity, and it wasn't until I came to this country that I used my real name. I know all about methods used in creating new identities, and there are probably scores of former Romanian Nazis guilty of zabernism pretending to be loyal communist carrying the name of someone deceased.

"My wife is a well-known executive in the business world, and when we were married she proudly took the name Pencovich as her new legal surname, a name that had been dead but was brought back to life through marriage. Unfortunately, someone in this country from Romania with a dark, disreputable past saw our wedding announcement and pictures in major newspapers in this country. Six months later, this person sent my wife an extortion letter with photos of a young blond male accusing him of capital crimes, and that if payment weren't made, he would go to the authorities."

Popescu's eyes registered an awakening. *He knew where Michael was going with this. It was all tied to what he told him when he was secretly visiting Ediniti. Up to this point, he'd been in the dark on details. Now, everything was falling in place.... This tree was going to be shaken for all it was worth, and if the man who sent him to prison turns out to be the extortionist, his own life would be in danger because he was a living witness to his former life as a Nazi party member. This was why Michael got him out of the country.*

"Mr. Popescu, I know I don't have to fill in the blanks for you. You are ahead of me and already know what I have to do."

"You are right on that, Michael. I'm keeping up with you, but I'm having to run to do it. I'll answer your next question so you won't have to bother. The Nazi officer who sent me to prison and threatened my life went by the name of Auton Lupel, and he always dressed in civilian clothes, but his language was sprinkled with military verbiage."

"Do you have anything in writing from him that carries his signature?"

"My dealings with him became strained toward the end of my confinement in prison. He used the soft treatment in the first few sessions I had with him, then stiffened his position with threats of violence and even wrote letters restating his threats, some of which I didn't even open."

Michael, knowing the significance of an unopened letter, asked, "Are those unopened letters still in your possession?"

"I'm sure there are some among all the stuff I packed in my luggage cases."

"It goes without saying, that the man you've named operates today with a different identity, and the process of finding him could be tedious because after the war Nazi officers did everything they could to become loyal communist and even took on the identity of deceased partisan resistors to evade the net of the new government. Therefore, we'll have to depend on your sight and memory for identification."

Michael saw the old man's eyes brighten with a look of challenge on his face. "You've given me purpose in my old age. When do we start on the project?"

"Tomorrow morning!"

Michael and the driver carried the old man's luggage into the house to a bedroom that had its own bath. Found on the nightstand was an evening snack the housekeeper and cook had left for the guest. Michael was closing the bedroom door when the old man said, "Michael, now may not be the best time to discuss what I brought along in two of those cases, but when I got your message requesting that I bring all the documents dealing with the authorities, I went to my old trunk where I kept everything and surprised myself at what I'd dumped in there over the years. Tomorrow, you'll find some very interesting papers."

Two men were seen getting out of a company vehicle in front of Katharina Enterprises each carrying a luggage case. Michael usually pulled into the garage and took the elevator straight up to the fourth floor, but today he wanted his guest to see the outside grandeur of the central headquarters building, the exquisite landscaping, and the centerpiece of the flowing fountain filled with Koi fish species. He also had another message for the old man. They stopped at the fountain.

"Mr. Popescu, do you see the name on the front of

that four-story building that takes up a city block? Katharina Enterprises has investments around the world, and do you know who owns it all? Rachel Isler's son, Jacob, formally Rachel Pencovich, my sister."

Up to this point, the old man knew Michael worked for a large company and was married to a very successful woman. But what he was just told pushed him into deep swirling waters. *Horrible history rushed through his mind. He remembered those dark, evil, days. What was Michael saying? They all perished on that fateful day!*

"You're confusing me, Michael. They all perished, none of them survived!"

"Do you remember the German General by the name of Bauman?"

"Of course."

"His wife visited him in Romania and was at Ediniti right after the massacre, found Jacob hidden in a wagon of hay. She returned to Germany with him, raised him as her son and made him the sole heir of all her wealth. Now, he's fulfilling her dream of supporting Israel by helping Jews return to their land."

The old man was speechless. He placed the luggage on the walkway, sat on the edge of the fountain and watched the peaceful scene of colorful fish swim about in the pond.

Michael didn't interrupt what was going on inside Popescu. He was making a journey trying to reconcile human heartbreak and tragedy with the gift of Providence. Still staring at the fish, the old man asked, "How could a saint live so close to an evil man as the general, let alone, be married to him?"

"Those were the early days. When she returned to Germany with Jacob after her visit to Romania, they soon separated and her wealthy industrialist father who opposed the government suddenly died under strange circumstances."

Still struggling over what he just found out, a mystery hung over the old man of how Jacob was saved—it had to be a miracle!

"How did Jacob reach the wagon of hay?"

"An angel carried him through a battery of soldiers and placed him in the wagon."

"Too much is coming at me in my old age. It's emotionally taxing. I feel like Daniel when he was weakened by exposure to the other world. I knew that boy when you used to pull him around in his little wagon. If I can't focus on our project for the day, you'll be the cause of it for telling me this unbelievable story."

Two old worn luggage cases carried by the man married to the lady running the affairs of the company elicited hidden glares from personnel as Michael made his way to his office. Alongside him walked an old man wishing Michael hadn't taken the luggage piece from him he'd been carrying.

Birdie, Michael's secretary, was seated at her desk when he and Popescu entered his office. The lady who ran his office like a sergeant stopped what she was doing and watched what was passing in front of her eyes. *It looked like a rescue operation with an old man coming in off the street and her boss carrying two tattered luggage cases. She wondered where he'd picked them up, and what this was all about?*

"Birdie, call maintenance and have them bring in a large folding table and set it up in my office. After it's up, you can help us sort out everything."

"Yes, Sir, I'll get right on that."

Chapter 6

Righteous Gentile

The two cases Mr. Popescu brought from his home in Ediniti containing what Michael requested appeared by age and condition to be of little significant value to Michael's cause: the units were old, faded, and marked with long-term use and rough handling. Everything inside the two cases was placed on top of the table for examination.

"Mr. Popescu, can you give us an overview of what's here before we start looking for specific information?"

"What we have here are items left at my home by Jews who were staying with me or were in transit to another safe zone. Not all Romanians were anti-Semites, and a few of us organized methods of helping Jews get into safe homes. We had a system of delivering food to those in hiding, and my house was used as a transit center. Over the months, people came and went leaving thank you notes and letters. Some left diaries, and I think there are two among what's here on the table. Much of it is heartbreaking and should be in a Holocaust museum."

Michael and Birdie saw the old man take from the top of the table a well-wrapped article. "This is what you requested me to be careful with, Michael. It's the notebook I showed you when you were with me in my home. And here are two diaries that will rend your emotions." When he handed them to Michael, his eyes showed pain, yet his face carried the purpose of his mission.

"One of those diaries belonged to a young lady who didn't make it and was brought to my place by a relative and left it hoping the world would read it someday. Both diaries, along with much of what's here on the table, belong in a museum."

Michael notice Birdie becoming disturbed from what she saw and heard. "Birdie, go to the coffee shop and take a break, then bring us an order of coffee and tea, and you don't need to be in a hurry, the two of us will carry on with the work here."

"Thank you, Sir."

By the time Birdie returned with a cart holding coffee and tea, everything on the table in Michael's office had been neatly cataloged and placed in large manila envelopes. Left outside on top of the desk were two unopened letters, sent by the Nazi identified as Auton Lupel, the man who imprisoned Mr. Popescu when the Nazi government was in power.

"Mr. Popescu, if you saw an old photo of Auton Lupel, would you recognize him?"

"I'm sure I could if it's a good photo!"

"Let's go to the records department! Birdie, would you please call records and request them to open up the vault room?"

Madge, the manager of the records department, was at the counter when Michael and the old man arrived. "Good morning, Mr. Pencovich. I got your message and all we need is for you and the gentleman with you to sign in.

"Are there tables inside the vault room where materials can be laid out?"

"Yes, there are two, and each has a couple of chairs."

"That will serve us well."

While the manager led the way to the vault, Michael dialogued with Popescu.

"Do you remember Colonel Funar?"

"He's bad news. I've been waiting to write his obituary in my book that's now in your possession. I will get it back, won't I?"

"It has to be examined for fingerprints first along with those unopened letters, and that will be done this week. Your task in this room is to examine photos of the living, namely, those who are in military uniform. You will be looking for a face as you remember it twenty years ago. Avoid looking at the dead; otherwise, we'll not get through this."

Michael placed out the table stacks of files filled with photos taken from the colonel's home. "If you find nothing in these photos, Mr. Popescu, we'll start on the documents and look for a name. However, a photo is far more important than a name. I have to make an important call. Can you handle being here by yourself till I return?"

"Michael, I wasn't born yesterday. It would serve me well if you brought me a magnifying glass when you return."

"I'll do that and bring lunch as well."

On Michael's way out, the records manager met him. "Mr. Pencovich, I overheard you citing the name of Colonel Funar. Everyone is riveted with that story, and I thought it might interest you to know that my brother works at the courthouse, and the news is that the prosecution will present its legal brief before the judges next week."

She saw Michael's tall frame stiffen. Expecting a response matching his body language, she was surprised to hear his reply. "Thank you for that information. I was in Israel with my wife on our honeymoon when I saw his picture on the front page of the newspaper announcing his arrest. That made our honeymoon special."

An hour later, Michael entered the vault followed by two workers from the coffee shop carrying trays of sandwiches, pastries, and fruit. The old man was found leaning back in his chair looking relaxed as if he'd discovered a solution to the world's problems.

"No need to bring a magnifier," said the old man. "Lupel came out loud and clear with military uniform in three of the photos you gave me to look over. Unlike Funar's photos, they don't show him next to dead Jews, nor by himself—just in a group."

Michael picked up the three photos from the table, looked at them, then at Popescu. "It appears he may have been a Lieutenant—not a high-ranking officer. That being the case, it would be easier to slip into hiding. However, it must be assumed he was an integral part of the killing team in view that his photos are found among Funar's things.

"Why would Funar want to keep all this genocidal evidence?"

Michael remembered that he was asked the same question when they first came upon the evidence in Funar's home. Time had not changed the answer.

"Genocidal war criminals only live in the present and are blinded to the consequences of actions. This person enjoyed a morbid kind of voyeurism of Jewish dead. He needed what's here in these boxes to feed his evil, sick nature."

The old man looked at Michael. "You've made a remarkable contribution to your people for their posterity. The battle is between good and evil."

"No, it's you, Mr. Popescu, who deserves honor and recognition of courage and bravery in helping my people. It was you who endangered your life when you didn't have to, and someday you will be honored by my people for your acts of heroism with the special title of Righteous Gentile."

"Knock, knock," came the words from the entrance of the vault. Madge, the manager of records, stood in the doorway. "Mr. Pencovich, I have a message here from your secretary." *She walked over and placed it on the table in front of him where he was seated. It read: Please call Eugen Tace.*

The old man was with Michael when his driver pulled into the Israeli Embassy. "Mr. Popescu, I have to drop off something here at the Embassy and will be right back." Twenty minutes later, they were pulling into Michael's compound, and for the first time, he got a full view of what was inside his walled compound. For a man who loved nature and the outdoors, the floral beauty was beyond anything he'd ever seen. Cloistered inside nature's floral bounty was another home near the guesthouse.

"Michael, how many homes are here inside your compound?"

"There are two homes and a guesthouse. There's also

a guard house in the back that provides sleeping quarters for those who have to stay over."

"Why all the security?"

"We have the reputation for supporting Zionism, and those who are enemies of Israel make us their target."

"Whoever thought that one day I would be here with you under these circumstances—will I get meet Jacob, the lad you pulled around in a little wagon?"

"That you will, my friend. Tonight, I'll pick you up at seven for dinner."

The old man managed a short nap, then bathed and dressed with the best he had knowing he would be among very important people. It was after six-thirty and he could hear vehicles coming and going inside the compound. Then came a knock at the front door. It was Michael.

"We're a few minutes early. Are you ready, Mr. Popescu?"

The two took a path leading to the home near the guesthouse that was shrouded with exotic plants and flowers. It was nature's best as birds sang and gentle breezes ruffled overhanging leaves. Michael was leading the way to one of the homes in the compound that the old man knew wasn't his. After reaching the front entry, He rang the doorbell.

The door swung wide, and standing in prominent view was a tall, angular, elderly man with furrowed hands and an aged face. However, when he spoke, his voice carried youthful vigor.

"Michael, you don't have to ring the doorbell!"

"I've brought a special guest I want you to meet."

"Well, bring him in so we can all meet the

gentleman."

Popescu saw a group standing behind the old gentleman who opened the door, moved inside behind Michael who took over the formalities that followed.

"I would like everyone to meet a very special person who has been a vital part of my life and the lives of family members. Were it not for him, Many Jews today would not be alive. He has been a friend to my family, was the foreman of my father's mill and furniture shop."

Popescu saw three ladies in the group, all stately looking. The man alongside the younger lady left him with a strange sensation. *He had the looks of a younger Michael and must be Jacob, the lad who was carried to the wagon of hay by an angel.* The old guest said nothing as Michael reached over and took his wife's hand. "Mr. Popescu, this lady is Sonje, my lovely wife, and allow me to introduce the other women with their husbands."

Michael turned to the elderly man who greeted them at the door who was now standing alongside his wife. "Mr. Popescu, this is Mr. and Mrs. Reznik, two beautiful people who led me to a spiritual birth. I was introduced to the Messiah, Jesus, by this man, and my faith made me a new person and gave me a new life."

Three elderly people stood looking at each other with common-life experiences: two had suffered as Jews in the Holocaust; the other had gone to prison for being a Zionist advocate.

At this point, Popescu couldn't escape his history—the young man in the group standing alongside his portrait-looking wife was a young Michael. *How could two people carry such identical looks at the same age?* Everyone saw

Popescu's eyes turn toward the man who was taken from the wagon of hay as an infant.

"And you are Jacob, the son of Rachel, who was taken from the bulrushes by the daughter of Pharaoh. I remember you as a lad when Michael pulled you around in your little wagon."

Memory pushed the old man's emotions back to the dark times of personal history. Tears came to his eyes forcing speech with staccato-ridden words: "We have all lost so much in life during those horrible times, my two sons in the war, and all your family by the tragedy of another kind of evil."

The old man took from his pocket a photo of him and his grandfather in front of the mill when times were good. "Here is a picture of your grandfather and me as a gift to remember him by. He was a wonderful man and my friend. Because of him, I came to love and appreciate the Jewish people."   .

The room lost its oxygen. The atmosphere needed punctuation of the right order—not words but an act. Jacob Isler, who was taken from the wagon of hay as an infant, grabbed and embraced the old man standing in front of him, weeping, whereupon others in the room gathered around offering support.

The evening climaxed around the dining table where gourmet delights were on full display. An upscale food-catering agency had provided the formal service with the evening being sealed with Michael fulfilling the promise he made to the old man.

"Mr. Popescu, in addition to proclaiming you a Righteous Gentile, I would like to honor you tonight by

71

fulfilling the promise I made when I was with you in Romania. Tomorrow, you will fly first-class with Mr. and Mrs. Reznik who will give you a personal tour of Israel and Jerusalem, the city from which Yeshua will govern the world."

The old man dropped his head, closed his eyes, and said nothing.

Chapter 7

The Nazi Hunter

A large vehicle equipped with special protective armor and darkened windows pulled to the curbside and stopped near a nondescript-looking man holding a briefcase. The driver's side rearview mirror showed the door flung open and the man at the curb jumping in. The vehicle sped away leaving the driver wondering whom the important pickup was and how long they'd be conducting business in the enclosed moving private chamber. His orders were to drive about town until told otherwise.

The man who boarded the up-scale vehicle was Eugen Tace, a survivor of the Romanian Holocaust and well-known Nazi hunter. The two men now conferring together had rocked the Western world with the news of an infamous war criminal being brought to trial for his crimes. Tace was first to speak.

"For the time being, I think this is the best way for us to meet," said Eugen, who was working with the state prosecutor in the Colonel Funar war-crime trial. "Michael, the compelling evidence you gave us left little doubt of a prosecution, and the witnesses testifying will move the judges to a guilty verdict and convince the public as well. I am working closely with the prosecutor, and the reason I requested this meeting is to inform you of what to expect in the trial and ask you to put it in your busy schedule to attend some of the trial hearings. I need objective feedback outside the legal framework on the way the trial is being perceived. Also, I need to know how factual the testimonials are and how provocative they come across to the public. The trial is not only a legal procedure but an historical-driven event that will long be remembered.

"Colonel Funar is a slick person having established his reputation here in this country and has become an anomaly being a Romanian Nazi tried in a West German court. The defendant, being non-German, will require the Judges to be over-scrupulous in court deliberations.

"In this country," continued Tace, "the court system operates on civil law, a judicial process without a jury. Judges investigate and are the principal agents who establish guilt or innocence. Other countries are known for the adversarial or common law system. Common law provides a judge as a referee, and a jury decides guilt or innocence. The biggest difference between the two is who decides facts and whether a defendant is guilty. The judge examines first, and there is no cross-examination. Therefore, you can see that there are certain limitations, and this is why strong public opinion may influence the judges. My role will be to work with the prosecutor in advisement. Unlike the common law provision, witnesses for the prosecutor cannot be coached prior to or during the trial session."

At this point, the man responsible for providing prosecutorial evidence for the Funar war-crimes trial interrupted Eugen Tace. "On the subject of evidence, what was found in Colonel Funar's home following his arrest that would be significant to his prosecution?"

"The only thing found that connected him to that era was a lot of jewelry, but there's nothing on the Jewelry to indicate the former owners were Jewish."

"I would suggest you arrange for Mr. Fine, the jeweler that broke this case, to view what they took from his home. There was a ring brought to him by Funar that had incriminating script. He knew the significance of that ring and filled in the inscription with a removable material. On its underside, it had a Star of David, a name, and a date."

"Yes, I remember hearing that story when Colonel Funar's identity was uncovered. Also, I remember asking you, Michael, if you 'were tempted to carry out avengement upon Colonel Funar after learning he was here in West Germany?'"

The Nazi Hunter saw Michael draw within himself—body language was showing a message of swirling ambiguity. Both Avenger and Hunter had histories of regret, each wishing they had worn the other's shoes—it was mutual guilt: Michael, for his avengement; the Hunter, because he didn't resist as did Michael.

"Yes," said Michael, "I was tempted after finding out where the man lived. It was one o'clock in the morning when my driver pulled into the parking lot of a car-rental agency, got out, went inside the office, returned, and opened the rear door handing me the keys to a rented car. I stepped out wearing dark clothing and entered the rental parked nearby. The driver continued watching me until I faded into the dark. The instructions I gave him were to wait until I returned.

"The chauffeur was not just a common driver. He

carried a concealed weapon, was a highly trained former special ops officer, and had the responsibility to protect the family members of a company that was a major supporter of the new nation of Israel. He was always reading a mystery novel in his downtime, and that night was no different. However, he knew another kind of mystery was underway with his passenger when I broke the rules by going off by myself. Some people know more than you think they do. Intuition told him I carried a mystery of a former life, and that I was about to re-enter that life.

"That evening it was dark with a heavy overcast. Streetlights dotted the community, and vehicles were not moving about at that hour. I pulled the rented car over to the curb, stopped in front of Funar's home and turned off the lights. I couldn't escape the scene across the sloping valley where a well-lighted community nestled itself. It was modern West Germany. The memories of Nazism with bombed-out buildings and factories had long been forgotten. This was the new free Germany showing its age of industrial and economic hegemony over old Europe, a nation unified with her former enemies. My hands that gripped the steering wheel reached over, took from a briefcase the photo of Funar and placed it under the subdued overhead street lighting coming through the window.

"Holding the photo carried a burden of memory, the memory of the Holocaust years in Romania, the time of my life when the only justice I knew was when I avenged the deaths of my family and the girl I was to marry. Thoughts of those morbid times pulled me into my old world, memories of having walked by open pits filled with dead

Jews, deaths caused by the orders of the man in the picture I held—a Nazi Romanian colonel in charge of genocide—and the man lived comfortably under the radar in the home across the street.

"I opened the car door, stood staring at the darkened home across the roadway. My hand tightened its grip on the photo. The heat from the clarion call of justice could be felt burning inside. The pain of history was awakening sleeping ghosts of my past, the years of surviving the Holocaust living in the mountains of Romania, using nature's brutal forces to enact revenge upon those who destroyed my family. Two dark curses hung over my life: the loss of family and the guilt of having to revenge their deaths. It was a time when Lady Justice had her blindfold, scale, and sword ripped from an ordered society—stolen by the evil forces of Nazism.

"I gave another look at the picture held in my hand, then took slow, deliberate steps to cross the street. When I reached the streetlight in front of the home, my past floated through me like a vaporous cloud—it was like yesterday.

"On that day when the Jews were massacred in my village, four Romanian soldiers raped the girl I was to marry. She, along with other women committed suicide rather than live. Three of those soldiers had already been executed, and the fourth, Colonel Funar, the one now living in this house under another name, had escaped my net. The last execution was still vivid in my mind.

"It was a clear day when we waited in the countryside outside an army encampment. Our target was an army officer, a member of the Iron Guard. That day he sat in the back seat of an open army jeep. My colleague Bub, avoided the sound of gunfire when he used his hunting bow to dispatch the officer's driver causing the military Jeep to crash into a tree. The man targeted for trial was pulled from the wreckage, his hands tied, then marched over rugged terrain to the execution site.

"Everything had the elements of a primitive court. It was designed that way. There would be no defense, no appeal, and no audience. The man would be given the same trial he gave others, the difference being they were innocent Jews and he was guilty of genocide.

"Our actions were intended to show order, discipline, and experience. Bub, the Bowman, walked over and cut the rope that bound the man's hands, turned, and walked back where he had stood, leaving Moshe to finish his part.

"'Strip off your clothes,' Moshe told the officer. The three of us watched the officer remove everything except his undershirt, underwear, and socks. Moshe continued: 'I said, strip off everything.'

"Standing naked with his clothes piled to one side, I remember watching my two compatriots tie the officer's hands together, then forcing him to kneel where he stood.
"We'd taken the man to a courtroom where nature looked on as the only neutral witness. There was no jury box, nor the presence of a defense attorney—that day I was the judge, jury, and the injured party.

"While standing under the streetlight in front of Funar house with his photo in my hand, I remembered another photo I held that day in the forest where a trial was being carried out—it was the photo of the girl I was to marry. I forced the picture in the face of the man who was kneeling and begging for his life. 'Look at this picture real good.

You raped her causing her to commit suicide.' Then I pulled from my pocket a piece of paper demanding, 'Read aloud what was written to me by the girl you raped before she killed herself.' The man's eyes sobered and his voice stammered through the words.

My Dearest Michael,

You have and will always be the love of my life. You will hear my story when you return. I cannot live with the memory of what's happened, and my body that was saved for you in marriage is no longer sacred and honorable. I would never want you to have this as a memory in our marriage, and I would never want to carry the memory of that burden, so when you return, I hope your sadness will not linger because of me. I am forever yours.

Love, Rebecca

"After the reading was over, I said to my two compatriots, 'Bub, you and Moshe can leave now.' When they departed, I continued with the man being judged.

"'I am a Jew and pose as a traveling merchant. I can move among Romanian civilian society and go unnoticed because I look Aryan with blond hair and blue eyes. I even visit your churches to learn your religious culture to be more efficient in what I do. Inside those churches on Sunday, I listen to your priests slander, berate my people, and teach anti-Semitism, then on Monday morning they lead the mass killers to the sites where Jews are hiding. My friends here with me move at night, I move in the daylight. You have seen me around different army posts plying my trade. This was why we knew you were coming this way at this hour of the day. Everyone has a price for information, and you of all people should know that. The man who put the arrow through the heart of your driver is a champion archer. This becomes useful when silence is needed, and people like you give him the opportunity to keep his skill up.

"Under your command and by your orders, my people have been made to strip off their clothes and stand naked before open pits and shot. However, you are not here today for that. You have been brought to my court because you were one of the four men who raped my Rebecca. She chose to die by cutting her wrists, rather than live with the memory of ignominy. You killed her and will be the third to die at my hands. Today, I'm your executioner to bring justice without mercy, and your naked body will be left here in the open field for wild animals to tear and rip apart and be eaten as carrion. You will now join others of your own kind with Colonel Funar soon to follow.' In the distance, it was the sound of a single gunshot that brought Moshe and Bub back to the court scene."

Michael stopped talking. The Nazi Hunter seated alongside him had the look of catatonic impalement. In his mind were the vivid pictures of his family members that died on the death train, and it was Michael now bringing those pictures to life by taking a personal journey into his own forbidden memory, that narrow strip of life's experience that demanded justice. Hearing his name brought focus back to Michael's story.

"Eugen, under the streetlight that evening in front of Funar's home, I put closure on the memory of those who raped the girl I was to marry, and after doing so, I felt the early morning blanket of chill hovering over the town lifted from my spirit. That night, I made an unpleasant journey into history in order to have a future.

"I chose to relinquish my sword to its rightful owner, Lady Justice, who now is fully restored in an ordered society with blindfold and scale. I turned and briskly walked full stride back to my rented vehicle across the street, drove to the car-rental agency where my driver was waiting. That night I made a philosophical and spiritual passage to the inner court of my conscience. I had passed the test and proven to myself that I could resist the temptation of avengement, a test of courage and validation of the work God had done in my life."

Michael's story had forced Eugen Tace to look into his own world. He wished for an avengement story of his own—like Michael's. Survivors of the death camps still heard haunting cries from families who lay silent in unmarked mass graves. He perceived himself a defeated victim, whereas, the man seated beside him had lived a noble life of valor.

Both men were quiet. They had taken a long journey and were now exhausted from emotional torments in their travels.

Finally, Eugen, the lawyer, spoke. "We all live with different forms of guilt. I have guilt for not having guilt. Hearing what you've told me makes what I do a bit trifling compared to your record. What you're doing in supplying evidence in a court of law to convict Colonel Funar should assuage any guilt you may have. You will go down in history with noble notoriety—you resisted—you fought back."

Michael said nothing. His thoughts were on how both bore the same loss but took different paths in pursuit of justice. "Eugen, you and I have experienced the same painful tragedies but have chosen different pathways in our quest for justice. The one I took has come to an end, but the noble one you chose has no ending. For as long as you live, you will be in search of those guilty of Nazi war crimes. However, someday there will be no need for people like us to bring justice to the guilty. It will all rest upon the shoulders of the Jewish Messiah who will reign over the earth from the city of Jerusalem."

Had these words been spoken by someone besides Michael, thought Eugen, he would've considered them inane and insulting. But he was sitting alongside a man of brave, noble character and smart beyond his own legal training and experience.

"And how did you reach this hopeful ending of mankind with the record of man's history of violence and evil?"

"Eugen, do you celebrate the Passover?"

"I celebrate the Passover only to the extent that it is part of my Jewish culture. It has little personal religious significance; however, I must admit that it does serve as one of the major key elements that bind together our Jewish ethnicity."

Eugen saw Michael's eyes turn toward him, eyes that carried the force of energy that would make any enemy lose courage. Today, they would be used to forge over the Nazi

Hunter another kind of energy, the kind that would pull a Holocaust survivor from the dark abyss.

"Disillusionment is a devastating nemesis," said Michael. "Both of us fell victim to the dark side of man's evil nature. The Holocaust tore from us the props that supported our Jewish religious worldview. We became confined to the prison of nihilism. If there were a God, and if the Scriptures were true, why did God allow the Holocaust? I became a dead man inside and the only thing that gave me feeling was when I rendered justice to those who caused my death. Then one day an old Jewish man threw me a rope when he asked me if I had ever read Isaiah fifty-three. On that day I opened a door behind which was a ray of light showing another Passover. I always knew and believe that the first Passover in Egypt was the prelude to the nationhood of our ancestors, but the second Passover of a suffering Messiah was intended to create another kind of new nation—one of the heart."

Michael Paused. Eugen's hands, now on his lap, showed nervous twitching fingers. He looked away.
"That was the day when new life was formed in me, Eugen, and today I live to make my life and other peoples' lives useful."

"You've taken me down a long narrow path, Michael, and all I can see is a vast sea of nothingness, and I haven't a boat to reach the shoreline."

"A boat is waiting for you and is found in Isaiah chapter fifty-three."

"Michael, you have convinced me to read that chapter when I go home tonight."

Chapter 8

Fingerprints

Michael's driver pulled into the Israeli Embassy and stopped at the front entrance where undercover security personnel opened the door for his passengers. Michael was first to exit, then assisted his wife. Up to this point, her husband had taken the lead in the extortion case by advancing investigative work based on the premise that the extortionist, who was demanding two million dollars, was part of the Nazi-led regime when Mr. Popescu was arrested and held in prison. Today, they would hear the forensic reports on the unopened letters sent to him, and the seized booklet showing execution dates.

They were met at the door by another security officer in plain clothes, then led to an elevator that took them up to the third floor. When the elevator door opened, standing outside was Ben, the forensics leader that formerly met with them at the vice chairlady's conference room at central headquarters. Michael detected a certain heightened exuberance.

"Welcome to our humble abode. Let's go to my office where we can get down to business." He opened a door to a room that held one desk and several chairs. Half the floor space was taken up with filing cabinets. Ben walked behind the desk. "Please be seated and I'll get Josh in here." He quickly placed a call to the party. "Josh, we're here and ready to go!"

Half a minute later, a man wearing a lab cap, rubber gloves, and a long white apron came through the door.

"You'll have to pardon the equipment I'm wearing. I'm in the middle of doing some lab tests. Ben can give you the report you requested, I'm just here to answer any question you may have in view that I did most of the lab work."

Ben walked over to a file cabinet and took from the top drawer a folder and a booklet belonging to Mr. Popescu. "I have good news for you, Michael. Your insight and intuition have paid off. We have lifted from this booklet and the sealed letters in the envelopes fingerprints that match the prints taken from the extortionist's letter. They are the same person. Some people excrete a greater amount of oil through their pores, and in this case, it was so, which helped preserve the prints over the years."

Ben and Josh saw Sonje take Michael's hand, lift it to her lips and kiss it. "My husband is a remarkable person. He possesses insight that the rest of us wish we had a little of."

"I believe I've already stated that about Michael in our last meeting," responded Ben. "We may have to request his assistance someday in helping us with a difficult problem."

Michael looked at Sonje. "There will be two approaches in bringing this case to a satisfactory conclusion, but first, we have to get Mr. Popescu back in this country for some yeoman work."

That night Sonje peacefully went to sleep in the arms of her husband, but Michael laid awake allowing familiar darkness to be his friend. Darkness opened the crevices of his mind and allowed creativity to have its freedom for deep thought. How strange his world had become. He was now using a different kind of sword for justice, and tomorrow he would begin the groundwork to identify and ensnare the extortionist.

Max, chief of security at Katharina Enterprises, known for his enormous size and shiny, glistening baldhead pulled up to the guardhouse leading to the underground garage reserved for company executives. It was eight o'clock in the morning and Max was wearing his early-hour look—a starched shirt and a pressed, dark, pinstripe suit. The security guard came out of the guardhouse, peered into Max's vehicle to confirm he was the only occupant. Though Max was his boss, had he not inspected the interior, he would've been written up.

"Good morning, Max."

"How are you today, Joe?"

"Couldn't be better!"

"Anything unusual going on," asked Max.

"Everything seems to be normal."

"Have the big people arrived yet?"

"The Chairman, Dr. Isler, and Michael…I mean Mr. Pencovich, arrived together today, and the vice chairlady came in a separate vehicle."

Max paused with a slight look of indecision, pulled forward, stopped, turned and looked back toward Joe.

"Joe… has Birdie arrived yet?"

Gossip was always a form of entertainment among

security people, and today the chief of security just provided something for the gossip Gristmill. That lady, Birdie, the overseas coordinator's secretary had done a number on this big man whose baldhead was already sweating at this early hour.

"She arrived about 15 minutes ago."

Joe watched Max move on into the underground parking garage thinking that perhaps something good was happening in Max's life with his interest in Birdie.

The first thing Max did when he arrived at Katharina Enterprises' headquarters building, was to check out all security stations. Being a former military officer, he maintained rigid standards of security. Part of the protocol in place was a stringent dress code. Drivers who were part of the crew that served the chairman and his family were allowed to dress informally but were required to wear a jacket to conceal the weapon each was trained to use. However, when it served the company's best interests in putting forth a favorable public image, drivers were required to wear a uniform and cap.

Max pulled into his parking space, went to the front security desk where he found a message waiting for him from Michael: "Max, I need to meet with you sometime this morning if you can work it into your schedule. Please let me know." Max tried to conceal a smile forcing its way across his broad face. He took a handkerchief from his pocket, wiped his face and slick, shiny, baldhead. It wasn't hot; the big guy just had a lot of mass that required a bigger cooling system than others.

The agent at the security desk saw Max displaying unusual giddiness, something out of character for the big man. He grabbed the phone at the security station and dialed Michael's secretary.

"Birdie, I just got the message from Michael that he wants to meet with me this morning. I'll come up to his office when it's convenient for him. I'm going to my office now, and you can let my secretary know what's suitable for him."

The front-desk officer took notice that when Max Left he had spring in his step and a slight whistle under his breath. He couldn't escape his history with Michael—rocky at first but personally grew from the conflict. The man was smart, always a step ahead of him. He possessed something he couldn't put his finger on; however, they had worked through their problems and were now good friends. Actually, because of Michael, he had met Birdie, and he would never forget that.

Chapter 9

The Assignment

When Max reached Michael's office, his dress still carried the early morning look. His starched shirt hadn't begun to wrinkle and his tight suit still showed a good, smooth press. Under normal conditions, his huge mass worked overtime to maintain its homeostatic balance, and stressful situations only increased the perspiration. Today he was nervous when he entered Michael's office. Birdie was sitting at her desk. Behind the scenes and unknown to him, certain employees used two sobriquets to describe his personality: the Enforcer, because of his rigid security standards, and the Sweater, due to excessive perspiration.

"Good morning, Birdie," said Max. Michael's secretary welcomed the attention Max had been showing her in recent weeks, but she was serious about her job and didn't want his attention to interfere with her work, especially here in the office. After all, she was secretary to the man who was married to the second most powerful person in Katharina Enterprises, and her office had the custodial care of some of the most confidential secrets the company had. However, she didn't resist tilting her head slightly so her glasses would slip down to the tip of her nose. It was then Max got an unspoken message as she looked over the top rims with the full force of her eyes accompanied by a smile. He knew the message of the smile. What she said and the way she spoke didn't match what she was thinking.

"Good morning, Max, I believe Mr. Pencovich is waiting to meet with you." Max saw Birdie light up Michael's intercom.

"Yes Birdie, what is it?"

"Mr. Pencovich, Max is here."

"Please send him in."

Max was taken to Birdie and had gone out of his way to arrange this meeting with Michael in his office rather than his own, hoping he would have a chance to visit with Birdie. That was not to be the case. Birdie rose from her seat at the desk, opened the door leading to Michael's office.

"Good morning, Max," said Michael. "Please be seated."

After Birdie closed the door and returned to her office, Max took a chair in front of Michael's desk that had no arms. It was a standing rule that those in the administration who dealt with Max always had a chair in their office without arms to accommodate the oversized man.

Once seated, Max was struck with the change in Michael's office. Its decor reflected a feminine influence with pictures and furniture complementing a theme. A large photo of his wife sat on his desk.

"Good morning, Michael!" No sooner had Max greeted Michael that he read the eyes of the man behind the desk: *they were serious, filled with intent. The man in front of him was always serious, but today he carried a special look of seriousness and he hoped it wasn't about him. This man could repeat verbatim anything he heard. His memory was incredible, and working with him in the past had been a rewarding experience as well as a challenge.*

Max was showing nervous tension with increased perspiration. Now he wished he had met with Michael in his own office where there would be a level playing field. He felt like he was starting a chess match against a champion player without the defense of the queen and a bishop.

"Max, I have on my desk here a folder with a report showing research on a man who was a member of the Nazi Iron Guard during the war. After you read the report, you will see that his name was Auton Lupel. When the communists seized power at the end of the war, Lupel, having access to confidential records, assumed a deceased person's identity. In all likelihood, the deceased party had no living close relatives, which made it convenient for the man to function at an unobtrusive level in the new communist regime.

"It is in the interests of Katharina Enterprises that we find Lupel's new identity. The man had associations with Colonel Funar, now on trial for war crimes. At this time, it cannot be determined whether Lupel resides in Romania, here in West Germany, or alternates between the two countries. Suspicion leads us to believe that he has low-level connections with the present government.

"Max, there's no one better than you to get to the bottom of this. Inside this folder are three photos of Lupel taken twenty years ago. Where we need to start is with an age-progression photo. We have a man in this country who was imprisoned in Romania during the war because of

Lupel, and this person could identify him if he is found. Take this folder, go through it, and get back to us with your insights on our options in finding this person. Today, I met with the chairman, and he has approved the necessary funds for our objectives in finding this man's whereabouts."

It became apparent to Michael that Max felt good about being made part of this mission. The big man relaxed, and after wiping his head and face down with a handkerchief, he stopped sweating. A project of this nature was his specialty, a challenge he'd gladly accept.

"Michael, this will be an interesting venture for me, and in view that the chairman is involved with this assignment, makes it all the more interesting. If history could be accurately written, cases of this nature where regime changes created stolen identities of deceased parties, books would be replete. I'll review this file and get back to you at which time a paradigm of action will be suggested. The age-progression photo with and without facial hair can be initiated right away."

After being handed the file, Max was light on his feet after closing Michael's office door. Birdie notice the difference. His aura left the message that things went well between the two. She could read Max like a book. Today, Max got two birds with one stone: he managed a dinner date with Birdie for the evening and was given an assignment in his area of expertise.

———————————

Near midnight, a large, dark vehicle pulled to the curbside of a seedy and neglected part of town. The area was atypical of Munich with dim lighting and bits of loose paper being pushed along on the roadway by a brisk, cold wind. A man seated in the rear seat used the outside overhead street lighting to check the time on his watch, then turned his attention to the driver.

"Driver, don't park the vehicle, keep it moving about until I return."

Passersby on the sidewalk saw a rear door open and the outline of a large man emerge with a hat pulled close to his ears dressed in dark clothes with a heavy outer coat. People nearby considered the big man, now standing alongside the upscale vehicle, to be out-of-place. He, nor the vehicle matched the neighborhood. Both were an anomaly in this part of town.

The driver pulled away leaving the big man casting his eyes in the direction of a nearby late-night café. A long, broad shadow from overhead lighting followed the figure as he made his way to the eatery still open to the public. Tonight he had an appointment with someone who lived in the shadows of justice, and the man was always known to be on time.

After reaching the front of a building that had survived the war, the man wondered why the person he made this appointment with had chosen this venue. The old building, with all the craftsmanship that went into it, now converted into a restaurant, showed the larger message of the country itself: West Germany was using its pillars of the past to build the future. His large hand pushed open the front door leaving the message that its hinges needed oil.

Standing in the open doorway, the big man felt he had a competitor vying for entry to the café. The rival was nature with its swishing, cold, outside air forcing itself in and around his big frame only to be morphed into a strong-scented smell of a soup kitchen.

Patrons at tables and those seated at an old fountain bar turned their heads in his direction. The imposing large figure, now looking about the dining room for the man he was to meet, saw faces staring where he stood with jaws paused. When eyes met his, they quickly looked away. From the moment the big stranger entered the neighborhood, he felt out-of-place and didn't belong. Now inside, he carried the same status. He continued scanning the large open dining room going from booth-to-booth. None of the patrons matched the description of the party meeting him.

"The person you're looking for is in my office in the back room," came the voice of someone nearby. The large imposing figure turned around. In front of him stood a person wearing a white apron wiping his hands with a clean towel.

"Come with me," said the man as he led the way through a side door. The big man had to turn sideways and dip his head slightly to navigate the door he went through. When the man reached where he was leading his guest, he stopped at a closed door on which was written: Office. After knocking on the door, someone on the inside pulled it open. Standing in front of them was a tall man dressed in informal clothes showing a thin face with a full head of dark, wavy hair. Neither said anything to each other until the man with a white apron left and closed the door.

"Hello, Max! It's been awhile."

Big Max extended his hand, saying, "Stellar, it's good to see you again. How have you been doing?"

"Conditions of the world make me as busy as ever, and it appears I'll be more so with the assignment you're giving me. Shall we get down to the matter of your project? I leave it with you to give me the finer details of your mission. As you well know, the group I belong to is an invisible entity that serves the interest of my people. Because the man you are trying to identify is a former Nazi, the mission comes under our purview, and for this reason, my organization is willing to help."

Stellar saw Max take from his briefcase a folder. "Needless to say, we are indebted to you for your assistance," responded Max. "Inside this folder is the information we have on a man by the name of Auton Lupel. He served as an officer under Colonel Funar, who is now on trial for infamous war crimes. It is believed that the man took on someone else's identity following the defeat of the Nazis in Romania. Included in this file are three pictures of Lupel taken over twenty years ago. Along with the original photos are several age-progression shots showing what he may look like today, with-and-without facial hair. We believe that he now holds a low-ranking position in the new government now ruling the country. These facts, along with additional information contained in this folder, I leave with you.

"Katharina Enterprises has the need to know this man's new identity. It is believed that he resides in Romania or West Germany and may alternate between the two countries."

Max took from the folder Lupel's photos, handed them to Stellar. "The man in these photos was one of Funar's central players, yet was low enough in rank to go unnoticed."

Stellar's eyes danced with intensity, pushing his memory back to the time when he served as a partisan fighter. With Lupel's photos in front of him, he looked at them one-after-the-other, saying in soliloquy, *"Your days are numbered."*

Interrupting Stellar's thoughts was a question from the big man: "I'm interested to know why you selected this venue as our meeting place?"

"With your pedantic nature, Max, I knew that question was coming sooner or later, and I'm glad you raised it. I asked you to come to this site for a special reason. Romania is opening its door for tourism as a form of foreign investment to aid in its failing economy. This is a slippery slope, and for a successful operation, we needed a network of people who know and understand the country and its people, people who carry foreign passports but understand the language, culture, and the lay of the land.

"The man who brought you to this office owns and operates this business and is a survivor of the Romanian Holocaust. He, along with others who hold West German passports use this site as a meeting place when called upon by my organization. With the country opening its doors to tourism to enhance foreign investment, we are able to take advantage by moving people who hold West German passports in and out of the country at will under the guise of tourism. They are willing and ready to be called upon at a moment's notice, and once inside the country their speech and cultural idioms put them under the radar of the watchful eyes of the government.

"Now let's get back to the reason of our meeting here

tonight. Our first step in this project will be to find the birthplace of Lupel and his living and deceased relatives. One major weakness in the country will serve to our advantage: bribery. It is rife in that country and money will loosen tongues and open doors like nothing else. Also, we are persuaded to be of help in your mission in finding this person because of the generosity of Katharina Enterprises…and for your information, I am being put on loan, apart from the assignment you're giving me about Lupel, to assist in a broad stealth operation under the sponsorship of your company."

"In that case," said Max, "you'll be serving double duty."

"Not to change the subject, Max, but there's global interest in the Funar war-crimes trial, and I understand that someone in a high position with Katharina Enterprises was responsible for providing the devastating photos and documents that forced this case into court."

"Word has a way of getting around," responded Max. "As much as I would like to discuss the matter, I am not at liberty to do so."

"That I understand," said Stellar. "After we find the identity of this person, what are your expectations in the final outcome of the matter?"

"I'm not privy to information at that level, though I'm sure I will have some input in the case."

Max's memory was churning inside. He knew of the smuggling operation in the Black Sea that carried the code word Operation Prince Henry, where ships at night picked up at sea Jews from Soviet Bloc countries destined for Israel, and that there would be an expansion of this program in the construction of a five-star resort center in the country of Romania. Apparently, Stellar was the key point man who would be part of the operation. Max interrupted Stellar.

"Stellar, when the Lupel matter is settled, will you be coordinating your stealth operations with a Marku Albescu?" A cold look of pallor came across the face of the man standing in front of Max. He said nothing, knowing he had stepped too far in the wrong direction.

"Max, both of us know more than what we should. I suggest we take a vow of silence and leave everything there."

"Those are words of wisdom," answered Max.

"Now, onto another matter," said Stellar. "After we discover the new identity of this person, you might consider allowing poetic justice to take its course. This man at one time was a Nazi and fought against the government now in power. With a much lower risk to everyone concerned, justice may be more quickly expedited by submitting our findings to the brutal dictator in power."

"That's a morbid thought," said Max.

"It may be an easy decision to make after all the evidence is in. However brutal that may be in its finality, it will never be as brutal as what he inflicted on others."

"Turning the man over to the dictator is a form of avengement justice, responded Max. "I lean heavily on the Idealism of Western jurisprudence."

Stellar chose not to retort Max's position knowing it was his penchant for protocol, going by the book, that was the driving influence in his life.

"Max, we can agree to disagree, but let's settle our

differences by remembering how things used to be by having a late-night dinner at the old-fashioned counter out there in the dining room.,"

"I'm game for that; Good memories and good food go together."

Max felt good after stepping outside the late-night café. Waiting for his driver gave pause to muse over first impressions of the area, a depressed and blighted part of town filled with people that carried the history of having lived under Nazism. With the success of his mission with Stellar and the food served at the old counter bar, gone were his first impressions of the area. People had made the difference—warm, honest, and hard-working people.

Max boarded his waiting vehicle making note that the weather had changed: the energy of strong-moving, cold winds no longer pushed against open doors, cracks around windows, and debris down roadways. It was a message that portended to a bigger picture of life. Another kind of weather-change was in the making, and Max would mark tonight being the moment when that change was put in motion for a man hiding from the blindfolded lady who held the sword and scale. When his driver pulled out onto the roadway, Max reflected on the old café's counter bar where he and Stellar ate and visited memories of the past, saying to himself, I just might return for another try at their menu, and if I do, I may even bring Birdie for an evening out.

Chapter 10

Clandestine Operations

In Belgrade, Yugoslavia, two men stood together in a line waiting to board a national airline with a scheduled flight to Bucharest. Both carried the looks of businessmen and could speak Serbo-Croatian as well as any native in the country. The leader of the two was taller showing a clean-shaven face with thick, coarse, dark hair. The shorter stood in contrast, and though dressed in a fanciful suit and sporting a slight beard, some might think him to be a professional bodybuilder with his bulging snug suit, tight lips, and balding head. Both men wore no rings, necklaces, or tattoos on their person. The only identity they carried was their DNA, fingerprints, and Yugoslavian passports. They had not been born in this country but had gained citizenship after fleeing the city of Bucharest during the Holocaust, escaping to Yugoslavia over the Carpathian Mountains and joining partisans resisting the invasion of the Germans. It was in those days living in the Serbian mountains among the partisans they learned how to perform as guerrillas, attacking German supply lines, munitions depots, and railway lines. The newly formed government after the war gave them special honor and awarded them citizenship. Today, they were honorary citizens of another order working under the radar defending the causes of Zionism and the state of Israel.

The taller of the two led the way as the line of passengers moved toward the loading gate where an official of the airline checked each ticket and passport holder. In a country deemed to be socialistic, the flight in front of them would be classless, and any deviation from this was reserved only for the bureaucrats in power.

On board the plane, both pushed their way through the crowded aisle of travelers negotiating bags and cases in overhead storage compartments. They always traveled light, and the cases they held contained everything for their mission. By the time their assigned seats were reached, the one in charge found his aisle seat occupied by a large, burly passenger already buckled-up and ready to go.

Using the widely spoken Serbo-Croatian language, he invaded the private space of the passenger. "Sir, I believe you're in my assigned seat."

A quick glance up at the man addressing him showed a disdainful expression. He appeared to be someone foreign to the country of Yugoslavia demonstrating rude characteristics of certain people in this region.

The man repeated the statement again, this time in German, and when no response was made, he used French. He remained unmoved by the demands put upon him. His friend standing behind him leaned to the side making his full presence visible. "Find another seat, this one has been assigned to us!"

The man's response revealed that the only thing he respected was power and strength. Eyes that once looked disdainful now yielded to the commands of the formidable now standing in front of him.

After settling in, the two on a mission practiced the

discipline learned when fighting alongside the partisans during the war: avoid mundane conversation that detracted from their assignment, and when in a crowd, practice the art of silence. Like two sentries standing guard, they entertained only silent musings.

The man in charge looked about the crowded aircraft. Everyone on board would shortly be landing in a country whose despotic leader held the grips of power with tens-of-thousands acting as his private police force. The country was a member of the Soviet Block but had softened its stance toward the West and was now eliciting foreign investment. He and his colleague on board were posing as entrepreneurial businessmen with special visas to get into the country to research investment options.

The man's musings turned to people on board the packed aircraft. Most showed Slavic-looking physical traits with broad round cranial and facial structures. He possessed a keen interest in the ethnic anthropological characteristics of people in Eastern Europe. He had studied anthropology at a young age at the University of Bucharest before being forced to flee over the Carpathian Mountains into Serbian where he found refuge among the partisans. It was in that land he learned warfare and how to survive on little. His interest in anthropology morphed over into his talent for painting and sketching. When not making surprise forays on German patrols, he spent his time sketching landscapes and portraits of male and female subjects. Painting faces required precise detail, and though today he did little painting or sketching, he couldn't resist profiling those who showed dominant ethnic facial features.

After the flight landed in Bucharest, passengers

deplaning were required to walk from the aircraft to the terminal building where they waited for the luggage stored in the belly of the plane. Because the two men on special assignment had only one piece of carry-on luggage each, they went directly to customs to be cleared. The level of inefficiency was showing everywhere, an indictment against a collectivistic government struggling to maintain its image in the Soviet Bloc on the surface, yet trying to promote limited Western capitalism.

The two well-dressed men were among the first passengers to arrive at customs. The one in charge was first to hand his passport to the attending officer. Outfitted with an official uniform that matched his dour-looking face, the government employee paid special attention to the man now standing in front of him. He rarely saw visitors to his country dressed in such an articulate manner. He opened the passport, looked at the photo, then at the man standing in front of him. Seeing that he had a special business visa, his eyes brightened and a smile softened the atmosphere.

"Your name, Sir?"

"The name is Stellar...Stellar Kraskov."

"Sir, our country needs entrepreneurs, and if you bring in or build a business here, I have relatives that would make good workers."

"I hope that becomes a reality," answered Stellar.

Out of the corner of the man's eye, he saw in the distance a casual-looking person waiting to take him and his colleague to a secret site for a planning session.

"Next please," said the customs officer. It was a repeat performance.

"Your name, Sir."

"Bram Katz," responded the man.

The officer took a serious second look at the man, saying to himself, he looked more like a bouncer than one who was an experienced businessperson.

Chapter 11

Pursuit of an Address

Bram had shed his business-suit guise and now blended in with the common folk on the streets of Bucharest, the place of his birth. He had lived here until the age of nineteen when he fled to escape the Holocaust, the time when he lost his mother and father along with many of his relatives. He and Stellar had the same story, and with nothing to go back to after the war, both made a life in their adopted land of Yugoslavia. However, being agents for a secret Zionist group, they were on call to go anywhere in the world to gain intelligence, and if necessary, act on the intelligence. Beyond the Lupel assignment, they were in this country on loan to Katharina Enterprises.

Bram had walked several blocks before coming to a large, stately building that bore architectural features of the early twentieth century. Cultured marble accentuated the front entrance with the design of an overreaching arch, above which was written with chiseled lettering: National Archives.

The man made his way up the stairs, pushed open one of the three heavy, solid-oak, double doors lining the entryway. Inside, a twenty-foot-wide corridor opened up from one end of the building to the other. On each side of the hallway were large open rooms, each showing a counter behind which state employees assisted the public. The building was cold and the ceilings seemed to reach upward forever. Footsteps heard in the large, hollow building reverberated to an almost echo sound.

Bram walked down the corridor until he came to a department that read: Vital Statistics. Inside, he saw four people seated at desks—all men.

After standing for what seemed like five minutes at the counter, one of the four men seated at a desk looked over where Bram stood, place the file he held in his hand down on the desk and rose to his feet. Age was telling on the old gentleman as he strode over where his customer stood.

"May I help you, Sir?"

"I hope you can, Sir. I'm doing genealogical research on a family tree and am in need of the birth and death records of a certain party that was born between 1915 and 1920."

"That may be a hard one to find, going back that far everything gets thin."

Bram lowered his voice. "Sir, if you're successful in this, I'll make it worth your while."

The man saw the customer take from his pocket two large leu Romanian notes. This is for your work, and if you succeed, there'll be a bonus."

The man said nothing. He reached for the gratuity, placed it in his pocket. "Here's a piece of paper. Give me the man's name and any information you may have on this party and check back in two days."

Bram was pleased how smoothly things went. He thanked the gentleman, was about to walk away when the man behind the counter asked, "Do you know if your party were in the military?"

"Yes, he was definitely in the military!"

"In that case," said the man behind the counter, "I might find some results for you. Anyway, check back day-after-tomorrow."

A rented vehicle had been on the roadway after leaving Bucharest for three hours with Bram at the wheel and Stellar alongside in the front seat. They had in their possession Auton Lupel's date and place of birth, and because there were more extensive records in his military file, they knew the military school he attended.

Much of their work in matters similar to this required intelligence gathering. Sometimes it became a puzzle and finding enough pieces to see the picture took time and effort. Today, they would be visiting Moreni, the village where he was born and where his parents lived, and in view that the population was not mobile, there was high probability they might find older people who knew the man and his family.

When approaching the town, Stellar said to Bram, "Our contact agent in Bucharest said that if we needed information after arriving in town, we should contact a certain party. No name was given, just an address. I suggest we go there after driving through Lupel's neighborhood."

"You know," said Bram, "people will be hesitant to respond because of the police state of this country."

"You're right about that, but with the dreadful economic conditions, generous gratuities often loosen lips."

After finding the neighborhood where the parents of Lupel had at one time lived, Bram drove to the address given him by the man at the official records department. Both were surprised to see that the site included a large amount of acreage with an old, large mansion.

"That was some home in its day," said Stellar. "It tells us that the Lupel family had clout and wealth at one time."

"Before we get a hotel," said Stellar, "let's talk to the party at the address our contact gave us. Information about the town from someone recommended could prove to be prudent."

They were surprised to find the address was less than a mile from Lupel's place and that the site itself was a Bed-and-Breakfast. The large, old home appeared to have two stories and a basement. Surrounding the building was spacious, manicured flower and rose gardens. Stellar, an artist, saw them as a scene he'd enjoy painting.

"The one in charge of finding Lupel was getting out of the vehicle, then turned and looked at Bram. "Do you want me to inquire about overnight lodging when I go in?"

"I'm game for that," replied Bram. "That will keep us under the radar until we're ready to ask questions."

Chapter 12

Bed and Breakfast

Bram remained in the vehicle while Stellar made his way to the front entrance of the large home that took in overnight travelers. The area was telling. It carried an upscale appearance with two and three storied homes and probably represented those who worked in higher levels of government.

From inside the vehicle, Bram saw Stellar walk up to the large, covered, front porch showing well-finished, park-like benches and an old-fashion doorbell that was activated by pulling a cord that reached into the house and jangled a manual bell.

After pulling the cord, someone opened the door wearing an apron and holding a dust cloth.

"May I help you, Sir?"

"I'm here to make an inquiry about overnight lodging."

"Do come in and have a seat in the office. I'll get the owner to help you."

He stepped inside and closed the door behind him. It was his practice when he went to a strange, unknown place, he never allowed people to have the advantage of coming upon him from behind. "I prefer to wait here, thank you." Standing inside the well-built, stately home gave him a sense of tradition, order, and discipline. He could tell the owner of this establishment ran a tight ship.

Stepping out from a side room was a tall lady dressed in a fashionable manner casting the image of a svelte model with smooth, light skin and long-flowing, wavy, dark hair.

"May I help you, Sir?"

"Good morning, Ma'am. My friend and I need two rooms for several nights. Can you accommodate us?"

"Yes, of course, please come into my office!"
Stellar followed her to a small side room used as an office. He could tell right away that the lady was nervous about dealing with strangers. Though he spoke Romanian as well as any, his Bucharest accent troubled her.

"Please fill out the form on the desk here and I'll show you the rooms we have available."

After completing the registration form, the guest asked the lady, "My colleague and I will be coming and going, and there may be people visiting us at night. Do you have a room with outside access?"

His question heightened her concerns over the state's intrusive secret police. Her eyes swept across the small office, then turning to him, said, "Please excuse me for a moment." Walking away, she scanned other rooms making sure nothing was left out that would show disloyalty to the state. Upon returning, she answered Stellar's question.

"Yes, we have one room that has access outside. Come with me and I'll show you both of the rooms I have available."

"We are not sure how long we'll be in the area, but I'm here on business, and there may be several people coming to see me at this site. Our staying here is contingent on these people coming and going. If this is acceptable, I'll give you a week's advance payment."

"That's very acceptable, and I hope your stay is satisfactory. Breakfast is served at eight o'clock every morning."

The guest took note that the front room had been made into a relaxing reading room with several bookcases well stocked with different genres. Coming at him from the rooms he had seen was a subtle theme of Russia: the pictures, books, and certain artwork all seemed to predate the twentieth century. Stellar reflected on his own family's oral and written history in Russia in the ninetieth century when they suffered in the pogroms causing them to migrate to Romania before the rise of Nazism.

The lady interrupted his thoughts. "This is the room that can be entered from the exterior. It has an outside light and sidewalk that leads to the front of the compound. The second room is across the hall which should make it convenient."

Her guest noticed while she was busy showing him the rooms, her stress seemed to have evaporated, but when he prepared to bring in his partner for the other room, her earlier condition returned. That was when she asked: "What brings you to this part of Romania?"

"We have come here to try to find a man who has become lost, lost to his family, and lost to his friends. His picture will be posted in public places for people to see with an address where we can be contacted."

"And what name does this person go by?"

Stellar took measures to fabricate his story. "The party that hired us for this project does not want his family's name out in the public. It is in his interests that the name remains anonymous. What the family wants to know is the name the person presently goes by and where he can be located. There will be a sizable reward for the person or persons who can supply this information."

The dialogue broke up when the lady heard someone ringing the front door. In the meantime, he inspected the room across the hall, and while the door was still open, Bram entered carrying their two cases.

"I assumed you booked the place, so I brought our luggage in. Do we have direct outside access?"

"Yes, it's the other room across the hall. You may want to check it out, and while you're in there take out a packet of Lupel's age-progression photos."

Stellar went to the room Bram was inspecting that had the outside entrance. The owner returned giving further instructions. "The showers and restrooms are located at the end of the hall. Towels are in a closet alongside the shower, and if there are any questions, please feel free to contact me."

"Madam, if you care to look at several age-progression photos of the man I made reference to earlier, they are included in this envelope. Copies of these will be posted at strategic places, and hopefully, good results will come in.

The lady opened the envelope and scanned four photos, two showing facial hair and two without, then read what was written at the bottom of each photo: *A reward is being offered to anyone who has information leading to the whereabouts of the man in this photo. Anyone providing information can do so at the following address:*

"As per our conversation," added Stellar, "the address

of your Bed-and-Breakfast will be added to the photos. If we are successful in this, you will be part of the reward."

"You sound generous!"

"The people who gave us this assignment are very generous."

"Sir, I don't believe half of what you told me."

"Are you saying the people who sent us here aren't generous?"

"No, what I'm saying is that the man you're looking for is not a lost soul that someone is longing over, and because you are so brazen and public about the man's photo, it tells me the person you are looking for has something to hide from the government now in power."

The lady saw Stellar glance at his colleague Bram, then back to her. "You are some clever person. Now I have a question to ask you: When did your family leave Russia for this country?"

The lady went blank. *Who were these people, she thought? What was she getting herself into with these two staying here? How did he know her family had their origins in Russia?*

"You're the clever one," responded the lady. "How did you know my family came from Russia?"

"I had an advantage. My family also migrated from Russia to Romania in the nineteenth century. It was your subtle cultural theme in furniture and decorations scattered about the rooms."

Stellar saw relief spread across the lady's face and a hand reaching toward him for a formal greeting, followed by the words: "Shalom...my name is Gavriella"

"And Shalom to you. I'm Stellar, and my colleague is

Bram."

The simple handshake gesture and Hebrew greeting caused an atmospheric pause to fill the room. They were in freefall. Lost were the walls of pretention. All three succumbed to the pain of common history—each had suffered the loss of family and friends in the greatest tragedy of modern times.

It was Bram who pumped oxygen back into the room. "Stellar and I were born in Bucharest and fled to Serbia in Yugoslavia, fought the Nazis with the mountain partisans. There we learned how to resist and fight back."

With eyes looking away into the dark world of yesteryears, the lady with smooth skin and flowing dark hair could be heard, saying, "You were very fortunate indeed, many didn't survive in the rugged mountains, and those that did tell of others that became a legend in their resistance."

Stellar, being the leader he was, pulled the conversation back on track. "History has its role in knowing where we've been, but for us to make a change for our people in the new world in front of us, we must appeal to our strengths and not our weaknesses. The Holocaust was a battle lost in the theater of conflict, but we will win the war."

"You two will have to pardon my show of emotional weakness. I have to watch every word I speak and every step I take to survive in this land. I don't display or speak of my Jewish identity. Anti-Semitism is rife, sometimes building to a breaking point, which you might accuse me of doing today. Shall we return to the seriousness of our conversation? I refer to the subject of the photos you gave me to examine. What is your real reason for trying to find this person in the photos?"

Stellar's assignment to this country extended beyond the search of Lupel's identity. He had been given the directive to set up an underground network whose efforts would be to organize a system for moving Jews to the coast where they would be taken out to sea and put on freighters whose destination was Israel. *This lady, thought Stellar, would be a perfect stealth operative working under the guise of running a Bed-and-Breakfast business. Agents could come and go without suspicion, but for now, Lupel was on the front burner.*

"Gavriella, What does the name Auton Lupel mean to you?"

Stellar and Bram saw history sweep across the face of the lady standing in front of them. To gain the courage to respond, she gave a deep sigh, slowly releasing her breath.
"The Lupel family was from this area and they were big in the military. They carried the pride of strong nationalism and joined the forces of the infamous Nazi Iron Guard. By the end of the war, the senior Lupels were deceased, and their only son disappeared without a trace leading some to believe that he was killed in the war. The family came into disrepute because of their alliance and support of the Iron Guard, and I need not remind you they were an extension of Hitler's Gestapo and SS. May I be impertinent and ask why you are seeking a man who is supposed to be dead?"

"I am not at liberty to tell you why we are seeking this person, but I will tell you that the man is alive and living with a stolen identity."

Stellar noted a veil of numbed hush settling over the

115

lady. Pain and fear registered on her face. He'd seen that look on faces of Holocaust victims.

"At the close of the war, it was rumored that he had died."

"Then there was no funeral, and a grave marker does not exist?"

"That is correct."

"Do you know what his specialty was?" asked Bram.

"It was well known that he supervised the intelligence gathering of partisan resistance."

Bingo thought Stellar! Now it was coming together. Lupel had files on partisan resistors and was using the identity of someone who had been executed or killed in a battle with no surviving relative.

Stellar looked at Bram, then at Gavriella. "A bombshell has just exploded. For the time being, we'll not make Lupel's photos public until we've shaken down something else. Lupel was in charge of all the records that were kept on partisan resistors. Had they been found at the end of the war, they would have been an indictment against him. It was in his interest to destroy or hide those records. However, it would serve him to keep them if he needed to switch to a different identity. Gavriella, why is it that you know what you do about the Lupel family?"

"In those days without radios and newspapers, everyone knew a lot about everybody, especially the Lupels who were in disrepute having joined forces with the Nazi Iron Guard."

"Did they own a home in this region?" asked Stellar. He already had the answers to some of the questions he posed, but he had the need to know what the average person knew.

"Yes, it was a large impressive upscale home with acreage surrounding it. It's not far from my place here."

"Do you know if Lupel has any relatives still living in the area?"

"I believe he has a second or third cousin who lives on the other side of the tracks, quite unremarkable, and who was an embarrassment to the family. He also has an uncle on his mother's side. This uncle was the closest living relative and was awarded ownership of the place after Lupel was declared to be deceased. The reason I know this is that in recent years, he's tried to sell the property and I was interested, but he kept refusing my offers. Actually, the old man always showed a kind and gentle nature and welcomed my inquiries. There were times when I thought he wanted to accept my offer, but something or someone seemed to be standing in the way. To show him what I wanted to do with his large home, I once brought him to my place and gave him a tour. I remember the exchange:

"Mr. Lunga, this is a business I started after my husband was killed. There are five guest rooms and we serve breakfast every morning. I would like to expand this operation at your place if we could agree on a price."

"Well, you know most of the old place has been made into apartments, and I derive some of my income from the renters living there. Where would I live if I sold my place?"

"You would be given life tenancy."

"I'd rather have life tenancy here at your place."

"That can be arranged!"

When discussing the old man, Stellar and Bram saw Gavriella's face flush with compassion. It stood in contrast to what they'd seen up to this point.

"That was the dialogue we had that day," said Gavriella.

Bram, the quiet one, took over the questioning. "It appears Lupel is smart. He allowed the property to fall into the hands of a family member after he was declared dead. Had it been sold prior to his disappearance, it would raise suspicions. We are now left with unanswered questions: does the uncle know his nephew is alive living under a false identity and does he make payment to his nephew for the home?"

There was a lull of quiet until Stellar spoke. "Well stated, Bram. This may be where we run up against the law to get what we need."

Stellar, looking at Gavriella, asked, "How many banks do you have here in this town?"

"The town has only one bank,"

"We need to connect with just one of the tellers," added Stellar, "and from that point on, we'll let human nature do its work."

"This sounds nefarious to me," said Gavriella.

"To make an omelet," remarked Stellar, "one has to break the egg. All we want is the name of a man who receives payments from the present owner of the Lupel property. This afternoon we'll make three stops: the bank, Lupel's cousin, and the old Lupel family home. We might even make the old man who inherited the mansion an offer."

"The two of you are not registered at my establishment," said Gavriella. "Do you wish to be anonymous or part of the patronage?"

Stellar looked at Bram, then back to Gavriella. "With our special visas, it is best we leave a paper trail.

It was one o'clock when two vehicles drove out of the Bed-and-Breakfast establishment with Stellar in one and Bram and Gavriella in the other. Ten minutes later Stellar was standing in line at the bank waiting to cash a large traveler's check with an envelope containing a gift with a note saying that if he wanted to earn extra money to meet him at the post office at five o'clock.

When dealing with government agencies, paying a gratuity upfront for services always expedited the process. Bribery was systemic and was exampled at the very top of government. In many cases, it carried over to the private sector. When Stellar reached the bank window, he saw an average-size man dressed in a well-used, dark suit. His tightly stretched skin behind thick-lens glasses gave the appearance he was as pure as the wind-driven snow.

"Good morning, Sir," said the teller. "How can I help you?"

"I would like to cash a traveler's check."

The teller's eyes followed his customer's dexterous penmanship in signing the check. Surprise was registered on the employee's face when he saw the amount.

"This is a sizable amount. Please wait until I return. I haven't enough in my tray to honor this payment."

Upon returning, the teller counted out the exact amount in front of his customer, then handing it to him, asked: "Is there anything else I can help you with, Sir?"

Stellar lowered his voice to almost a whisper. "I'm

leaving with you a gratuity in this envelope, and inside is a business offer you might be interested in."

The bank employee saw Stellar stuff in an envelope a sizable amount of cash, then handing it to him, said, "I'm looking forward to your response."

The man took the envelope and placed it under the counter where he stood. Stellar walked away, hearing the bank teller say to the next waiting customer, "I'll be right back, Sir." *On his way to his vehicle, Stellar thought that the egg he had just broken had a high potential of being made into an omelet. That would be determined today at the post office at five o'clock.*

Gavriella waited in her car for Bram to finish the transaction with Lupel's cousin. Meandering thoughts rushed through her. She had been challenged by her inclusion in what Stellar and Bram were about. Though it was an added expense, she had brought in help at her Bed-and-Breakfast business to be available to help in what was going down. Her strong-willed nature equipped her for what she was doing. It reminded her of younger years when she was married to a Romanian Goy, a good and decent man killed in the war, and who left her the property she now owns. During those times, both risked their lives helping Jews and destitute families. Today everything made her feel younger than her years. If this were a dream, she wished not to be awakened.

In the rearview mirror, she saw Bram coming up from behind the vehicle and after getting in the car, asked, "How'd it go?"

"He accepted the envelope, opened it, and looked at the photos. He seemed dazed, and without speaking, he closed the door—let's drive out to the old Lupel home and wait for Stellar. Today, we hit two soft spots, and if we come up dry we'll have to dig deeper and hit harder."

"You mean you'll have to break more eggs?"

"That's the idea!"

"Do you ever run out of eggs?" asked Gavriells.

"Not as long as there's a demand for omelets."

"Sometimes levity has its place in times of seriousness. Do you know what you're going to be served for breakfast this week?"

"I like omelets, especially for breakfast," said Bram.

Chapter 13

The Mansion

Stellar was waiting in his vehicle when Gavriella pulled into the driveway of the old Lupel family home. It had a commanding aristocratic aura. What used to be beautiful pasturelands behind the home now showed neglect and ruin. Scattered around were parked cars of tenants who rented a room or a combination of rooms. In its heyday, the old home was a diamond that glistened with pride; today, it bore the ugly marks of time and neglect.

Stellar got out of his car, walked over to Gavriella still seated in her vehicle with windows rolled down.

"Gavriella, it's time for your stage performance. You lead the way and Bram and I will be your supporting cast by pretending we are investors. If he still wishes to sell the place, tell him we'll have to inspect the rooms, especially the basement."

The three walked up the old, squeaky, wooden stairs, stood in front of a solid oak door that had withstood the ravages of sun, weather, and time. Gavriella used the door-knocker, waited, and was about to knock again when someone slowly opened the heavy door.

"Is that you, Mr. Lunga? This is Gavriella. You remember me, don't you?"

The door opened wide. "Oh, it's the beautiful lady who wants to buy my place," said a frail, gaunt-looking figure that carried the frame of strength and vigor of yesteryears. Gavriella jumped right into the matter of why they were at his front door.

"Mr. Lunga, are you still interested in selling your place?"

"I'm always interested in selling my place at the right price."

"I'm here with two investors, and if you don't mind we would like to look your place over and perhaps make you an offer that you can't refuse."

"That's acceptable to me. However, some of the rooms are occupied and the tenants are not at home. I live in an apartment here at the front on the first floor."

Standing alongside Gavriella was Bram with clipboard and pencil in hand. "We'd like to get an idea," said Gavriella, "of how much income is derived, and how many units are in the old home? Also, it is important for us to know if the changes that have been made conform to city code and if permits were obtained for the alterations?"

The old man's eyes turned downward searching for an answer that would best position him for negotiations. He attempted to evade a direct answer. "The monthly income in Romanian leu is equivalent to fifteen-hundred dollars on the international market. Regarding permits, everything was done with city approval."

The old man's attention was drawn to Bram taking notes on his clipboard when the note-taker asked, "How long has it been since there's been a pest inspection?"

The owner of the old mansion dryly introduced the humorous side of his nature. "The only pests I have here are the tenants I have to live near."

"May we now look around?" said Bram.

"Oh, of course," mumbled the owner.

"Let's start in the basement," requested Bram.

"The basement…you want to see the basement?"

"Yes, it's a vital part of the house!"

"Well…I don't know…I haven't been down there in quite a while, and I don't know what it looks like."

Stellar paid close attention to the old man's reservation about inspecting the basement. Running through his mind were the secrets that this old house would tell if it could talk. No telling what mysteries lay hidden and buried in the silence of hush. If Lupel had hidden his secrets somewhere about this home, he would know he had little time left to retrieve them with the old uncle now reaching the precipice of his mortality. *That alone, thought Stellar, would imply if something were buried it would never be found unless one was looking for it. The question remaining was: who inherits the property upon the old man's demise?*

Stellar's ruminations continued. Lupel and his family were avowed Nazis, committed to a cause with a religious fervor. People with this kind of inordinate ideological belief system sometimes took measures to be remembered in strange ways, like burying what they are for others to find in the next generation. Fanatical Nazis believed that Fascism would rise again.

Stellar pushed his meandering thoughts further. *What did this old man know? Was he also a closet Nazi?* How did he figure into Lupel's scheme? Gavriella offered to buy the place on several occasions, but he rejected the offer. How many other offers besides hers were rejected? It might be that he was listening to two voices: His own calling to rid himself of the burden of the place; the other being Lupel's from some dark chamber waiting for a revived world order of Nazism.

All three followed the old gentleman to the door that led to the basement. After opening the door, he turned facing his guests. "You'll have to go down by yourselves, I have trouble navigating stairs. At the bottom of the stairs is a door that opens to the basement. You'll find the wall light switch alongside the door."

Stellar and Bram had brought along flashlights and by the time they finished the inspection of the basement, they knew little more than when they started. It was a large room with odds-and-ends, nothing of significant interest. It was when they were preparing to return upstairs that Gavriella saw an antique china closet on one side of the large open room reaching all the way to the ceiling. The masterful smooth finish carried a certain style she'd seen on pieces that came out of old Russia. She took Bram's flashlight and walked over to examine its finer details. The two men followed. While Gavriella inspected details, Stellar saw a bigger picture. On the cement floor at the base of the large piece of furniture were scuff marks indicating it had been moved in-and-out from the wall. Going to the end of the cabinet, he pointed his light between the wall and china closet and saw something that compelled him to enlist Bram's help. Together, they pull one end of the cabinet away from the wall. Gavriella thought they were making it convenient for her to inspect the backside, but when she moved to where they were, she stood in awe at what they'd discovered: behind the beautiful, classical antique china closet was a heavy, metal-locked door. None spoke. Stellar pointed to the scuff marks on the floor.

The old man was waiting for them at the top of the stairs. "Let's inspect the attic before going through individual rooms," suggested Bram.

"That also involves stairs," said the owner, "so I'll let you navigate them without me."

When they returned from their attic inspection, they found the old man waiting. "Good news on the basement and attic," said Bram. "None of them showed signs of termites."

"As I said, the only pests I have in this house are the two-legged ones."

"Are there any children staying here," asked Stellar.

"No, and that's too bad. I like kids!"

"Then you don't make decisions on who your tenants are?" asked Gavriella.

"No, there's someone I've chosen to do this for me. He also collects the rents from the tenants and does my banking."

"And who might that be?"

"It's Sorin Dalca. He's been around for several years."

"Is he one of your tenants, and is he by himself?"

"There's a woman that comes to live with him from time to time. He says, 'she's his wife,' but I rather doubt it. Because he manages the business end of the place, I give him reduced rent for what he does."

Gavriella found the old man in a talkative mood. She took advantage with additional questions. "Mr. Lunga, do you have any living relatives?"

The three of them saw the old man give pause. Looking away, they could see his history flowing through his mind by the expressions showing on his face and in his eyes. With eyes, still fixed, sad, somber words rolled from his lips. "I have no living relatives…at least any that I can be proud of."

With a show of compassion in her eyes and on her face, Gavriella moved closer to the old man, placing her hand on his shoulder. "Mr. Lunga, if you don't sell your place, who will you give it to in your will?"

The old gentleman lifted his head with tears showing in his eyes. "I never had a daughter, only a son who died in the war. However, if I did have a daughter, I would wish that she would have turned out like you. You are one of the few people who has shown me kindness through the years. The person who inherits my property will be a person who will make it a better place, an honorable place, unlike its recent history. For me, it has been an albatross around my neck. It was a gift that came with a curse, a curse for over twenty years, and I blame no one but myself. I dealt with the devil, and he always wins. But God has given me the opportunity to reverse the curse in my death.

"Every time you came to see me, I wanted to sell you this property, but I couldn't because I had chosen the albatross. I have let other people direct my life instead of being in charge of myself, but I will shortly be free, free of the curse, free of the albatross, and those who follow me here at this place will change the curse into a blessing."

The old man's guests saw an abstract picture that didn't need explaining."

"Mr. Lunga, I am inviting you and these two

gentlemen with me to my flat for dinner tomorrow afternoon at six o'clock, and if you agree, I'll pick you up at five-thirty."

"I am honored by your invitation and will look forward to it."

The three visitors left the Lupel home without speaking. Their minds were swirling, not for the need of answers to questions but from the experience of seeing the power of the human conscience acting upon the will of man. Integrity was returning to the throne of an old man's life. It was four-thirty. Gavriella and Bram drove to her place and Stellar went to the post office.

Everything had moved so fast with such intensity at the Lupel home with Mr. Lunga that Stellar struggled shifting into his next assignment. He knew the bank closed at five and that if the teller chose to act on his proposition, he would be at the post office a little after five.

He arrived at five sharp. The post office had few customers and traffic was light. He had hardly entered the building when he saw the man coming through the front door. Stellar moved toward him and extended his hand.

"I'm Stellar!"

"Under the conditions we're meeting, just call me John. I'll not give you my name, though I know if you thought it important you could easily find that out."

"John, the less we know about each other, the better off both of us will be. First, let me say thank you for responding. For privacy, it would be best that we take a walk for the matter I want to discuss with you."

Both moved outside the building and commenced a slow stroll down the sidewalk.

"John, I'm in need of the name of one man. I'll preference my proposal to you by first asking a few questions. Does a Mr. Lunga do business at your bank, and if so, to what extent?"

"To my knowledge, the gentleman of which you speak has no account but does rent a safe-deposit box. However, he does come in from time-to-time to purchase a bank check. Sometimes he shows up with another person who attends to some of his business."

"Is that man's name Sorin Dalca?"

"That sounds right."

"How is it you know Mr. Lunga when he has no account at the bank?"

"Everyone knows Mr. Lunga. He has been an important figure in our community for many years."

"What I need is the name of the party that the bank check is made out to and any pertinent information associated with that name, such as a city, village, or region."

"If you want to go back and wait at the post office, I'll run over to the bank and see what we have on this party. We still have a couple of people working."

"I think that would be best for both of us. I'll be waiting at the post office."

Things were moving faster than Stellar thought they would. If only a name were given, it would be a start. He found the post office closed at five-thirty, so he stood nearby and hoped for the best. Fifteen minutes later, he saw John walking down the street toward where he stood. He held an envelope in his hand.

"Inside this envelope, I have listed the bank-check

purchases made this last year by the two gentlemen of whom you spoke earlier. They all have the name of the same payee, and there is no address, only the city."

Stellar took the envelope, opened it and read the name of the party: Teodor Popa. Stellar reached into his pocket, pulled out a sizable amount of Romanian Leu and handed it to the man called John. "It's been a pleasure doing business with you, John."

"Thank you, Sir!" Both parted ways. Stellar now had the name of the party believed to be Lupel. His project for big Max in this land was coming to a close. However, there was lingering mystery hanging over Lupel and the old mansion that could keep the big guy involved in this country.

Gavriella's Bed-and-Breakfast operation was on the home's bottom floor. It consisted of five bedrooms, a separate reading room, and a large dining room adjacent a small kitchen. She lived on the spacious, self-contained second floor. It was accessed by two sets of stairs, one from inside on the first floor, the other on the outside that led up to a large veranda overlooking a beautiful floral outlay of flowers and shrubs. Tonight she would have Stellar and Bram assist Mr. Lunga up the outside stairs. Help was brought in for the evening event.

Stellar and Bram were relaxing in chairs on the veranda outside Gavriella's flat when she drove up in her private driveway, got out of her car and assisted her elderly guest who carried something in his arms. They all met at the bottom of the stairs where Gavriella took what the old gentleman carried while Stellar and Bram helped him up the stairs.

After the dessert was served, everyone saw the old man stand, walk over, and take a violin from the case he had brought into the house. While holding the musical instrument in his hands, he looked at Gavriella. "This classical piece is dedicated to the beautiful lady seated at the table whose life has had tragedy in this land."

When he began to play, the three seated at the table were astounded at what was coming through in his performance. With the quality of music coming from the old gentleman, they wondered if he had been a professional musician. Gavriella noted Stellar had closed his eyes meditating on something of his history. Soon, tears appeared on his cheeks.

"Please favor us with another beautiful piece!" asked Stellar."

"Before I do another," said the old man, "I want to say that music is a language all to itself, a force of energy that communicates to people like none other. I brought this over tonight so my dear friend will have something to remember me by when I'm gone."

Again, they sat with tranquil amazement listening to his quality performance. This time it was Gavriella who was teary-eyed, and when the evening was over, Stellar helped the old man down the stairs, then carried to the car his case holding the violin.

He watched the taillights fade in the distance, turned to go to his room and retire for the evening when he heard a voice coming from the tall shrubbery near the driveway and a man walking toward him holding something in his hand.

"Sir, Yesterday someone from here delivered some photos to my place. I would like to talk to someone about them."

Lightning may have struck again, thought Stellar. "You've come to the right place. Come with me and I'll get the man."

"I don't want anyone to know I'm here."

"I understand. No one will see you."

Both entered the room that could be accessed from outside. Inside the well-lit room, Stellar saw a man having been beaten up in life, evidenced by his physical appearance and lack of self-esteem. "Wait here! I'll get the person you saw yesterday. You can have a seat if you like."

Stellar returned almost immediately with Bram following. Bram took charge. With a friendly tone in his voice and a hand extended, Bram introduced himself.

"Hi, my name is Bram. Are you comfortable talking in this room, or do you wish to go elsewhere?"

"It doesn't matter as long as I'm not recognized."

"By your being here, we must assume you know something about the party in the photo we gave you."

"That's correct. How much are you paying for the information I'm willing to give you?"

"That depends on what you can tell us. We need to know the name the man goes by today, where he works and lives, and any other pertinent facts about his activities. Without giving specifics, how much can you tell us?"

"I have not brought a lot of details, but what I have might be a pathway that could lead to a treasure trove. Mr. Lunga, the old man, has always treated me well throughout the years. I walked over to his place at night about six months ago to visit him, and when I arrived, I saw a vehicle that showed a government license plate. I wondered if Mr. Lunga was in some sort of trouble with the authorities and hid in the shrubbery. I noticed a light on in the basement and after waiting for an hour, two men emerged from the old house and walked to the vehicle parked in the driveway. The overhead light inside the vehicle clearly revealed the driver. The next day, I talked to Mr. Lunga about what I saw and was told that 'they just came to look around and left.' I wrote down the vehicle license plate and never gave it another thought until you gave me that photo yesterday—the one showing facial hair."

Stellar registered approval in the way Bram was handling the interrogation. He practiced fundamental principles eliciting information from a willing informant by making him feel respected, accepted, and that the information being given was important. At times, a good interrogator might use words and body language. Today it was both.

Bram continued: "We want you to know that we appreciate your response. You are insightful when you say this could lead to a treasure trove. However, we need more information. You said that you wrote down the license number. Do you still have the number?"

"I wouldn't be here tonight if I didn't," replied the man. "If I had the money, I could've paid people to do the footwork to get that information on the man who drove the government vehicle, and by doing so I would be in a better bargaining position with you. As you know, this government specializes in keeping records, and it's just a matter of getting at them."

Bram looked over at Stellar. "I'll ask my colleague to respond to what you are offering us."

"First, let's get acquainted on a first-name basis. I'm Stellar. Your name is...?"

"Nicu...I go by Nicu."

"Nicu, we'll make a deal with you. We'll give you in Romanian Leu the equivalent of one hundred dollars tonight, and if the license number of the vehicle you now have in your possession reveals the man's name and his place of employment in the government, we'll give you four times what you receive tonight."

Nicu became silent. Stellar and Bram saw a change come over their visitor. The man who had come to barter looked about the room showing reservation in giving his response to the offer. They were surprised in his statement.

"This won't hurt the old man, will it? I don't want him to get hurt because he's been a good friend to me over the years, even assisting me with finance. I'm a rejected distant cousin to the Lupel side of the family. Mr. Lunga's connection to the family came through his sister's marriage to the Lupel senior. When the Lupels rejected me, it was the old man who became my friend, and I could never forgive myself if he were offended because of my actions."

"Why don't you think on this for a few days?" said Stellar. "That'll help you know what you should do."

"I believe you're right. I'll get back to you later."

Stellar and Bram heard Gavriella's vehicle pull into the driveway soon after Nicu departed. Both went to bed early wishing for quiet among the guests on the bottom floor. *About to fall asleep, Stellar heard someone playing the violin. It was the same classical number that the old man played tonight that brought tears to his eyes. My, what a talented lady! The quality was superb, equal to that of the old man. Tears came to his eyes again. That piece of music was his sister's favorite, and she played it often in the concerts where she performed. Tonight, she was somewhere in an unmarked grave, a victim of the Romanian Holocaust.*

Chapter 14

The Inheritance

At eight o'clock Stellar and Bram joined other guests in the dining room for the buffet breakfast. After serving themselves at the buffet, they found an empty table and soon found Gavriella seated with them.

"I think I told one of you that this week's menu would include omelets. I see both of you selected omelets instead of the hot cereal."

Stellar added a bit of humor. "Things always have a better flavor and go down better when they're broken."

"Well, you've certainly done a lot of breaking since arriving here!"

Stellar looked at Gavriella with a serious stare. "You play the violin beautifully. Do we get charged extra for that?"

"For you, it comes with the nightly charge."

"How old were you when you took up the violin?"

"I was very young...six years of age."

Uncomfortable memory made its swath over Stellar. He removed himself and went back to the buffet without saying anything.

"Did I say something wrong?" asked Gavriella

"You said nothing wrong. His sister was a concert violinist and perished in the Holocaust. They were very close and he rarely ever goes to concerts where violinists have a prominent part."

"I guess we all have those special places of pain from those horrible years."

When Stellar returned to the table after having picked up a fresh cup of coffee at the buffet table, he sat looking at Gavriella whose eyes met his at the halfway point, that tiny strip of neutral ground where something electric happened between them. To avoid embarrassment, Stellar spoke.

"We want to thank you for everything you've done for us. It remains to be seen, but we think that most of our objectives have been achieved here. However, something lingering may require us to stay for another two or three days. In the meantime, we need to send a coded message out of the country, and this can only be done in Bucharest."

"Whether it's today or tomorrow," said Bram, "it should be a round-trip, same-day event."

"I agree on that," said Stellar.

Breaking into the conversation was one of her help coming to the table. "Madam, someone is in the office wishing to speak with you."

"You gentlemen will please excuse me."

Near her office desk stood a well-dressed man. When entering the room, eyes that carried a somber look turned toward her. "I have a highly personal and confidential message to you from attorney Vlad Serban."

She saw him take from his pocket the lawyer's card, and handing it to her, he continued his purpose of being at her establishment. "Mr. Serban is sorry to be the bearer of tragic news in the passing last night of Mr. Lunga, your dear friend. Because you are included as an heir in his estate, he would like to meet with you in his office this morning."

The messenger could tell the lady was left speechless. "I'm saddened by this news. It was expected, but it doesn't ease the pain of the loss of this special person."

"Please accept my condolences," responded the messenger.

"I don't understand. Why does the lawyer want to meet with me?"

"Because you are one of the heirs, Madam."

"Mr. Lunga never talked to me about this."

"He never talked to anybody about it."

"And you say the lawyer wants to see me this morning."

"That's correct."

"I'll be at his office at eleven."

When Gavriella returned to the dining room, she walked and looked like a zombie. "What happened to you in the office, you look like you've seen a ghost?" asked Bram.

"Mr. Lunga passed away last night." Her two guests gave respectful silence. "And he made me an heir. I'm to meet his lawyer this morning at eleven."

Hush was as cold as ice. They all expected the demise of the old man, even remembered him discussing it himself. It was the mystery the old house carried that sent intrigue through them. For the moment, the matter of going to Bucharest was put on hold.

"I need one of you to be with me in this meeting with the lawyer."

"Take Stellar with you. He's had legal training and will be a great help."

Gavriella looked at Stellar. "He may not be willing since there will be no eggs to break."

"I'll choose to go because before this thing is over there'll be lots of eggs to break. Besides, how can I refuse such a talented, beautiful lady."

"Is Stellar always this helpful to women in his ports of call?"

She watched Stellar stand and leave the room. It was the second time within the hour that Stellar left the table after something she'd spoken.

"It seems that I'm always saying something wrong," said Gavriella.

"Stellar is a complicated person. He's bright, intuitive, and wounded," responded Bram. The girl he was going to marry died alongside his sister according to eyewitnesses. You should feel honored. I have been with him for many years and I have never heard him address or refer to a woman being beautiful. The only beauty this man has seen in life has been his artwork and acts of justice for his people."

When Stellar and Gavriella arrived at the lawyer's office, they found his secretary seated at a desk and one client waiting to go in.

"Good morning, I'm Gavriella. Mr. Serban has requested that I meet with him this morning. Would you please tell him that I am here in the waiting room?"

They remained standing while she went into the office and returned. "You may go in now."

Rising to his feet from behind his desk to greet his

client, Gavriella and Stellar saw a plane, broad-faced, burly-looking man without glasses extending a hand of welcome.

"Please be seated," said the lawyer. "May I ask who your friend is?"

"This is Stellar, my legal adviser."

"Legal advice is always recommended, but the matters that we have in front of us are simple and don't really require legal help."

"I'm concerned more about Mr. Lunga than his legal affairs. Who's handling his memorial and burial rites, and how did this news reach you?"

"Those are very noble statements. I am the executor of Mr. Lunga's estate, and a Mr. Sorin Dalca acted on written instructions that if anything should happen to him he was to contact me and that we together would plan his final rites. He is presently being prepared for burial in three days at the site he chose and paid for prior to his demise. The public memorial service will be announced in the local paper two days prior to the internment.

"Now, the matter of his estate. Within the last month, Mr. Lunga revoked his old will and hired me to rewrite a new last will and testament. I will leave you a copy of his old will he gave me when he came in. It was a will drawn up by a law firm in Bucharest making the heir of his estate a trust, an ingenious way of hiding ownership from the public. He said. 'the original was with the firm that drew it up.' I have taken the time to stamp nullified on each page.

"This morning I have three packets with me that are yours for the keeping. One contains his final will just drawn up making you the sole heir of everything, another contains keys to the residence and safe-deposit box that you have instructions to act on, and the third packet is the copy of his old will. As your attorney, I will file a copy of his new will with the court.

"You are now the legal owner of Mr. Lunga's property. He told me when the will was drawn up that he was leaving his property to a wonderful lady who would make it beautiful and honorable."

The lawyer stood to his feet, handed her the three packets, saying, "Congratulations and best of luck!"

Before reaching her vehicle, Stellar heard Gavriella say, "Would you please drive me home. I'm numbed over this event, and I'm not sure I'm in complete control of myself."

"My advice to you is to secure what's behind the metal door in the basement before you do anything. You have replaced the intended heir, a person with a violent history, and though he may not come to this area, he has henchmen to do his work. Tonight, we need to move on this and remove what's behind that door in the basement. We have to factor in the unknowns. Some of the tenants may have loyalties to Lupel, and if that's the case, all the more reason to get on this as soon as possible."

"Why don't we act on it this afternoon instead of tonight?" responded Gavriella. "I'll bring in extra help at my place. With what's happening in my life, I'll have to keep permanent help."

"I'm sure none of the keys in your packet will unlock the metal door. We'll have to pick up special equipment to drill through the thick metal door. Bram is good at these things, so we'll let him take the lead in this."

Chapter 15

The Metal door

It was three o'clock when Stellar, Bram, and Gavriella arrived at the old Lupel place. Someone standing at a window on the upper floor was looking out at two men carrying boxes and a woman struggling with what appeared to be canvas bags.

"Don't look up," said Gavriella, "we have a pair of eyes peering down at us."

"This is something you'll have to get used to," remarked Stellar.

"I feel guilty and out of place coming here like this claiming ownership with keys in my pocket that open every door."

"Not every door!" said Stellar.

Gavriella found that the old man had everything organized and in place for the property handover. The keys were labeled and notes were everywhere describing what worked and didn't work. Even antique furniture and paintings carried a description of its age and origin.

Everyone became tense as they approached the door that led downstairs. Bram found the door unlocked, pushed it open, and led the way down a flight of stairs to a small anteroom containing a locked door that opened into the basement. The box of tools he carried was placed on the floor.

"Do we have the key for this door?"

Gavriella was prepared, handed him the key, adding, "Mr. Lunga's organizational skills were as keen as his music."

Bram took the key, opened the door, and switched on the light. Everyone followed. Stellar close the door and locked it from the inside. They quickly moved where the old china closet sat. Everything appeared to be as it was when they were last here.

Stellar and Bram slid the china closet far enough away from the wall to gain access to the heavy metal door. The covered-up door now exposed in full view intensified the mystery. Gavriella watched Bram and Stellar work like journeymen putting everything together to commence their drilling and metal cutting. Once underway, noise and flying sparks were horrendous for five minutes. Everything came to a sudden stop.

"We've broken through," said Bram. "Let's put everything away."

"Do we draw straws on who opens the door?" asked Stellar.

"I think Bram should, he did most of the work," responded Gavriella.

Bram pulled the door open. The dark mystery room released a rush of damp, musky air. Flashlights penetrated the room. At first glance, it appeared to be a large, walk-in closet with deep, pullout drawers on both sides. Boxes sat on the floor at the end of the room. "Is there a light in here?" someone asked.

One of the flashlights pointed to the ceiling showing a light bulb fixture with a string hanging down. A hand was seen reaching up and pulling the light switch. With a well-lighted room, nothing was seen in the open, just deep drawers on both sides and stacked boxes at the other end. The first drawer to be opened was the one next to the door. Three jaws dropped at what they saw. The drawer was full of jewelry: gold rings, rings holding diamonds, gold necklaces, and watches. Some showed inscriptions with Jewish names and others bearing the Star of David, all taken from Jews during the Holocaust. A blanket of eerie hush covered them. Silence paid respect to those who once wore what they saw.

Stellar saw the need for a photo record of what they came across. "Bram, get the camera we brought and get photos of the room and the contents in these drawers.

"This could be evidence that Lupel was a central figure in the commission of war crimes," said Stellar, "and there's no telling what's in this room. We can't spend time going through it now. Our energies must be spent boxing it up and removing it to a safe place until we can decide what to do. If we go to the authorities in this country, it will only end up in the accounts of government people and would bring attention to ourselves, which we don't want. For now, let's pack everything we can in those large canvas bags Gavriella brought in. Remember, don't spend time looking over the stuff as you pack!"

"May I offer a suggestion?" asked Gavriella. "The most unsuspecting place is here in this building. Why not divide everything up, leaving the valuables in the attic and the boxes in my basement?"

"Good suggestion! Let's go with that," said Stellar. "We'll put the canvas bags in the attic, and take the boxes

144

with us in the vehicle."

It was four o'clock when Gavriella watched Stellar and Bram take the last box from her car. She followed them to the basement.

"What do you think is in those boxes?" asked Gavriella.

"Well, let's open one," responded Bram. "We need a reward after all that heavy lifting."

"I'm not sure it will be a reward considering what we already know," said Stellar.

All the boxes were uniform in size with half of them taped close and half left unsealed. Most were identified by month and year, but all carried the word reading RESISTORS. Pulling the cardboard flaps back on one that sat on the top, they found it full of standard-size file folders. Upon close inspection, they saw that they were records of war detainees captured, killed, or executed. Many showed extensive personal histories. Personal items were in some.

"Lupel chose one of these file victims over twenty years ago to change his identity," said Stellar. The irony is that he had to become what he despised to escape punishment. There are probably scores of former Nazi war criminals living under the radar with stolen identities from these files."

"Why would he keep these files?" asked Gavriella.
Bram, the quiet one, offered an opinion the others thought plausible. "Most likely, Lupel sold identities to Nazis trying to hide from the new government coming to power, and

because of the volume of jewelry found in that room, they may have used stolen wealth from Jews as payment. In time, he became secure in his new role and allowed reason to yield to false invincibility."

"That's a logical conclusion," responded Gavriella. "Since there is nothing of monetary value in all these boxes, I think we should leave them here for now. I have one more requests to be made. The bank is still open and I have the deposit key to the safe deposit box. Do I have a volunteer to go with me?"

"We'll both go with you," said Stellar. "You may have a problem without documentation to show that you are the new owner. They may require a death certificate. I suggest you take Mr. Lunga's will and a briefcase to carry everything."

Chapter 16

The Safe-Deposit Box

When Stellar and Gavriella entered the bank, few customers were waiting in line to be assisted. The employee that had previous dealings with Stellar wasn't working the window but seated at a desk.

While waiting in line, Gavriella saw Stellar lean toward her, and expecting him to say something related to the matter of business at hand, she was left gripped with strange weakness: "Gavriella, may I call you Gav?"

Before answering, she heard the teller say, "Next please!" She felt confused. Voices were coming at her from two different worlds at the same time: one was business, the other carried signals that elicited strange feelings.

Stellar took her arm. "Let's go to the window."

"May I help you?" asked the teller.

"I would like to get into my safe deposit box!"

"And your box number is?"

"The number is one hundred thirty."

"And the name is?"

"It's under the name Gustav Lungar."

"Please accept my condolences in his passing. I read in the paper today of his scheduled memorial service. The teller went to a drawer and pulled out a book containing the names of those renting safe-deposit boxes, placed it on the counter and asked, "Your name please."

"My name is Gavriella, but the box is under the name of Mr. Lungar."

"It looks like Mr. Lungar just added your name to his box about a month ago. Do you have a key?"

"Yes, I have a key."

"Please go to the end of the counter, and I'll let you through the gate."

"May this gentleman go with me?"

"Yes, that will be fine."

Inside the inspection room, Gavriella lifted the lid off the box. Staring at them from inside the box were stacks of neatly bundled Romanian Leu notes. After removing the paper notes, they found underneath two sealed envelopes marked, "GAVRIELLA, my special friend."

Stellar watched Gavriella open the envelope and take out two hand-written pages. Immediately, her countenance changed. Soon, her jaw drop, her hand went up to cover her mouth, an unconscious gesture that sometimes people do when they see or hear an unexpected tragic event. Coming from her lips were the words that sealed her thoughts: "My…my…my…."

After reading the first page, she quickly went to the second, and when she finished both pages, she handed them to Stellar, then stared into space trying to collect herself.

Dear Gavriella,

As you now know, you are the sole heir of all my estate and I came to this decision based on several things. First, because of whom you are as a person, and second, I had the need to expunge guilt from my conscience of unknowingly protecting someone guilty of war crimes.

I made an unwritten agreement with my nephew to take title to the property with life tenancy and signed a will giving the title to a trust through which he could hide true ownership upon my demise. This was why I would not sell you the property, but things changed when a photo of a certain Colonel Funar, arrested for war crimes, appeared on front pages of newspapers. It was like a light thrown on my history here at this place. I remembered seeing that colonel on this property at night on several occasions after I had occupied this place under the agreement I made with my nephew.

There are secret hidden chambers in that old house, put there by his father. For twenty years, I lived in that house and never took the time to search them out. Sometimes, one learns to compartmentalize his life, and in doing so he can choose which compartment to live in. I lived there with the memory of my sister and her son carried the memory of his father. Both he and his father were devout and committed Nazis. My nephew presently works for the communist government in the Department of Foreign Service by delivering vital information as a courier to this country's embassies in Europe. He goes by the name of Teodor Popa. I hope you will not see me as a bad person, and this is not intended to be a deathbed confession. Perhaps my story of turning on a family member for

what's right will somehow touch people that need to hear it, people who need to have the courage to stand for what is right.
Your friend,

A. Lunga

When Stellar finished reading the second page, he looked up at Gavriella who now had her face covered with the palms of her hands weeping. She felt his hand on her shoulder, then heard him say, "You are a strong person, and I admire your strength."

She turned and faced him while wiping her eyes with a tissue. "Thank you. Those are kind words." Then showing a slight smile, added, "You may call me Gav, if you like."

"I would like," said Stellar, "but only when others aren't around. We better put the other envelope with everything else in the briefcase and get out of here before they close the bank on us."

On their return from the bank, Bram drove while Gavriella and Stellar looked over the second envelope found in the safe-deposit box. It was a one-page, handwritten document by Mr. Lunga:

Gavriella,

Below are my wishes for the distribution of the cash contained in my safe-deposit box, the total amount being approximately ten thousand dollars in Romanian Leu:

1. Three thousand paid to Nicu over the period of

150

thirty months.

2. One thousand to my community church.
3. The balance to be spent at your discretion on needy people in the community as needs arise.

Chapter 17

The Rule of Faith

The next morning Gavriella walked Stellar and Bram to their vehicle for their round-trip drive to Bucharest. Their mission in this country for big Max was almost closed. The only thing left to do was to send the details in code form. However, their work in this land in moving Jews to Israel had just begun.

"We'll be back tonight for overnight lodging," said Stellar. "We don't want to miss the funeral tomorrow. Bram got behind the wheel while Stellar and Gavriella stood and talked.

"I like being around you Gav."

"The feeling is mutual."

"I don't have a beautiful woman in every port you know."

"I know, I was just making conversation."

"But I found one in this port."

"You know how to embarrass me, don't you?"

Bram drove out of the parking lot as Stellar waived bye to a woman that had opened a floodgate that had been locked inside him for years. Each experienced special energy from the other. Gavriella had dared to yield her feelings to a line she said she would never cross. Something about Stellar had swayed her emotions and was being pulled away from her moorings. This had never happened to her since the passing of her husband years ago. Rather than yield to the temptation of what she felt surging inside, the man would have to know what was more important to her than anyone or anything.

It was six o'clock when Bram pulled into Gavriella's driveway. Other cars filled the parking lot, an indication they were fully booked for the night. They saw Nicu leaving the compound and Gavriella standing on the front porch.

When they neared the porch, Stellar was first to speak.

"Did Nicu come to see us?"

"Yes, he did, but I talked to him about certain matters in helping me at the old Lupel home. He'll be a watchman at night monitoring the activities inside as well as the outside compound."

"That's a wise decision," said Stellar. "There's no telling what could happen there when Lupel finds out the property has gone to you."

"How did things go for you in Bucharest?"

"We accomplish what we intended?"

"Have you two had dinner?"

"Yes, we ate about an hour ago," said Bram.

"Stellar, can you come up to my flat before you go to bed tonight? I need to talk to you about a matter."

"Sure, give me ten minutes and I'll be there."

Stellar thought Gavriella had turned cold, something atypical of her recent display of warmth and friendliness. She had the air of entering a serious business arrangement with intense negotiations in play.

Stellar walked up the outside stairs leading to her flat admiring the beautiful flower garden below. It showed order, symmetry, and design. He admired the beauty of ordered nature. It served as a salve for the healing of the ugliness of man. Perhaps this was why he was drawn to this lady he was meeting tonight—she carried an aura of goodness with purpose and design—like her flower garden that gave inspiration to others. After reaching the top of the stairs, he was surprised to see Gavriella sitting outside in one of the veranda chairs. The orangey atmospheric prism of sunset gave a soft touch to the evening's ambiance. She was a beautiful woman. He had been around beautiful women before, but this person was different. The woman he was taken with interrupted his meanderings.

"I'd like to go inside where there is greater privacy." She opened the door and allowed him to go in first, then followed. After being seated, she opened the conversation with the purpose of meeting with him at her place.

"Stellar, there are some things that you should know about me in view that we have come to know each other better. I am a widow, married for two years before my husband was killed. He was not Jewish but a devout Christian believer who provided sanctuaries and hiding places for Jews. My family and I were among those he saved. At our hiding place, he would come weekly with food provisions, and one day I asked him, 'why do you help our people?' His response was, 'Jesus was a Jew and was the Wounded-One in Isaiah fifty-three, and would return to rule the world from Jerusalem.' I thought the man to be honorable, noble, a righteous Gentile, but of course, I believed nothing he said. I had been taught otherwise all my life. But that night when I went to bed I was awakened in the middle of the night, and standing beside me was someone in white whose feet and hands showed deep wounds. I lay awake the rest of the night trembling, knowing an intelligent being had visited me from another dimension. I remembered the righteous Gentile telling me about the man of Isaiah fifty-three. I did something I had never done before—I read the prophet Isaiah for the first time in my life, and when I came to chapter fifty-three, I read it over and over, then came to believe that the historical Jesus who was rejected by our people was the Messiah and the Passover Lamb fulfillment. I married the righteous Gentile who died two years later along with Jews he was helping.

"Stellar, I'm a person without a country in more than one way. The land I live in has rejected me being Jewish, and the people among whom I belong reject me for having converted, so I have become a lone island afloat in the open sea.

"This is my story, and I hope after tonight we'll still be friends." Gavriella paused, then gave the punch line of the evening. "Because of what I am and what I believe, I can only be your friend, and I hope after tonight our differences will not abridge that friendship. Would you care to stay for tea?"

She saw Stellar in deep thought. He was an intelligence analyst who examined and acted on collected information totally outside the touchy-feely domain, but the lady's statement of faith required a response.

Stellar was good at framing responses. He had passed the bar exam in Belgrade after the war and excelled in the art of polemics within the legal system, but when a secret Zionist organization learned of his partisan resistance during the war, they asked him to join their group. He could speak five languages, go anywhere in Europe and the Middle East on assignments and was a highly regarded intelligence officer. However, for the first time emotion interfered with his adept polemical role.

"Of course I'd like to stay and have tea with my special friend."

She smiled. "I'll put on the hot water."

"Let me help," responded Stellar

Throughout the evening, the mental images she had painted for him kept fading in-and-out like a phantasmagoric torment. She had built a fortress with a high wall with only one entrance to gain access to her life. Yet, it did nothing but present a challenge. To Stellar, she was a living expression of the idyllic scene of her postcard flower garden.

Gavriella awoke to the sound of her musical alarm. Rushing through her were the day's activities, but hanging heavily in the background was the memory of her walk to the line she'd drawn in the sand with Stellar. She had imposed a sudden stop, and the extent of their friendship would be tested today.

Gavriella dressed, proceeded to check in on the kitchen help who was now preparing the morning breakfast for her patrons and was surprised to see Stellar and Bram seated at one of the tables drinking coffee. Upon her entry, Stellar stood to his feet. "Are we honored to have the lady of the house sit with us?"

Stellar was not only a top intelligence officer, thought

Gavriella, he was also a diplomat. His adroit use of pretension was showing, and Gavriella knew he was smarting from what she told him last evening.

"Are you gentlemen up to going with me to Mr. Lunga's memorial gravesite service this morning?"

Stellar was still standing when he answered. "Only if you wish us to do so."

The carefully framed statement carried legalese and intent. It was all about her line in the sand.

"Yes, I would be honored to have you with me."

"In that case, please be seated and I'll get you a cup of coffee."

The morning was balmy outside. Wind gusts ruffled the loose, outer clothing worn by the party of three now walking toward the vehicle that would carry them to the city cemetery for Mr. Lunga's memorial service. Bram sat at the driver's wheel, Stellar assisted Gavriella into the rear seat carrying a violin case. Neither spoke, yet voices were loud and clear inside the two now seated behind the driver. Though the solemnity of a funeral justified the dearth of verbiage, both wondered if another kind of passing was underway: he, to what he was before he met the lady who turned his world upside down, and she, to her reclusive state of helping Jews in a land with a history of pain.

Trees that lined the narrow roadway leading to the gravesite showed that autumn was in the air with tumbling colorful leaves falling to the ground leaving branches bare—another kind of death, a metaphoric symbol of the larger picture of human life. The day seemed to carry the theme of mortality.

The car came to a stop behind the hearse that brought

the late Mr. Lunga to his final resting place. Bram got out of the vehicle. Stellar and Gavriella sat looking out the window across the soft, green turf dotted with headstones. *Stellar couldn't escape what rushed at him when his eyes caught the scene of the canopy-covered, open grave over which rested a closed casket containing the cold, lifeless form of Mr. Lunga. Funeral rites were closures for the living, something that eluded him with his family that lay buried in a mass, unmarked grave somewhere unknown to him, an open wound that never healed.*

Gavriella saw pain in his eyes. Compassion compelled her to reach over and placed her soft hand on his. "I know this is hard for you, Stellar."

His heart trembled. It was a hand reaching beyond her fortress wall, a touch that weakened him, leaving a feeling of euphoria. But it was short-lived with Bram knocking on the window.

"They're waiting for you to begin the program."

Stellar wished Gavriella's hand still held his as they walked together where vacant chairs awaited them alongside the bier that held the closed casket, now covered with floral arrangements ordered by Gavriella. Everything was highly organized and attendance was above expectation. Soon, they were joined by Nicu, one of the beneficiaries of the Lunga Estate who now worked for the new owner of the Lupel mansion. Though not related to the old man's side of the family, he came to pay his respects to a dear friend. After the clergyman finished his homely, he requested closure with Gavriella's performance on the violin. For ten minutes, the lady who had played the violin from her youth captivated the crowd under the canopy with

Mr. Lunga's favorite religious and classical pieces. Hearts not moved by the message of the pastor found their eyes moistened by the persuasion of music.

Stellar walked back to their vehicle alongside Gavriella carrying her violin case, glancing from time-to-time at the tombstones jutting up from the ground. The lady beside him noted the need he had to read headstones.

Taking the musical case from Stellar, she handed it to Bram, saying, "Bram, take this and wait for us. I want to show Stellar the cemetery."

On their stroll, Stellar verbalized his meditations when first arriving. "Cemeteries carry closure for the living. They are like libraries with records, records with names, dates, and expressions of written feeling about the departed. The headstones are always there year-after-year without variability of message because everything is written in stone.

"Cemeteries are as much for the living as for the dead. They provide closure, a form of emotional healing for the living. But across this country, there are Jews who have family members, friends, and acquaintances buried in mass, unmarked graves without markers, without a site to place a flower in remembrance of life. The living needs closure for their dead and cemeteries with headstones serve that purpose...and I have neither the cemetery to visit nor a headstone at which to place a flower."

Gavriella was weeping inside for Stellar. Neither looked at each other—both had stepped into a dimension not requiring the need of sight. A lady who carried herself as a pillar of strength reached across her line in the sand and took his hand for the second time. But unlike her earlier touch inside the vehicle that carried only an expression of sympathy, she now felt the energy of a different kind, the kind that is normal when two people are attracted to each other. If he were a believer in Yeshua, she would open the floodgates of her feelings, but one of faith must not be unequally yoked. While still holding his hand, Stellar contributed to her inner struggle.

"It's strange," said Stellar, "that I have come today to the place of the dead to find life, and by that I mean life that comes to me from what and who you are."

Gavriella, for the first time on their walk, looked at the man whose hand she still held. "Stellar, because of my faith in Yeshua, I have to reinforce the line I have drawn in the sand, a line I cannot cross."

Stellar felt the soft hand he'd welcomed slowly drop from his, and after a long pause, she heard him say, "I hope you will always be my friend?"

Another long wait ensued. "Stellar, I'll be your friend till the day I draw my last breath."

Chapter 18

The Trial

In Munich and throughout Europe, major news agencies were carrying the lead story of Colonel Funar's upcoming war-criminal trial. Three judges had been appointed to investigate the evidence presented by the prosecution and upon a thorough examination made the determination that a criminal trial should go forward. When the trial reached the stage where the prosecution would present its evidentiary findings and its witnesses, Eugen, the Nazi Hunter, arranged for Michael to meet him at the courthouse where he would be given an official pass to sit in as an observer. Not wanting to be dropped off in front of the courthouse, he instructed his driver to let him out a block away. Eugen was waiting for him at the steps of the courthouse.

"Glad you could make it, Michael. Today, the judge will guide the prosecutor through the prosecutorial stage, and if time permits, allow the witnessing process to begin. If everything goes as I expect, the man will leave the courtroom, unlike the way he enters."

They parted ways, Eugen to a side room with the prosecutorial team and Michael to the section inside the courtroom that accommodated observers and reporters. Michael was one of the first to be seated in the visitors' section, and when a young man about the age of thirty passed in front of him, he stopped momentarily, stared at Michael as if he had seen a ghost, and was about to say something, then walked on with a void look on his face.

Seated around the man responsible for the war-crimes trial now underway were reporters and writers from major newspapers of Europe. Chatter among the group abruptly stopped and silence fell across the press corps when two guards were seen leading the defendant into the courtroom. The man carried an arrogant, defiant look. It reminded Michael of the sneer captured in one of his photos taken alongside massacred Jews. *How strange, Michael thought, that the man aroused in him no feelings of animosity and revenge. The burden of justice now rested upon the state.*

Attention shifted to the three presiding judges being announced in a formal manner by the court recorder. Everyone stood to their feet as the magistrates entered from their adjoining chamber. The lead judge, shrouded with the German judicial customary red robe, was tall and thin with thick glasses and a graying full head of hair. Those familiar with the inner workings of the legal system knew the judges had already done their judicial review of the evidence, and by the countenance showing on their faces, some might think a verdict had already been decided. But for the sake of equity, justice, and compliance with the law everyone would be on an equal legal footing.

Reporters and journalists identified themselves by activity seen in their note-taking. Photos were prohibited, and the young man who earlier gave Michael an intense stare was part of the pack.

Charges of war crimes were read to the court and after lengthy legal innuendo and formalities, the judge declared a thirty-minute recess. At this point, nothing earth-shattering in the way of evidence or witnesses' testimonials had been presented by the prosecutor.

Michael stood, and before he could leave the observers' room, the young man who previously gave him an engaged stare came up to him.

"Sir, pardon my indulgence in the use of your time, but I have the strange sensation I have seen you before."

"We all have lookalikes," said Michael, "and I hope my lookalike in your experience was a pleasant one."

Michael spoke with a heavy Romania accent, and when the stranger heard Michael speak, it mesmerized the man. A vortex of swirling memories flowed through the man's mind, experiences he had as a Jewish child in Romania fleeing Nazi soldiers in search of Jews in hiding.

"Sir, it wasn't your lookalike I saw, but it was you! I will never forget what I saw that day and what the tall blond man with blue eyes did for my people. It was in the mountains where we had fled, and the SS soldiers were rounding up fleeing Jews, and I was but a child when it all happened."

The man was remembering his experience in the mountains of Romania when he was but nine years of age. Michael remembered everything—like it was yesterday.

"So you were one of the two lads we found that day hiding in the brush?" said Michael.

"Yes, and because of you, we managed to survive those terrible times."

Those were the days when Michael was the lone figure in the dark shadows of a dense forest in the mountains watching two young boys running down a dusty, well-used mountain pathway, veering off to one side of the trail and crawling under a large clump of thick bramble. He knew the cause of their flight. Hidden under the thicket of scratchy bramble, he could almost hear their hearts pounding and lungs gasping for air. Wrapped in the cloak of nature, they were out of visual sight of those coming down the dust-laden trail. Raw nature had become their friend and protector. Neither spoke. Communication was the silent script written on their faces, punctuated by fear. The Soft ground underneath prickly brush was the gift of comfort after the struggle of forcing their small, thin, cylindrical bodies into hiding. They were hidden from Nazi soldiers on patrol.

Lying side-by-side in quiet, fearful torment, the two Jewish lads who had escaped the SS troops on patrol heard nothing but each other's heavy breathing. Gentle sounds of wind rustling the leaves in trees and birds giving intermittent overhead chirpings went unheard. Time froze for the two in hiding. Though concealed in nature's cocoon, it offered no protection from what they heard coming down the pathway—the noise of soldiers yelling and women and children shrieking. The two boys took hold of each other's hand. They had known each other all their lives, but today, there was a special bonding that went beyond companionship. The cauldron of fear forced to the surface a heightened human experience, a bridge formed between them over which the two would cross throughout their lifetimes, a bonding friendship made forever.

Closer and closer came the sounds of soldiers yelling and women and children weeping. The two young lads hidden on the roadside couldn't resist forcing open a small crack in the wall of foliage. They saw mothers, fathers, and children terrorized, threatened, and pushed along like herded animals. Under the cover of nature, they watched a human tragedy unfold in front of their eyes: the strong and brutal terrorizing the weak and innocent. Legs and feet that passed in front of their eyes struggled to keep bodies from falling. It was their walk of death. Then something happened. A blanket of eerie quietness settled over the scene with the sound of a loud thud accompanied with an agonizing groan. A soldier clutching his rifle fell nearby, then another thud broke the atmosphere with the collapse of a second soldier across the roadway, both hit in the chest by lethal whizzing deadly arrows. The two soldiers left standing had no immediate response. They were hardened men trained in the use of modern warfare, conditioned to the sound of gunfire, not the invisible, silent strokes of lethal arrows. Taken by surprise in the silence of death, they were helpless when two men with bayonets came from the brush.

In a moment's time, four soldiers who had brutalized the innocent lay dead. Victims being marched off to death camps now huddled together in silence. They looked on in fright not knowing their fate.

Fears soon quelled when one of the men said to the group, "Take all valuables off these bodies and remove them from the roadway. All of you will have to move quickly to a more secure place here in the mountains, and be sure that others in the area are informed."

Women and children watched the men remove the bodies of their Nazi tormentors out of sight, and turning to thank their rescuers, they found them gone—as if they had vanished.

The two boys remained in hiding under the bramble. Quietness returned, but the event left them in catatonic numbness. There was no energy, nor will to move. Then came a voice breaking the calm quietness.

"You two under the brush can come out now. You have nothing to fear."

The two lads looked at each other with faces showing fear. They said nothing in their struggle to free themselves from under the prickly bush, and while still on their hands and knees, another fearful sight showed itself: in front of their eyes stood two boots—German boots! Eyes struck with fear followed the outline of the figure in front of them from boots upward. A young friendly looking man with blond hair, deep blue eyes, and a heavy beard reached down and pulled both of them to an upright standing position. He carried a sidearm and held a rifle equipped with a bayonet dripping with blood.

"So you saw everything that went on?"

The boy who chose to speak, said, "Yes, Sir, we saw everything."

"Where are your parents?"

"They're up in the mountains at a hidden campsite."

"They were not among the group that just left here?"

"No, Sir."

"You must tell everyone to move farther into the mountains. Someone has informed the SS of the campsites in this region, and you are not safe."

The boys saw the blond man reach into his pocket and pull out several hundred Romanian Lei notes. After dividing the amount between the two, he gave instructions for its use. "You are to give this to your families. It will help them stay out of reach of those seeking to do you hurt."

Before the boys left to find their families, they saw two other men join the tall blond man, one holding a large bow with a quiver full of arrows.

Inside the courtroom in Munich, the young reporter was left looking at the tall blond figure standing in front of him. He and Michael had allowed memory to walk through a dark day in history. He would never forget those steely, deep-blue eyes he saw in the mountains when he and others were rescued from the SS troops.

"Sir, I'm a firsthand witness to the legend you became, and when this trial is over your notoriety will be global."

"What is your name?" asked Michael.

"The name is Simeon."

"Simeon, notoriety is not in my interest, only justice."

"But our people need to have access to the records of individuals like you as examples of heroism, someone to look up to, someone who demonstrated valor and sacrifice for our people."

"Simeon, our Sacred Books that carry the voices of the prophets should be our heroes, and it is David's offspring, the Branch, to whom we should look as an example of heroism?"

"Sir, I share your larger picture of Zionism and its place in the modern world. I am a reporter and writer and would be pleased if I could arrange an interview at a convenient time."

"I'm sure that can be arranged, providing I remain an

anonymous figure. The name is Pencovich, and I can be contacted at Katharina Enterprises."

"Thank you, Sir, but you need not tell me your name, most survivors of those evil days in Romania know your name as a household word, and I will be contacting you."

Michael returned and found his seat in the visitors' section. He noted that the prosecutor had set up a large screen and slide projector for his evidentiary presentation. For the defendant, it was a repeat performance. When upon re-entering alongside two guards, he carried the same arrogant, defiant sneer, followed by the entry of the three judges. The defendant was being tried for war crimes based on the evidence Michael had taken from Funar's home during the war, and it all lay dormant until the man's identity was discovered this year. The prosecutor and Eugen had transferred damning photos and documents onto slides to give visual impact to the news media. The judges themselves would have already reviewed firsthand the original pieces of incriminating evidence. Cold silence settled throughout the courtroom as the prosecutor narrated the slides showing the defendant standing among the dead. The press sat on the edge of their seats. Michael paid special attention to Colonel Funar. His defiant look remained fixed on his face slide-after-slide, while others inside the courtroom looked away to avoid the carnage of the dead. Even reporters seated around him, those who were paid to report on such events, closed their eyes to what was being shown.

The court scene showing the defendant's arrogance

pushed Michael into the throes of personal history. *Did he do Western society a favor by disposing of others like Colonel Funar? Just when he thought he was in control of his past, voices of justice were calling from dark shadows.* But Michael's melancholy would be short-lived.

Following the pictorial slide presentation that included Colonel Funar himself among massacred Jews, documents appeared on the screen showing written orders signed by the defendant himself requiring the wholesale slaughter of villages. Stupefaction gripped the courtroom. The last bombshell came from two witnesses who had experienced firsthand Funar's selection of those who would die and those who would go to labor camps. The denied and hidden evils of genocide in the country of Romania were being made public for the world to see. It was a trial showing how those guilty of war crimes could slip into dark shadows and hide from the arm of justice.

Michael kept his eyes on the defendant, and by the time the two witnesses had finished giving their personal testimonials of Funar's atrocities, the defendant's countenance was showing stone-face fear. He also noticed the media seated around him were treating the trial as an event of the decade with some having brought stenographers for an exact transcription of the trial. Even news people that were not admitted to the courtroom were gathering on the courthouse steps to hear the judges' verdict.

The prosecution rested its case. The leading judge looked across the courtroom now covered with a cold blanket of somber numbness. Every eye was on the leading magistrate.

"The court has determined that there is insufficient time on today's calendar to hear the defense's arguments. Therefore, the court orders a resumption of the trial tomorrow morning at which time the counsel for the defense will make his arguments. Be advised that those in attendance inside this courtroom are to remain seated until the defendant is removed."

Everyone's eyes turned from the judge and fastened onto the defendant being lifted from his chair as if he were dead weight. The proud zesty sneer and arrogant image he carried into the courtroom had morphed into a cold, empty image of granite. He had succumbed to unexpected blatant incriminating evidence taken from his home. Standing judicially naked, he would be judged based on truth and justice, and the evidence presented would serve to strike fear in those still in hiding.

Michael remembered that in ancient times when the victor returned from battle, he rode aboard his steed parading those he defeated and captured through the streets of towns and villages for public viewing. Today he was the victor, and the world awaited the humiliation of the defeated. *The mill of justice sometimes grinds slowly, but it grinds very fine. Eugen was correct when he said, "The defendant will leave the courtroom, unlike the way he enters."*

Michael's driver was pulling into his compound when his phone rang. He was surprised to hear who was on the phone.

"Hello Michael, this is Eugen I have news for you and I don't know whether it's good or bad. After the defendant was taken from court, he was rushed to the hospital with serious health issues. Under these conditions, the judge ruled that future court sessions are put on hold until further notice. The prosecutor did a superb job today in court articulating the case against the defendant and I will keep you informed as things progress."

"Thank you. I'll wait to hear from you"

Chapter 19

Mailroom

When Karl Biggs left his home for work, he never expected to be at the center of a major event happening under the radar. After showing his employment badge at the front entrance, he walked down a long corridor leading to the isolated mailroom, entered his passcode, and began his day inspecting mail from around the world. He first sorted the larger pieces from everyday general mail. After five minutes of sorting, he came upon a large manila envelope showing the name, Sonje Shuster Pencovich. It had been posted in Bucharest, Romania. A large red flag waved in front of him—early-morning zest came to a stop.

He had been hired by Max, the chief of security, and under protocol regulations for incoming mail from the country of Romania, Max was required to review and approve its delivery to the party addressed. Biggs found himself stressed. He remembered the telephone call from the vice chairlady: *"Please be aware that I'm expecting a package from Romania, and I want you alone to deliver it to my office."* This implied Max was not to know. He felt an uncomfortable vise tightening. Max was called the Enforcer for a reason. Protocol was now placing him in a precarious position if Max ever found out. He had only one option. After examining the item for hazards, he left the mailroom for the fourth floor hoping he would not see Max on the way.

Karl Biggs had an assistant who did all the footwork mail deliveries, and he personally had never been on the fourth floor where all the administrative people conducted business. When the elevator door opened, an aura of affluence signaled to the visitor that this floor was a world unlike his lowly mailroom. *He couldn't escape comparing his special delivery to the second most powerful person in the company to that of a serf appearing in the presence of the Lord of the Manor.* He knew the elevator he had taken was for regular employees, and for security reasons, there were several private elevators that only the administrative team used.

The man from the mailroom was lost in a maze of offices, and unless he soon got directions people might consider him someone that didn't belong here. *Tension accelerated at the thought of meeting Max here on the fourth floor. What would he say—how could he justify being here? Perhaps he should have called before coming.*

It was his luck to see someone coming out of an office door wearing informal clothes and dressed in a manner that looked more like him. It was a bigger surprise when the man spoke first.

"It appears you are looking for someone up here on the fourth floor," said the man who wore no visible sign of an employee badge.

"Yes, I'm from the mailroom and have something to deliver to the vice chairlady."

The eyes of the man stared down at what Karl Biggs held in his hand, then said, "Follow me, and I'll take you to her office."

What a strange experience, thought Biggs, that a person who looked to be off the street would be leading him to the office of the lady who ran this international company and was known to be a fashionable dresser, unlike the man he was following.

When entering the front office of the vice chairlady's secretary, the man in front of him leading the way seemed to own the place. "Good morning Freda, is Sonje in her office?"

"Yes, Sir, she's in, and no one is with her."
Everything was becoming more confused. Who was this man who took command and seemed to have the run-of-the-place?

"I didn't ask your name, but since you are from the mailroom, I assume you are Karl Biggs?"

The man making the delivery wondered how a person he had never met would know his name. He thought it wise to respond with the same respect that the secretary gave him.

"Yes, Sir, I am Karl Biggs!"

Both now stood at the door over which was written: Vice Chairlady. Mr. Biggs saw the man give a strange rap on the door and then wait.

"Come in."

The man leading the way opened the door and allowed Mr. Biggs to enter first. The nervous tension gripping the man making the delivery interfered with the visible affluence about the office. Seated at the desk was a person he had never seen or met, a lady who wielded the power to run an international company. Her image fit the description of her reputation: she was beautiful and wore smart, fashionable clothes.

"Madam, I am complying with the request you made of me on the phone about any mail that comes to you from the country of Romania. I have with me something that just came in today."

The lady behind the desk rose to her feet, walked over where Mr. Biggs stood and took from him the manila envelope he held in his hand.

"Thank you, Mr. Biggs, for acting on this as I requested. It is to be understood that no one is to know about this piece of mail you have delivered, and in the future if a problem arises because of breaking protocol, I assure you there will be no problem."

"I was apprehensive about that matter, but what you have said has allayed my concerns."

When the man left the vice chairlady's office, curiosity forced him to stop at the secretary's desk. "Miss, I didn't get the name of the gentlemen who brought me here."

"Oh, everyone knows who he is. He's the company's overseas coordinator and husband of the vice chairlady. His name is Mr. Pencovich."

Inside the vice chairlady's office, Michael and Sonje opened what Karl Biggs delivered. What was predictable was laid out in front of them on the desk. The large envelope contained a letter, photos of a young blond man on a crowded street, and a six-inch section of an arrow tip. The letter read:

Madam, enclosed are articles of evidence that connect your husband with the deaths of certain Army personnel. In my possession are weightier pieces of evidence that will prove your husband's guilt. As per my demands in the previous letter, all evidentiary materials pointing to your husband's guilt will be given to your courier upon the delivery of two million dollars. The next letter you receive will give directions on how and when to make the exchange.

"Michael, you made the right diagnosis—he's giving us the slow, soft touch. Do you think these materials should be sent over to the forensic team?"

"At this point, I can't see how that action would serve to advance our efforts. Let us secure them, and if further lab work is required, it can always be done later. At this stage, we have a lot to go on, and with Max on top of this, everything could move fast."

Sonje saw that Michael was preoccupied with something going on inside. "What are you thinking?" asked Sonje.

"People who engage in nefarious activities invariably slip up and show what I call blind spots. This happens when the energy of untruth interferes with seeing the whole picture. It's yet to be proven, but the man who wrote that letter may have shown us one of his blind spots when he used the word courier."

"Michael, I want to talk about us going on a picnic tomorrow. We need some relief from some of our stress!"

"You must have something special in mind."

"It's a surprise event, all because of you coming into my life."

Chapter 20

Restoration

It was a beautiful Saturday morning when an older, nondescript vehicle carrying a man and woman pulled off the main highway onto a single-lane, private roadway shrouded with tall overarching oak trees. It was a private driveway leading to what looked like an older upscale farmhouse with a large hay barn and several equestrian stables. Beautiful, magnificent horses dotted the pasture. It was the kind of estate where at one time German aristocrats lived and hired others to do the manual work. Today, it was a place that would fit the lifestyle of a downtown executive who would go home to his family after a long day at the office and relax in country-style living.

The vehicle pulled off the private roadway and stopped under one of the large oaks. They had driven for two hours to reach this site. A lady driver got out of one side of the vehicle, her passenger exited the other. The person who drove wore oversized sweats and tattered, walking shoes. The man matched the woman's down-dressed appearance. They took from the boot of the vehicle a large picnic basket and walked hand-in-hand over a velvet-green pasture under a deep blue sky while country air effused its lusty, smooth fragrance. Together, they made their way to a grassy knoll overlooking a pond stocked with fish. In the shade under a towering lone tree with overreaching, foliage-filled limbs, they laid out a large blanket. Today, nature's calm was serenading two people who had found fulfillment in each other. Both sat on the soft, unfurled blanket; the lady was first to speak.

"Michael, I'm glad you agreed to come here today without being told why. We're the only ones here on this property. The owners agreed to vacate the ranch just for today so you and I could be here alone by ourselves. I was brave taking this step, and you were brave to come without reservations.

"My father owned this piece of property before we were all taken off to the concentration camp. When I was a child, I played under the tree where we are presently resting, fished the pond, and rode beautiful horses about the property. Those were fond times of my life until the night the Gestapo came and took us all away. After the war, I tried to re-create myself without the memories of my past. This included what you see here. Michael, you have brought healing to my spirit and it is still ongoing, and for that reason, I gained the strength to bring you here today to tell you about my early childhood."

Sonje saw Michael with tears in his eyes. She took his hand, brought it to her lips, and smothered it with kisses. His tears were from seeing a banished memory restored, the evidence being that she was willing to visit the home her family was taken from in the middle of the night before being sent away to the labor and death camps. Michael put his arm around his wife, pulled her close.

"Would you like to own the property again?" asked Michael.

"You're always one step ahead," responded Sonje. "I

would consider purchasing the property only upon your approval."

"Well, you have my approval which you certainly don't need."

"Michael, I live my life to please my husband who has made me a stronger person. When the Gestapo took us away, the Nazi government confiscated and sold our property, and though I could take legal action, any settlement would be only for its current value. Therefore, I sought an agent to do my bidding with the present owners. As it presently stands, a contingent offer has been accepted and the contingency is that my husband would approve of the purchase. Would you be willing to live here at this old ranch, Michael?"

"I would live with you anywhere."

"You make me tremble inside when you say things like that."

The two strolled hand-in-hand about the property in their peasant-looking clothes inspecting horse stables, the barn, and even took a tour of the house.

"What are you going to do with the place after you purchase it?"

"If you're with me on this, we'll renovate the home, build a caretaker's residence, and come here every other weekend to ride beautiful majestic horses and fish at the pond's edge"

"I'm interested to know," said Michael, "how you managed enough nerve to down-dress and acquire the old vehicle you drove here."

Still holding hands, they stopped. "First, you know that I broke the chairman's protocol. His family is required to be protected by highly trained security people serving as drivers in armor-protected vehicles. Michael, I arranged everything for privacy so just the two of us could be alone. When I'm with you, I don't have the need for upscale clothing, because you accept me for what I am."

Michael embraced his peasant-looking wife, held her tight and smothered her face with kisses, then whispered in her ear, "What about the old vehicle?"

"I let Luis, our driver, handle that for me."

"And where did he get it?"

"That, I will probably never know, but he was rewarded well for his effort."

They resumed their walk with Michael speaking. "I look forward to our visits here on weekends. Will I have the pleasure on those occasions to be with a beautiful woman dressed in sweats or a beautiful woman in her normal fanciful attire?"

Sonje stopped, looked up at Michael with a facetious smile. "I'll come packaged in the wrappings that you choose."

"That being the case, it won't matter, because you are beautiful either way."

"Michael, you're a sweet doll."

Chapter 21

The Mount

A vehicle carrying three passengers moved slowly alongside pedestrians crowding the streets outside the old city of Jerusalem. On their left, they could see Mount Olivet ascending twenty-five hundred feet above the Kidron Valley that connected two of the most revered sites in Israel. For the three passengers, this visit to the top of the mountain would put closure on their extensive tour of Israel. Inside the vehicle sat two survivors of the Romanian Holocaust, an elderly couple whose daughter had married one of the wealthiest men in Europe, and who was now chairman of Katharina Enterprises. Family members and friends honored the husband as a spiritual leader and modern-day prophet. Seated alongside the couple was a man who had earned the title of Righteous Gentile because of his efforts in saving many Jewish lives during the terrible years of Nazi rule.

Heavy traffic and pedestrians clogging the highway encouraged the driver at the controls to join the fray of competing for space on the roadway with frequent use of the horn. It reminded him of ancient times when Coliseums were packed with subjects of Rome to be entertained by the grand events of chariot races. The highway soon cleared, and the driver found himself on an upward winding road to a point on top of the mountain where pilgrims go to get a panoramic view of the Old City. It was the last site the three passengers would visit before flying out of the country. Arabs in the area paid special attention when the driver opened the door and two men and a woman emerged with a vigor that didn't match their age. The lady among them showed signs of having entered senescence more gracefully than the men.

The three visitors to the site were greeted with swirling gusts of afternoon wind rippling across an ancient mountaintop ruffling the face of nature. Trees gently swayed in rhythmic dance giving life and meaning to an ancient hill symbiotically linked to the city that lay at its feet across the Kidron Valley. Both, the city below and the mountain where they stood, were flanking partners interwoven in history, and like a sleeping giant, the mountain would someday be awakened by the feet of Him who would rule the world.

Three visitors welcomed the cool breezes flowing across their furrowed brows and aging faces. They had come to this site to reflect on the mountain's history and the message it held for the future. For thousands of years the mountain was known for its production of high-quality olive oil, but its wider popularity came from those who walked its crest leaving footprints of a changed world.

The old prophet felt his wife take hold of his hand, followed by a question: "Mr. Reznik, at what are you looking?" His wife was always insightful about the man she had been married to for most of her life. She knew the look on his face when he was inspired with deep thought. He had been in life a diamond cutter and knew where to place his cutting tool to get the best results.

"Mama, sometimes it's what we don't see that bears greater meaning." The old man raised his hand and pointed across the Kidron Valley toward the city of Old Jerusalem. "David, the great King, fled that city barefoot three-thousand years ago to this spot where we stand on this mountain to escape the sword of his own household. Some considered him a defeated King and would soon perish in the Judean desert. Even Shimei, a relative of the late King Saul, found strength and courage in David's plight to curse and throw stones at him as he fled from Absalom. But David would later return over the same pathway to rule the city again, and it was on his return that we have a message for the future.

"History repeated itself in a transcendent way one thousand years later when another figure in history, David's prominent offspring, the Messiah, was rejected and driven from the city. Outside the city walls, David's descendant, the rightful heir to his throne, was offered as the Jewish Passover Lamb as described by the prophet Isaiah.

"With wounds in his hands, feet, and side, He departed from where we stand with the assurance of returning. Zachariah says, 'His feet shall stand on this mountain and it shall divide itself into two parts.' And from the top of this mountain, He will descend to the city of Jerusalem to be king over the whole world."

Mr. Popescu's face brightened. It carried a look of enlightenment. Truth from the old prophet had opened his eyes to something he'd never seen before. The old Gentile had a history of tears in his own country, but today his tears carried a smile across his face. The prophet's wife, who was always prepared for any eventuality, showed her fastidious nature by handing him a tissue. After drying his eyes, he turned to his guests.

"It took this site for me to see a truth I've overlooked. Do you see that old nearby olive tree knurled by age and time? It shows me a bigger picture. As a Gentile and not part of Abraham's sand-numbered posterity, I'm one of those limbs grafted-in by faith from a wild olive tree."

Mrs. Reznik saw her husband put his arm around the old enlightened Gentile, then heard him say, "Mr. Popescue, truth always hangs on truth. Abraham was promised two numerical kinds of descendants, those who were numbered as the sand on the seashore, and those who were numbered as the stars of the heavens. The sand descendants were measured by what one saw and felt under one's feet. Abraham's star offspring was heavenly and mortals on earth could only see the lights of those numbers in the distance by looking up. Sand was unstable, it shifted and changed, but the stars were always permanent. Down there in that city called Jerusalem, the Roman governor heard David's descendant say, 'My kingdom is not of this world, else my servants would fight.' Abraham's star descendants are those composed of Jews and Gentiles who have been birth into a new spiritual order where there is neither Jew nor Gentile.

"Being Jewish, my wife and I are members of the sand offspring and are numbered with those who occupy geographical boundaries. However, the three of us standing together as Jews and Gentile represent the new star kingdom from above and are a picture of fulfilled prophecy."

"Mr. Reznik," said the old Gentile, "we are building a chain with links of insightful truths up here on this mountain. Were it not for faithful Jews who were the first members of the star kingdom who went into the Roman world to preach the message of this new order of faith, I would not be standing alongside you today."

A broad smile came over the old prophet's face.

"Well spoken my good friend and brother...well spoken."

The old righteous Gentile looked across the Kidron Valley as if he were seeing the future. "The mountain upon which we stand once carried the footprints of Him who changed history. His footprints will again mark this site when He returns to make His coronation walk into the city from which He will rule the world."

Somber, quiet moments settled over the three. Each had edified the other with truths more fully perceived because of the location from which they were spoken.

The old Gentile broke the silence. "For three weeks, you have given me the greatest experience of my lifetime, and I thank you! Tomorrow awaits our return to the throes of doing battle in the trenches of a dark world. I got news today from Michael with the message that vital information has come in on Lupel, and he's waiting for my return."

Chapter 22

Reports

Inside Michael's walled compound a company driver was seen walking up to the guesthouse where the old man, Mr. Popescu, was staying. He had arrived late last night from his flight from Israel and was scheduled for a meeting in Michael's office within the hour. After ringing the doorbell several times without a response, the driver began knocking on the door. He was surprised to hear a voice from behind.

"No one's inside, he's out here taking a walk in the beautiful floral garden. It makes one younger...you ought to try it sometime, It'll make you younger!"

"Mr. Popescu, I'm supposed to have you at Michael's office within the hour, so we better leave as soon as possible!"

"Where is Michael?"

"I've already taken him in."

"What about his wife, Sonje?"

"She went in with Michael today."

"I know I shouldn't ask you this question...but is Michael happy in his marriage?"

"If you were around them for any period of time, you wouldn't ask that question. Both are very happily married."

"I'm glad to hear that. Michael has had a lot of pain in life."

"Both have had more than their share of hurt. She may be German, but suffered in the camps just like the Jews."

The old man showed a startled look. "Really! I wasn't aware of that. What a beautiful picture of the law of mathematics in human relations when two negative experiences come together to make a positive. I'm happy for both of them."

"Mr. Popescu, why are you so clever when your looks and dress don't match your cleverness?"

"It's not what's on the outside, my boy, it's what's on the inside!"

"You'd better get in the vehicle so I can get you to Michael's office."

The old man was dropped off in front of Katharina Enterprises. He stopped at the beautiful flowing fountain, the landscape centerpiece in front of the massive four-story, city-block complex. The colorful Koi fish still gave relaxing entertainment to the eyes that took the time to stop. The early sun had cast the old man's shadow across the water giving varied reflective hues coming from the fish as they swam in and out of his shadow. He saw loneliness in the fish. Like people, they seemed to need companionship from others, but those who passed this way rarely took time from their busy schedules to show them attention. His tranquil state suddenly shifted back to the real world. Someone had stepped behind him whose enormous shadow now covered his in the pond.

"Mr. Popescu, Michael is waiting for us in his office."

The old man turned around and saw someone more than twice his size carrying a briefcase showing the image of a large, slick, baldhead with arms the size of his legs, all embellished with a starched shirt and pinstripe suit. He was something to behold.

"I'm Max, and we need to get to a meeting to go over some important matters. I was waiting at the entrance for you, and you kept dawdling around out here, so I came out to get you."

Max took him by the arm, pulled him along through the front doors and over to the security desk.

"We have to sign you in before we go up." Max had protocols from which he never deviated. His people behind his back called him the Enforcer, was never late for a meeting, critical of those who were, and would write anyone up who failed to meet protocol standards. Today, his treatment and handling of Mr. Popescu showed the man's enforcer side: he wasn't going to be late in his meeting with Michael.

Once in the elevator, Max let go of the old man's arm. Mr. Popescu thought the big man was much too tense. "What do you do around here, Max, besides acting as a bouncer? Max took the statement in stride allowing a slight grin to show on his broad face.

"Right now, Mr. Popescu, I am a delivery boy and have an important package to drop off."

"I didn't know I was that important."

Max looked down at the aging man. "Sir, you are the cause of it all."

Max and Popescu sat across the desk from Michael with the big man's clandestine report in front of him.

"Max, the chairman and I reviewed your report together, and he requested that I highly commend you on what you have collected with your undercover contacts outside this country.

"Mr. Popescu, I've asked you to be part of this meeting because you are a central figure in this operation by making it possible with the information you gave us. For your safety, I arranged to get you out of the country, and with your help, we found photos of Lupel. We may need your help before this issue is finalized, but you will soon be able to safely return to your relatives and home in your village in Romania.

"With Max's help, we have discovered the identity of Auton Lupel, the man that ran the Nazi anti-partisan intelligence operation and who also imprisoned you. Up to this point, he has successfully hidden himself using someone else's identity. Presently, he works for the government of Romania as a courier delivering diplomatic mail to Romanian embassies in Europe. Everything is being brought to a close and we want you to stay with us until that time comes when Lupel is exposed."

This ends the matter of extortion, thought Popescu. "And what name does Lupel presently go by?" asked the old man.

"Max was able to get that information through the agent he assigned for that mission. It came from two sources: his uncle and a local banker. Lupel passes himself off now as Teodor Popa."

Michael saw the old man give a sudden grimace.

"Memory always comes back to haunt you," said Popescu. "A faceless man with the name of Popa was in solitary confinement at the prison where I was sent. He was faceless because no one ever saw him, but we managed to communicate when guards weren't looking. I found out all of his family was killed and he took up arms with the partisans, was captured and Locked in solitary confinement. One morning he turned up missing, and we assumed at the time that he was executed."

Max had been silent up to this point. He remembered what Stellar said about poetic justice—exposing Lupel's Nazi connections to the brutal regime now in power. At the time, he thought it a violation of Western judicial idealism, but hearing what the old man said put another face to it.

"Michael, how does the chairman want to handle this in its finality? Lupel would probably fall under diplomatic immunity and escape prosecution here in this country as a war criminal, so perhaps it would be best to take direct measures and deliver the evidence straight to the authorities of the Romanian government."

"In the final analysis, that's where it will end up, but for now, we're waiting for a special message to come through before we act on it. In the meantime, Max, if your contacts can secure for us Lupel's embassy delivery schedule, it'll get us prepared for our next move. I want Mr. Popescu to see the face of the man who sent him to prison."

"I'll get in touch with them tonight and get back to you when something comes in. It'll take several days, but when I hear, I'll call you."

The following week, Mr. Popescu spent his time at the guesthouse in Michael's compound. During the day, he worked with Mr. Reznik in the flower garden, discussed theology, and learned elementary Hebrew greetings and phrases. He prepared his own breakfast and lunch, and for the evening dinner, it was at the Rezniks or with Michael and Sonje.

The old Prophet and Mr. Popescu were having their daily afternoon tea in the garden gazebo when they saw Michael and Sonje's driver pull through the iron gate of their walled compound, followed by big Max's vehicle. Michael got out, saying to his driver, "Luis, take my wife up to our place."

Michael waited until Max parked and walked over where he stood. Together, they strode through the floral garden where nature flaunted its beauty under the umbrella of overhanging flowering limbs swaying gently in the afternoon breeze. Both of the old men sat at the table in the gazebo watching them walk in their direction. They knew Michael well, and with the look he carried, they knew he was there on business.

Still standing, Michael was first to speak. "Mind if we have tea with you?"

"Please have a seat and help yourself," replied Mr. Reznik.

Both pulled up chairs and sat at the table. Max was fortunate to find a chair without arms. Unknown to the four men were the eyes of Mrs. Reznik watching from inside the old Prophet's home. It was her innocent, impertinent nature that contributed to her colorful personality, and today she was true to form—she had the need to know what was going on out there in that gazebo.

Mr. Popescu was first to speak. "What news have you

brought me today, Michael?"

Before Michael could answer, Mrs. Reznik was in the gazebo carrying a tray of freshly brewed tea and a container of hot coffee.

"I happen to know that Max prefers coffee over tea, and no one comes to my place without being served what they want! I brought some freshly brewed tea and a pot of hot coffee for Max."

Looking directly at Max, Mrs. Reznik asked, "How's Birdie doing, Max?"

Max was taken back. He was bold as brass in everything except in personal matters of discussing a lady he was interested in. He looked embarrassed, wishing, on one hand, the question hadn't been asked but at the same time welcoming it. He knew the inquisitive nature of this lady, and if he didn't give a meaty answer, there would be no end of her probing.

"Birdie is doing fine. In fact, she and I are going out to dinner tonight. It's a weekly event nowadays."

"Oh…how wonderful! I hope good things happen between you two…both of you together make a fine-looking couple."

Though Max was pleased with her statements, he didn't show it. He did feel good about others knowing of his interest in Birdie without having to bring up the subject himself.

Mrs. Reznik's husband, the spiritual leader of the clan, was always an arbitrator between her and the company they were with. She had the need to know trivia about people, and he had the need to ameliorate her meddlesome manner in getting her need satisfied. Today, he didn't have to pick up after her, and in a gentle way had served as a matchmaker. She chose to stay and have tea with the expectation of hearing trivia.

After everyone had finished their drinks, Michael turned to Mr. Popescu. "I'd like you and Max to take a walk with me in the garden. We have some things we need to discuss with you."

Turning to Mr. and Mrs. Reznik, Michael said, "Please excuse us for a few minutes, Max and I need to discuss with Mr. Popescu matters of his return to his country."

The husband and Michael saw the downcast spirit showing in Mrs. Reznik's countenance. She knew by Max being present in their meeting, important subjects would be discussed that had high intrigue.

"Dear, we must invite Mr. Popescu over for dinner tonight, don't you think?"

The old man's smile showing on his wrinkled, aged face wasn't nearly as large as the one inside his thoughts. "Yes, Dear, I think that would be a good gesture, because he may not be with us much longer."

Once the party of three had removed themselves from the gazebo, Michael opened the conversation.

"Mr. Popescu, our plans have been changed because of sudden drastic events that have taken place in your country. Max has a report to give us about the status of Lupel."

"First, let me say," said Max, "Lupel is a slippery person. Information has come to me that he had an uncle who recently died and left in his will the revelation of his nephew's identity, but it was his attorney, as instructed by

193

the uncle, who delivered Lupel's identity to the authorities.

"Somehow, Lupel was given advance warning and disappeared from the scene. My contacts tell me he most likely assumed another identity that was already in place and probably has property registered in that name which gives him instant cover. It's a known fact that Nazi officers stole a lot of Jewish wealth in the Holocaust, and in that country, if one has money he stands a good chance of staying hidden. His greater threat will come from an avenger who has personal reasons to take him out.

"That's been done before," said Michael.

"Michael, if you were a betting man, what are the odds of Lupel not making it to a court of law for his crimes?"

"I defer to Mr. Popescu. He and I both lived in a lawless, genocidal country, a land where today hundreds guilty of murder and war crimes walk the streets unmolested and will never stand in front of a judge on this side of mortality. Lupel is only one among many and would have gone undetected had it not been for his extortionary attempts."

Both waited for Popescu who had yet to give comment on the subject.

"Michael has told it like it is. Lupel became vulnerable when he played the game of extortion and lost. The man moved outside his safety zone and became exposed. Reference was made that he may already have a new identity, and if that is the case, he will continue to go undetected unless an anomaly occurs. Michael will never have to worry about extortion and I will never have to be concerned about his presence in the area of my village. He may even attempt to get out of the country, and who knows but that he already is? I consider the matter closed."

Max, for the first time, saw the whole picture of the mission surrounding Lupel. It was a matter of extortion—something tied to Michael's past and was dealt with at the very top of Katharina Enterprises.

"Mr. Popescue, when do you want to return home?"

"When it's convenient for you. I look forward returning to our village, the place where both of us were born. For you and me, it carries many painful memories, but it's all I know. I'll pick up a new bike in Bucharest with the money you gave me and visit a certain town on my way home."

"Be sure to get one of the new larger models on the market today, and I might add, you'll not have to make a garden every year because you'll be receiving a monthly retirement stipend from Katharina Enterprises. When you arrive in Bucharest, someone will be there at the airport to take you shopping. We'll schedule a flight for you tomorrow morning."

Unknown to Popescu, plans had been made to honor an unsung hero. The evening was finished off in a small banquet room at an upscale diner in Munich. Around the long, floral-decorated table were the Israeli Ambassador, Hans Isler and his wife, Michael, and Sonje, the elderly Rezniks, Max, Birdie, and the honored guest, Mr. Popescu.

The evening had the closure of a professional photographer taking photographs of the Ambassador awarding Mr. Popescu an engraved plaque honoring him as a righteous Gentile who risked his life in saving hundreds of Jews during the Romanian Holocaust. The chairman was last to speak.

"I have with me tonight the enlargement of a photo given to me by a special person who gave himself to my family in service and friendship. It is a picture of Mr. Popescu and my grandfather standing together in front of the lumber mill he managed and made successful."

After unwrapping the framed photo and showing it to everyone at the event, he continued. "I made two copies of this photo, one which now hangs in my office, the other for the man who has given life and joy to many people. Mr. Popescu, please come and accept this framed picture as a memory of our event tonight."

When the old man stepped forward, embraced the chairman he knew as a one-year-old, saying, "Tomorrow, I return to a country that is known for its historical pain on a people who were chosen by God to bring His light to this world through the Messiah. Thank you, Jacob and Michael, for what you have done and what both of you have become. Thank you, Mr. and Mrs. Reznik, for your kind hospitality and friendship. Thank you, Sonje, for making Michael, who is like my own son, a very happy man."

The old man sat. Everyone in the room stood to their feet and applauded.

Chapter 23

The Uncrossable Line

Stellar and Bram had been on the road in the country of Romania for one week pretending to be businessmen in search of potential business opportunities when all the time they were doing research on how to best create an infrastructure of moving Jews to the coast who would be smuggled aboard freighters. This was their assignment with everything coordinated through the front operation of a first-class, five-star hotel resort now under construction on the clean coastal sands of the Black Sea.

For Bram, the time spent on the road was boring but took it in stride as part of his assignment. It was made more difficult by Stellar becoming withdrawn and quiet. He had been like this from the moment they drove out of Gavriella's driveway at her Bed-and-Breakfast. Even at night, he tossed, rolled, and talked in his sleep, sometimes getting up in the middle of the night and slipping out for a walk. He was Stellar's best friend, and up to this point had shared nothing with him, but had suspicions it was all about the woman he'd met in Moreni. Their return to Gavriella's Bed and Breakfast was on schedule and would occupy the rooms they had prior to their mission.

"Bram, let's drive by the old Lupel place first and see what's going on there." The atmosphere inside the vehicle lacked energy, and after a long lull of not speaking, Stellar looked at Bram behind the wheel and spoke like he was making a confession. "You know I called her several times while on this road trip."

Bram was taken aback with Stellar's lack of specificity. "You called whom several times this week?"

"Gavriella."

"What was the purpose of that?"

"I don't know, perhaps I was just lonely."

"I've never known of you being mesmerized by a woman before. You've always had friends that were women, and still do but never anything like this. You don't sleep at night, you talk in your sleep, and sometimes you take walks. You've never done this before."

"Yeah, I know, I come ill-equipped for this."

"It appears, Stellar, there are some hurdles that you're trying to figure out how to overcome. Are they hurdles that you've created or do they come from her?"

"Now, you're trying to be my counselor."

"Well, it seems you are in dire need of one."

"I can think of nothing else but her. It's like she fits that part of me that's been missing."

"I've been there a few times in my life but not to the extent of your experience."

"She's built an impregnable fortress with only one entrance."

"And your problem is you don't want to walk through that door?"

Bram saw Stellar look out the side window showing body language of avoidance. A direct answer to his question was a bridge too far to cross.

"I am not a good person," Stellar said, "but I'm

honest, honest to myself and others. The only subterfuge I engage in is in the ploy of our work. To do what we do, we perfect deceit in every form to defeat our enemies but outside that domain, my devotion to honesty is pristine. A challenge is facing me from Shakespeare in the character of Polonius who said it well, 'To thine own self be true.' My struggle is not in knowing what moral truth is, God has penned it on every unseared conscience. My conflict is with pretention, that of being something I'm not to get what I want, and that is the highest level of deceit, and to not recognize it puts one on the path of self-delusion, and specifically to my case, hurt to someone else."

Bram saw Stellar's courtroom skill in skirting a direct answer to his question by mixing philosophical truisms within the context of human experiences. His dissertation was a clever way of avoiding a direct question and at the same time deny his cry for help in his struggles over something he lacked the strength to go through? Bram thought it was turf he would avoid.

"It's one o'clock, Stellar. Do you want to find a place to eat before we go to the old Lupel place?"

The question from Bram pulled Stellar, who was lost in his thoughts, back to the mission in front of them.

"Yes, I think we should eat before that event."

Before leaving the restaurant outside Moreni, Bram insisted that Stellar drive knowing it would help get his mind out of his melancholic state. He had never seen him in this condition before.

When they pulled into the driveway of the old Lupel

estate, it could hardly be recognized. The shrubbery had been trimmed, grass cut, the open land mowed, and vehicles belonging to tenants had been assigned to a parking spot. Everything had a disciplined look about it. Stellar was first to speak.

"That old house has a lot of hidden mystery. The uncle who gave it to Gavriella said there were chambers he'd not seen. We've already opened one which wasn't really hidden, which leads me to believe that everything we found inside had been recently moved there from another area."

"You may be onto something," said Bram. It's a massive structure, and if there are concealed rooms, they were probably put in before the uncle moved in."

Stellar opened the door at his side, then turned and looked at his partner. "I'm sorry I've been out of it on this trip. My condition hasn't been too helpful and I apologize for it. Let's get out and walk around the old house. I've been mulling over some ideas about this place. I'll run it by you and see what you think."

After reaching the backside of the old mansion, Stellar asked: "Wouldn't you say this old place has a lot of aesthetic value?"

"It has that and even more, but how does that factor into where you're going with this?"

"This town is an oil producing area. Romania has privatized its oil industry, which has brought in professional people from Europe and the Middle East, and because of the grade level of existing hotels in this town, these people patronize hotels in other areas. If we went into partnership with Gavriella and remodeled this old place into a luxurious hotel with riding stables and equestrian recreational facilities, it could have wide patronage appeal and would serve as a gathering site for those being collected to board the freighters off the coast."

Stellar saw a hard look coming from Bram. "I must say that it has potential, but the person who can better assess its viability as a successful business is the one who is presently in control of the Lupel estate. However, I must ask how much of this has come about from your fixation with the woman who owns everything?"

"You have every right to think that, but I did consider this before we left on our tour. Everything warrants further research before we approach Gavriella."

"I would suggest that before we spend time on research that we see what Gavriella would want to do."

"I'm glad you said that and not me," replied Stellar. "This is why we're here on this mission, and we may as well start at this point and see where it goes."

Bram was feeling good about Stellar becoming engaged with issues outside his obsession with Gavriella. He appeared to be returning to his old self. He wished for it to remain so.

Gavriella now had the responsibility of managing both sites, the Bed-and-Breakfast establishment and the old Lupel place. Stellar and Bram were impressed with her aggressive managerial skills. In a short time she had put a new face on the Lupel place, and for Stellar, he saw it only strengthening her position inside her fortress leaving him the message that she was no weak damsel in need of male chivalry. Her line drawn in the sand was clearly defined: he had to become what she was before that door of her life would open. No man would ever step beyond that threshold and enter her life without first believing as she did—that Jesus was from God and was the promised Jewish Messiah. This was beyond his reach. He was the next thing to a secular Jew, which was one step away from being an atheist. The Holocaust had ripped from him any vestige of faith he had in Judaism, and now she was requiring a leap, not to the fundamentals of Judaism, but to something that had been rejected by his people for centuries. This was a leap beyond his reach.

Stellar and Bram didn't speak a word from the moment they pulled away from the Lupel estate to the time their vehicle entered Gavriella's driveway.

"Stellar, you go on inside, I want to go over some notes I made at several of our stops."

Stellar knew what Bram was doing—Bram wanted him to see Gavriella alone. He pushed his door open and began a walk he wasn't sure he should take. Rejection had only whetted his drive to get what he couldn't have, and her presence would only intensify that energy. Courage, thought Stellar, was not enough as he walked toward the front door—he needed luck! But luck fell under the law of mathematical probability which offered little solace, the odds being what they were.

Unknown to Stellar, the person's beautiful face he wanted to put on canvas with her long, flowing dark hair was peering at him from the office through a crack in the window shade. After hearing his car pull into the driveway, she couldn't resist the temptation to look and wait. She had walked up to the line, the line forbidden to be crossed, and though she had the freedom to step over, and was tempted to do so, she could never share her life with someone outside her faith.

The doorbell rang. She stepped away from the curtain, briefly looked at herself in a mirror, and opened the front door. Each stared at the other without speaking. Messages were exchanged, not on the lips in the form of words but through the energy of the eyes.

"Do I get to be invited in?" asked Stellar.

"Oh, I'm sorry, please come in! Your rooms are ready if you would like to bring everything in."

"Bram will be in shortly with our stuff."

"I missed you and Bram while you were away...especially you. It was good of you to call me. It made me feel like I was part of what you are doing."

"I was lonely. I've never been like this before and it makes me insecure in my responsibilities here in this country."

"I'm sorry if it's my fault. I didn't intend it to turn out this way. Perhaps, we shouldn't see each other if it means I'm interfering with your mission?"

"If you imposed that on me, I would leave this country and return to my law practice."

"I wouldn't want you to do that."

"Bram and I have a business proposal for you to consider and it involves the old Lupel estate."

"Speaking of the estate, I believe it should rest with you to make the decision on what's to be done with what we found behind that door in the basement. The jewelry items should go to a Holocaust museum, and I leave it with you to act upon this matter."

The conversation was interrupted by the sound of the

doorbell, followed by the door being opened by Bram holding two cases. But with the door open, her attention was drawn beyond Bram to someone pulling into the driveway on an upscale, late-model bike.

"I see a patron arriving. Why don't you two get settled in your rooms? You might say I'm celebrating your return by inviting both of you to my flat tonight for dinner. If there is business to be discussed, that would be the appropriate time."

"I'll accept your invitation," said Stellar, providing you perform for us with your violin."

"I'll accede to those demands if you help with the dishes!"

Stellar and Bram retired to the reading room adjacent the office to pick up reading materials for the evening.

Chapter 24

The Fountain of Wisdom

Gavriella opened the front door to her establishment and found standing in front of her a medium-height, robust man showing a smooth, elderly face, crowned with a full head of thick white hair. Held in his arms was a new bike helmet.

"Good afternoon, Madam," said the man, "do you have a vacancy for a couple of nights?"

"Yes, we have a vacancy. How many nights do you wish to stay?"

"I'll pay for two nights, and if I decide to stay longer, I'll let you know tomorrow evening.

"Please fill out the registration form. Sir, it's none of my business, but what conditions would change your mind to stay longer?"

The man said nothing. She took the form, looked at the name and his city of residence. Her face registered a slight grimace, followed by a second glance. She, like any Jew in this country, knew the history of his town.

"I see that you're from up north, from the town of Ediniti. What brings you here?"

"Just flew in this morning to Bucharest from Munich and wanted to see what Auton Lupel's town looked like."

Gavriella froze. It was the name Lupel. Words that flowed with warm, friendly fluidity came to a sudden stop.

Still holding the registration card in her hands, only her eyes moved between her guest and the man's name. Then appearing near the office entrance were Stellar and Bram having overheard the entire conversation in the reading room. After composing herself, she braved her way back into the conversation.

"What would be your interest in Lupel and the city he's from, and besides, it's been many years?"

"Many years from what, Madam?"

"Since he disappeared."

"Then you don't believe he's dead?"

Stellar, looking on and hearing the dialogue, thought the old gentleman to be clever. He even had a juridical self-confidence about himself knowing the power of silence and the weakness of talk. For a non-professional to cast that kind of disciplined image without formal training comes from the school of life's hard knocks.

"Sir, what is your interest in Lupel."

"Madam, I'll strike a bargain with you. You answer my question, then I'll answer yours. Is Lupel alive?"

Stellar saw Gavriella look over at him, then back to the old man.

"It is my belief that the man is still alive."

The old man up to this point had not seen Stellar and Bram standing nearby outside the office. The scars from the pain of the Holocaust ran deep with those who survived, and not all survivors were Jews. To answer the Lady's question, the old man stepped back in time. Gone was his self-confident-looking image. Emotion was never lost in the memory of pain. It was a time of his life when what he went through made him what he became.

"Madam, I have no interest in Lupel—just questions. I wanted to see the town that allowed a man to become the evil creature he was. Lupel arrested me on suspicion that I was part of a partisan resistance movement, was sent to his prison filled with innocent victims and saw men taken out on a daily basis for interrogation and never returned. I was there for six months and would have joined others who never returned had it not been that the war was coming to a close."

Those listening saw the old man forcing his mind and emotions on board a personal memory train that came equipped with large viewing windows. His faraway look yielded to a voice in soliloquy.

"I wasn't a Partisan, nor was I guilty of the accusation of lending assistance to those who were. My resistance came in the form of helping Jews after seeing scores massacred in my village. I took the names of the guilty, those who plundered, murdered and raped, and gave them to three young men that became legendary for their acts of avengement on army officers and civilians guilty of war crimes. Today, their celebrated names are written in stone in the minds of those who know the history of a people who had no justice in this land."

Gavriella saw the old man step off his train and board another with a different destiny. Strong, clear eyes showing purpose and resolve spoke words that warmed her spirit.

"I just returned from Israel where I stood alongside two Jewish Messianic believers on the Mount of Olives overlooking the city of Jerusalem. All three of us, Jews and Gentile, gave pause reflecting on the event when Jesus, the historical descendant of David, would enter that ancient city to rule the world.

"Madam, this was why I gave support to the Jews in those horrid times of Nazi rule. They are God's chosen people and were promised geography for the coming of David's Descendant who will rule the world from there."

Stellar saw Gavriela turn her back to the old man, take tissue from a box on her desk and wipe her eyes of the tears now showing on her cheeks.

Stellar was impressed with the old man's valor and noble commitment to Jewish causes. However, the effect it would have on Gavriella would be a greater resolve of strengthening her fortress, leaving him on the outside.

With moistened eyes still showing, the Lady who pushed the old man into conversation asked, "Sir, what name do you go by?"

"Just call me, Popescu...Popescu will do."

"Mr. Popescu, do you have baggage to be brought in?"

"Yes, after I make payment, I'll get them."

"Just don't you mind, my two friends will bring them in for you while I show you the room."

"Tell them to be careful with the smaller packages, they contain very important items!"

Bram and Stellar didn't have to be instructed by Gavriella to bring in the man's luggage. Once out the door, Stellar was first to speak.

"Cool waters have gently flowed our way today. Mr. Popescu is the perfect fit for what we need here in this country. That old man is a very clever person. You can tell he has been a leader of men, and if we can't enlist him, we'll do ourselves a big disservice."

"I agree," said Bram.

"He said to be careful with the smaller packages, but I don't see any small packages, only a couple of bags, one with a newspaper about to fall out."

Bram watched Stellar refold the newspaper in a neat manner, was replacing it when he saw something of interest on the front page.

"Let me see the paper you have in your hand," said Bram. Taking the paper and opening it up, both saw a startling photo on the front page. It was a Munich newspaper and carried the headline: "Israeli Ambassador Bestows Special Honor on Righteous Gentile." The photo included the Ambassador, Mr. Popescu, chairman and Vice-chairwoman of Katharina Enterprises.

The two men stared at each other with dropped-jaw looks. "Stellar, we need this man in our operation in this country, but his notoriety would be a disservice, requiring him to go underground and a person of his caliber needs to be a visual operative. He is not Jewish and could move freely among people and he fits the profile of those we need to build our operation around."

"I suggest we act on this quickly in two ways," said Stellar. "You make the proposal to Mr. Popescu, and I'll see where Gavriella stands with a partnership as we discussed. The reason for acting quickly on this is to seal off the notoriety that could come from Mr. Popescu's exposure to the public. Therefore, you need to meet with Popescu as soon as he is available."

Gavriella was waiting for the two men when they came through the front door. "Is Popescu settled in his room?" asked Stellar.

"Yes," answered Gavriella.

"Bram needs to see him right away."

"Follow me and I take you to his room."

Upon reaching Popescu's room, they found the door open and the old man waiting for them. His luggage pieces and personal effects were placed on the floor.

"Thanks, fellows!"

"Mr. Popescu, are you up to talking with me for a few minutes about a very important matter?" asked Bram.

The old man put a slight grin on his face. "If you're not selling me anything, I can manage that."

"Great!"

Appearing in the doorway was the kind lady who had registered the old man's overnight stay. "Mr. Popescue, I'm inviting you along with these two gentlemen to my flat tonight for dinner at six o'clock. The outside entrance is up the stairs just outside."

"I'm honored by your invitation and will to be there on time."

On the way to the office, Stellar broke the news to Gavriella. "We have a celebrity among us in Mr. Popescue.

"A celebrity among people in this country, or elsewhere?"

"We'll see. Popescu has a newspaper from Munich showing the Israeli Ambassador bestowing on him the honor and title of Righteous Gentile. Standing among them are the chairman and vice-chairwoman from Katharina Enterprises.

"Do you know anything about Katharina Enterprises?"

"Only that the company is in many countries."

"They are a major supporter of the organization I'm with. I want to extend an offer to you as the new owner of the Lepel estate. My assignment in this country is to build an infrastructure for moving Jews to the coastal region where they will be smuggled aboard freighters that will take them to Israel. To do this, Bram and I must hide under the guise of being a foreign investor.

"Your town is an oil-producing region, and since Romania has privatized the oil industry, workers, investors, and professional people come from all over Europe and the Middle East to work here. However, because there are no first-class hotels available, they patronize hotels in other towns.

"The Lupel property with its massive home and large acreage has a lot of aesthetic value and could be made into a scenic wonder by upgrading and remodeling the old home into a luxurious hotel with riding stables and equestrian recreational facilities. This would attract the business and professional elements coming to the region and would serve as a cover for our operation by giving us a business investment face.

"If you are willing to go into partnership with the stated goals, we will bring into the country the necessary financial backing to make it a reality. You would be the sole manager and responsible party for making it a financial success. Bram and I will carry the responsibility of overseeing all construction and improvements. In time, it could make you well off."

Stellar gave a short pause so his question would have a greater effect. "So what do you think?"

"It goes without question, the proposal heavily

benefits me."

Stellar saw Gavriella look away. She was a woman nearing the age of forty, yet looked to be ten years younger. Both carried the vigor of youth. Each had awakened the other to the natural instincts of compatible attractions. Her hands were placed on her lap in such a way that each finger was distinguishable. Her widowhood had not discarded the gold band on her ring finger. For the first time, the thought came to Stellar that perhaps the ring was part of the fortress she had built to keep him out.

"There's a matter that concerns me," said Gavriella. "Though this partnership arrangement would serve both of us, how will it influence us being so close together day-after-day? I don't want to be a contributor to an environment that would impede or endanger your success in what you're doing in this land."

"I appreciate what you are saying, and it's apparent that you carry the greater strength between the two of us."

"I would not laud my strengths, but if I have strength, it comes from what I believe the Scriptures teach. However, I will admit as a confession to myself and to you, that for the first time since my late husband's passing some years ago, I have been moved to walk to the line that I cannot cross. I need not explain again what keeps me from stepping over that line. You saw my tears I could not restrain when Popescu spoke of the coming Messiah. Those were emotions of faith and are the emotions I want in the person who meets me when I choose to remove the ring I wear."

A long pause of cold silence settled in the room. Stellar saw himself in a dark corner, forced into a fetal position without anyone to reach toward for help. His heart pounded inside, felt helpless, alone with a pain he didn't know could exist until he met this woman. Then came the surprise of his life. A hand was placed over his. It was her hand, one of warmth acting as a sword fending off the cold, bitter feeling of rejection. The hand stayed spreading warmth, followed by the balm of words: "Stellar, we can remain, friends, if you can live with that kind of relationship between us."

The hand that brought warmth and comfort was slowly lifted. Stellar wanted to hold and caress it, but it was a chasm beyond his reach.

"Gavriella, when my family and the girl I was going to marry died in the Romanian Holocaust, a certain part of me died inside, and I lived with that death until I met you. You have resurrected something in me that I never knew I had. I admit, even being a Jew, I was tempted to pretend to be what you are, a Christian convert, to win your favor. However, though I come up short on a lot of things, I'm honest and not deceitful, and I would never in my lifetime do that."

"Perhaps this is one of the reasons I'm attracted to you—your honesty. But one does not become what I am by converting. I am what I am because of what I believe. Belief is an active, ongoing living process, not a formal document one signs or a ritual one goes through that allows membership. Do you remember the serpents that inflicted pain and death to those Moses led out of Egypt? Healing was provided when Moses exalted a brazen serpent on a pole, and all that was necessary for healing was to look up at the raised, brazen serpent. 'Look and live' were the keywords. The brazen serpent was the symbol of the Messiah being made a curse for us, the sacrifice for our sins that separated us from God."

Stellar saw himself in a different kind of courtroom, one that forced a retort with a sophistic bent. He could think of no other defense.

"I never stayed on Moses' desert long enough to be bitten by serpents—I returned to Egypt, an Egypt that had a different kind of desert where I learned to survive without the miracles of Moses."

She saw pain showing itself in Stellar's intellectual ploy. It was his only defense. "My hope for you, Stellar, is that you will find the strength to return to Moses' desert floor, find healing in the raised brazen serpent, the gateway to the promised land."

"Gavriella, those are sobering words. When I see the light of truth as you see it, I will come knocking at your heart's door."

A silent lull followed Stellar's statement. The atmosphere was like two opposing forces having retreated to a safety zone, neither carrying a white flag for surrender. The quiet demanded response.

"Stellar, when that time comes, my door will be open."

That evening after dinner at Gavriella's flat, they were entertained with her performance on the violin with classical numbers causing tears to show in Stellar's eyes. Moved by what she saw, it left the message that his feelings about her hadn't changed. Then came a surprise of the evening—a request from Popescu.

"Madam, a lady of your talent can surely play my favorite, *Nearer My God to Thee*."

"Mr. Popescu, I'm glad you requested that piece. It's my favorite too!"

The old man closed his eyes and meditated on the words he knew from childhood. *Then to her surprise, she saw Stellar showing quiet, meditative repose. Could this be the first step in his return to Moses' desert where the brazen serpent awaited him?*

After her performance, she placed her violin in its case, saying to everyone at the table, "Stellar will be conducting important business that involves all four of us, but before he commences, I must exert my authority. All three of you are to help me do the dishes before the meeting begins."

Chapter 25

The Room of Darkness

Stellar stood in the driveway of the old Lupel mansion with Gavriella, Bram, and Mr. Popescu. The old man, Popescu, had been gone a week having agreed to return and join Stellar and his team as a supervisor over the workmen in turning the Lupel place into a first-class hotel. He knew how to manage men, was a skilled artisan and committed to the operation of moving Jews to their homeland. The workers at the site would be under his direction and he would be answerable to Bram, a civil engineer. The exterior of the existing building would be refurbished. Most internal walls that were not bearing walls would be removed or replaced with a modern upscale aesthetic appeal. Polished oak would adorn handrails, doors, cabinets, and coves. A morning breakfast would serve the guests in a modern dining room. The twenty-acre estate would be fenced with outbuildings, walking trails, equestrian stables, and eventually stocked with quality riding horses. His first phase of involvement would be at the hotel site, and upon its completion would move north as an advisor to key operatives who would be working undercover with the Jewish population.

Stellar was first to speak. "I want to thank Mr. Popescu for agreeing to join us in our mission here in establishing a base to move our people to their ancient land.

I have asked Gavriella to read an excerpt from what Mr. Lunga wrote about this place, and the challenge it presents to us, and this goes directly to you, Mr. Popescu. You will be the first to see what's behind those walls and under those floors. All the Lupels were devout Nazis and the house is mystery-laden with a lot of unknowns, some of which we've already found."

Gavriella unfolded a piece of paper and proceeded to read words written by the man who left her the Lupel estate:

There are secret hidden chambers in that old house, put there by the father. For twenty years, I lived in that house and never took the time to search them out.

Stellar continued. "All the tenants will be out by tonight, and tomorrow Mr. Popescu and Bram will have the freedom to commence their work. Gavriella has agreed to keep us as her only guests because secrecy is vital in what we're doing, and I have arranged for her to bring in household help with cleaning and cooking."

"I want to take Mr. Popescu through the house on a quick walk-through," said Gavriella.

Interrupting Gavriella, the old man asked, "My question to you is, what mystery have you already found?"

"You'll see when we go through the old mansion," answered Gavriella.

The former owner's apartment was first to be inspected. "This house was a beautiful mansion in its day," commented Popescu. "Who were the original occupants?"

"We always knew it as the Lupel place," answered

Gavriella.

"Knowing who the people were that built the original structure might give us insight on any anomalies we may find. People in history who had a lot of money had strange ways of hiding their wealth."

The next place they inspected was the basement. Gavriella went straight to the metal door where the china closet still sat in front of the mystery room. Stellar and Bram pull the beautiful piece of cabinetry away from the wall revealing a metal door that now had a repaired lock.

"I see someone has repaired the lock," said Bram.

"Yes, I brought a locksmith down here to repair the door when you were away. Let me open it!"

"Is there a light in this room?" asked Popescu.

"Yes, it's overhead," someone said.

Everyone saw the old man reach up and pull the string that turned on the light. The light showed a room that looked as it did when they last left it, but something strange came over the old man. He stood still, turned his head slowly like he was trying to hear something that went unheard by others.

"There's something strange going on here. I can feel it." The eyes of the old man were drawn to the floor. "Someone has built a floor covering over some stairs leading to a cellar below, and it was most likely done when they installed the metal door."

All three standing alongside the old man said nothing but looked at each other with a show of askance. Gavriella placed her hand on the old man's shoulder, saying, "Mr. Popescu, we better get you home and leave everything here for another time. You've been on the road all day and look quite weary."

"I agree with that. Tomorrow is another day. But I concur with you, Stellar. This place carries a lot of mystery.

The engineer among them, Bram, saw in the old man genius that he couldn't put his finger on. He carried insight that reached beyond formal training, but what makes him think there's a cellar below the closet floor?

The next morning Stellar waited in his vehicle for Bram. Their schedule would take them to a small coastal village near the port city of Constanta where they would confer with field agents and Marku Albescu, the visible undercover front man for Katharina Enterprises.

Seen coming toward the vehicle was the lady who had turned his world upside down.

"Stellar, if you have a chance, would you please bring back some fresh fish? I'm creating menus for our cook?

"If I return with fish, will you do something for me?"

"If it's within my power."

"I'm an artist, and I want to sketch your beautiful face that I dream about every night. Will you pose for me when I return?

"You know how to weaken my knees! Of course, I will sit! Do I have to take a vow of silence?"

"Most of my subjects are allowed to talk; however, for optimal results, I'll request your silence. Your lovely eyes sparkle when you speak and would be a distraction. I'll be doing two sketches, a frontal and your best side. You have two best sides, and I leave it with you to make that decision.

"You're not to know where I go when I drive out of this town. Perhaps this will change in time, but for now, this is the way it is. I can't promise I'll find fish, but I'll do my best."

"And I'll pose for the sketches whether you find fish or not."

"Bram and I will be available to help in the project at the Lupel place when we return. After the construction project is completed at the old mansion, our time here will be determined by the intelligence we gather on this trip."

Gavriella and Popescu found the workers hired for the old mansion project waiting at the work site when they arrived. Gavriella watched the old man organize eight men in the dismantlement of interior walls on the first floor.

"Mr. Popescu, I'm having duplicate keys made so you can come and go at will."

"That would be a big help—thank you!"

"Before we go to the basement, I want to show you what we took from the closet after cutting through the metal door. We stored it in canvas bags in the attic. Follow me please."

The old man followed Gavriela to the third floor of the mansion, went to a door that appeared to be a closet. After using two keys to open the two locks, she opened the door and switched on the light.

"The stairs behind this door," said Gavriella, "lead up to the attic. Prepare yourself for the startling things you will see—I'll lead the way."

The stairs were narrow without banisters telling the story they were rarely used. Popescu thought of the big man, Max, in Munich, and the struggle he'd have traversing these narrow, tight quarters. Nostalgia hit the old man. His experience with Michael and the team he worked with at Katharina Enterprises was a memory he'd cherish until the evening of his earth's journey.

When they reached the attic floor, eyes that rarely missed anything scanned the room. It was spacious, used through the decades to store memorabilia, heirlooms, and secrets. *The old house was full of mysterious unknowns, and this room would begin his journey into the dark mystery of its past.*

Gavriella walked where bags filled with stolen Jewish jewelry were stored, all covered with a canvas sheet. She pulled the canvas covering off the nine bags, took one, and poured its contents on the canvas nearby. Both knelt and examined wealth taken from Jews, stolen before they were murdered: gold rings, watches, diamonds, and pearl necklaces.

The old man stood to his feet holding several pieces in his hands. Memory caused him to look away. He was seeing history, his own history of watching local townspeople carrying sacks of valuables from Jewish homes after they'd be massacred. His lips gave expression of what was rushing through his mind.

"Heinrich Himmler, head of the SS troops, had trained people that followed his killing teams and were responsible for collecting stolen wealth. The collectors would melt down the gold and silver, package it, then ship it out for storage in Swiss banks and safe-deposit boxes. This old mansion bears the record that something disrupted the process causing it to end up here at this site."

"Mr. Popescu, do you think there could be more stolen

Jewish wealth hidden around here?"

"I can't answer that at this stage, but what we have to do is be sure workers don't find it, see it, or hear about it. This is why we have to be ahead of the tear-outs, floor-after-floor.

"It might be helpful knowing who occupied this place during the war years? Was it requisitioned for Nazi SS officers? If the SS occupied this site during the war, and were forced to retreat, they would not have carried evidence of their crimes with them. Under these conditions, it is possible that Jewish wealth is hidden somewhere on these premises. Whatever the history may be, we still have the question, *why was it stored in the closet behind the iron door?*"

Gavriella saw in the old man a keen analytical depth. His thick, heavy head of snow-white hair was his trademark of wisdom.

"Let's go down and get on with the job of taking out the closet floor," said Popescu.

Two workers were taken to the basement followed by Gavriella. "How long were the items in storage before removal?" asked Popescu. "If you have an answer to this question, it would tell me when the flooring was installed."

"I don't have an answer to that question."

"When the workmen remove the flooring, we'll find stairs leading down somewhere. Over the years, there have been alterations in this to this old place and we need to find every hidden closet, cove, and cellar.

"What gives you the clues to believe that?" asked Gavriella.

"The first one is the filled-in flooring we're about to

remove. Walls have been added and moved to accommodate the creation of new rooms and apartments. Then there's the major point: committed Nazis lived here for years."

Gavriella unlocked the metal door and both watched two skilled carpenters rip up the floor and remove the debris from the room. The old man pulled out his flashlight and cast its light down into a dark hole showing stairs leading somewhere. Gavriella leaned over to get a better view and felt the old man's hand holding her back.

"This is dangerous in more than one way. Let's lock everything down. I'll send the workers to join the others. Only you and I should be the ones who know what's down below."

She watched the old man lead the workers to the door leading upstairs with instructions that he would join them later. The old sage then locked the door and returned where she stood.

"Do you feel brave?" asked Popescu. There's something not quite right—I have an eerie feeling about what we've opened up. The stairs have a banister and I'll test them using my flashlight, and if they prove to be stable you can follow."

"Just be careful, Mr. Popescu."

"It'll be a miracle if there is a light switch down here, and even a bigger miracle if there's power to it," said the old man.

When the nimble feet of old Popescu touched the bottom of the stairs, he moved the light back to the flight of stairs.

"The stairs seemed quite sturdy. Do you feel up to

coming down here? If you do, go very slowly and keep a grip on the banister."

As she neared the bottom steps, he reached up and took her by the hand. Popescu moved his light around where they stood, found a wall switch nearby. Upon hearing the click of the switch, both covered their eyes from sudden blinding light that filled the room. Then came into view what they'd entered. The stairs had dropped into a large open room with finished walls, carpeted floor, and expensive hanging lamps. Arranged in different parts of the large room were beautiful pieces of oak furniture with leather-patted cushions. Then came the unexpected scene of horror from another time: a large Nazi flag pinned flat against the wall over which hung the pictures of Adolf Hitler, Heinrich Himmler, and Dietrich Eckard, architects of Nazi occultism. Tables below the pictures held books and materials used in occult practices.

Strange, unnatural, icy feelings that gripped them coming down the stairs returned. The old man reached over and took hold of Gavriella's hand, led her to the middle of the room, lifted his face, closed his eyes and said a prayer: "In the name of Yeshua, Creator, and Life-Giver, we rebuke the evil in this room and forbid it to return."

He released her hand, then heard the old man quote a scripture. "These signs shall follow them that believe; in my name shall they cast out devils...." Silence, like a cold blanket of ice, wafted itself throughout the room moving Popescu to reflect on the sinister nature of Nazism.

"The people who occupied this secret chamber used it to tout and energize the spirit of Nazism in themselves and others and have kept it hidden from the public through the years. Nazism was a religion to those that entered this room.

"Some are led to believe that the basis of Nazism was inspired by black magic and the occult, and is not just a political dogma as many are led to think. And it is also commonly believed that the people in the pictures you see hanging on the wall were the leaders of these occult practices.

"Madam, do you know what we're missing down here?"

"What would that be?"

"Your violin playing *Nearer My God to Thee.*"

"Mr. Popescu, you are something else! I'll make that a reality. I'll run home and be right back."

"Bring a camera. We need to take photos of everything in this room as it is, then destroy the evidence by burning it.

"We don't want anyone down here, so both doors in the basement must be locked at all times. What we have found must be kept among ourselves. News of this reaching the public would have deleterious results on your business and effectiveness in moving your people to Israel. I'll go with you to your place. Bram left me drawings I should have with me here at the building site."

Workers saw the lady who owned everything carrying a musical case navigating her way through the maze of debris strewn about in the first-floor tear-out, followed by the man in charge of the project.

"Gavriella, wait for me at the metal door. I want to go over a few things with the men." She said nothing as she moved on. *The old man watched her elegant, willowy frame move on across the broken and disrupted first floor of the mansion. His thoughts took him back to his late wife in her younger years. She had the same beauty and command of herself as lovely Gavriella. He would pray for her. He knew what emotions were in play between her and Stellar. He had seen the eyes of both interacting together in the throes of emotional exchanges. He would pray for two things: that Gavriella would remain strong and Stellar would come to see and believe in the Passover Lamb.*

When he reached the basement door, he heard the quiet sound of beautiful violin music. He closed and locked the door, walked slowly toward the stairs that led to what had been a habitation of evil. By the time the old man reached the bottom of the stairs, he saw Gavriella's eyes closed playing her favorite, *Nearer My God to Thee*. Then to her surprise, she heard a voice singing the lyrics to what she was playing. He had been a vocalist in earlier years in his fundamental community church before the state shut them down. For ten minutes, he sang from memory the words of old hymns as she played.

"Madam," said the old man, "the voice of music is one of the last things to go in senescent decline."

"And with you, Mr. Popescu, the quality of your voice will be around for a long time. You have more than made my day by requesting what we have just done."

"I see you have taken all the pictures from the wall and laid them face down on the table. That noble act was appropriate before the music was played."

"For the record, I took photos as you requested. Also, close-up snapshots were taken of the books and paraphernalia laid out here on the table. There is an adjoining closet behind one of the doors that contains materials in boxes you may want to examine. There never seems to be an end to what went on in this old house over the years, and it all validates what Mr. Lunga, the man who willed this place to me, said about the chambers of darkness hidden behind walls and locked doors. What are your thoughts about this room? Why was it left as we found it—the floor over the stairs making the room inaccessible? Needless to say, I'm confused."

"Most likely what happened here was that Lupel's father, an avowed Nazi with occult beliefs, created this room for occult practices. When the father died, Lupel sealed it off with the metal door and left it as a memorial. As Lupel's uncle grew older, he removed what he wanted from down here, built the floor making it appear to be only a closet. Conjecture can be made that at some point Lupel expected the soon demise of his uncle and was in the process of removing what you found behind the metal door to another location. I can't see him leaving in permanent storage what you have removed."

"Where do you think that location is?" asked Gavriella. "At this site or elsewhere?"

"That's hard to say, but that's the reason we have to be ahead of the workers. What you don't want is the news of this reaching the public. The sudden death of Lupel's uncle, and you being the only heir, interrupted the removal process. It never entered Lupel's mind that his uncle would change the will they'd drawn up."

"Then we must assume he came here at night from time-to-time to do what he needed to do."

"I'm sure you're correct on that."

"Mr. Popescu, God has sent you to this place, and I

want you to know you are a pillar of strength for me. My marriage record shows I have a Romanian name. I could get an exit visa tomorrow to most any European country, then fly immediately to Israel as a new immigrant. Though rejected by my own in this land because of my belief in Jesus as the Messiah, my leaving would make me feel I was abandoning them."

Gavriella saw compassion on Popescu's face. The old man looked away like he was seeing something out of his own history. "When we have to stand alone, events that go against us will either weaken or make us stronger. For you, family rejection has made you stronger. We have similar experiences. I have been rejected by my people for helping Jews. However, you and I must remember that struggles also embellish our rewards in the world to come."

Chapter 26

The Conference

A driver with two passengers pulled into a small coastal village on the Black Sea, stopped in front of a residential-looking home showing a worn look from its frequent use by those seeking the pleasures of boating, swimming, and beachside swimming. It came fully furnished and was rented to patrons on a weekly basis. Its major asset was the ocean view from the front porch overlooking the sea's calm, blue waters that were interrupted from time-to-time with white-foaming breakers streaking the coastline.

Two passengers in the back seat exited the vehicle, each carrying a piece of luggage. The vehicle drove off leaving two men standing alone. They quickly moved to the front door that opened before they had a chance to knock.

"Come in! I'm Marku Albescu."

"It's good to meet you in person—I'm Stellar, and with me is my colleague, Bram."

The two moved inside, closed, and locked the door. Stellar was first to engage in the purpose of their visit.

"I understood the big man at Katharina Enterprises, the overseas coordinator, was supposed to be present in our meeting today."

"Those were the original plans, but he sent someone in his place—someone you know! He arrived early this morning and is in the bedroom taking a nap."

The sound of a gravelly voice coming from a bedroom down the hall interrupted their conversation: "Marku, has our company arrived?"

Coming into view from the bedroom was the figure of a staggering, sleep-deprived, oversized man wearing a starched shirt that had the appearance of being slept in the whole night. The trousers he wore matched the appearance of his shirt.

"Hello, Stellar! Good to see you again! Pardon the way I look. I think I feel worse than I look."

"Yeah, you look like you had a bit too much to drink last night."

"I don't drink. If I drank, Birdie would cast me aside."

"Are you serious with a lady?"

"Serious enough to consider marriage!"

Marku saw the conversation between Max and Stellar becoming personal and thought it best he and Bram remove themselves to the kitchen.

"Bram, let's go to the kitchen and put on some coffee"

Max and Stellar were left alone with personal issues common to both.

"Have you asked her to marry you?" inquired Stellar.

"I don't have the courage."

"Afraid of rejection?"

"Yeah, probably," answered Max.

Turning to Stellar, he asked: "Do you know what rejection is?"

Stellar thought the big man didn't waste time getting where he wanted to go. He was big, blunt, and in most cases always right.

"That's a daily experience for me. Both of us are Jewish, but she believes like Christians, that Jesus was the Messiah."

"And because you don't believe, she won't allow you into her life?"

"You said it all, Max."

"Stellar, you don't know what's going on out there in the real world. The man you were to meet, Michael Pencovich, the overseas coordinator, is a Jew but a believer in Christ. The chairman of Katharina Enterprises, Hans Isler, his Jewish wife, and her parents, are all Jews who believe in Christ. Stellar, I'm going to leave you my Bible that has the Book of Isaiah. If you want to know God's love for man and what he did to reconcile man to himself through the death of his son, read Isaiah fifty-three. They are words written by a Jew for the Jewish nation.

"Gentiles didn't spread Christianity. Its message came from Jews who saw Christ's death and witnessed His resurrection. He was the Passover Lamb who covers us and will pass over our guilt. He who knew no sin became the Passover Offering that we may be saved."

Stellar recoiled inside. He resented hearing and seeing the pushy, self-confident Max lecture him on a subject he was taught against all his life. It was less abrasive when it came from Gavriella than from this oversized man whose wit matched the size of his frame. Shaken by Max's words, he had the need to escape the mysterious feelings of conflict going on inside. Everything Max said was as powerful and forceful as he was in size and strength. Forces of two worlds were gripping him. One came from Gavriella and Max, the other was his being Jewish. History was on his side—the centuries of being brutalized by the Christian church—even down to the Holocaust years that he had lived through. He was a Jew, and to become what Gavriella and Max were would make him a quisling to his people's history and what he was. However, it was the other voice of energy coming from Gavriella and Max that spoke the loudest and had forced him onto this open field of battle. He had the need to flee.

"Perhaps we should get on with our purpose of meeting today," said Stellar.

Max knew it was a move to avoid an inner struggle. It was showing with his sudden lack of confidence. Gone was Stellar's image of courtroom erudite poise. *Big Max remembered the historical encounter of King Herod and the prisoner Paul, before being sent to Rome: "Do you think that in such a short time you can persuade me to be a Christian?"*

The objectives of the conference were to establish parameters of accountability, working relationships between the entities involved and reports of progress at the two sites. Marku, the figurehead-owner of the Constanta resort, was first to speak.

"The directive we have at the Constanta resort is to carry the image of a successful business operation. The government wants foreign investment, and the resort will provide this by bringing in tourism from Europe. In conjunction with upscale lodging and sandy beaches, the resort will provide deep-sea fishing and boat rentals. Boats used during the day to entertain tourists will be used at night to make coastal pickups for freighters waiting at sea.

"Today, I am pleased to report that the first operational

phase of the luxurious Constanta hotel is scheduled to open within three to four months. Our agents in Europe are on a big campaign to promote the enterprise."

As Max interjected himself into the deliberations, the three men alongside him at the table acknowledged his wealth of experience. His reputation of being an enforcer didn't go unnoticed.

"I think we need to understand," said Max, "that we are creating business fronts that are long-term ventures. They are designed to be successful, progressive, and at the same time provide a cover for being in this country. Once a system is created and protocols are established for the transfer of people, it must never be violated. Trial and error will force protocol changes but must always be done with serious forethought and collaboration."

Stellar was preoccupied with what Max said and had little to offer. Bram was aware something was going on with Stellar, his lifetime friend. The articulate, courtroom lawyer was not himself. Bram took over.

"It is our intent to have several boat operations going on at the same time when prospective immigrants are taken out. Passengers will wear a life vest but carry no luggage. All baggage will be loaded on a boat inside a cargo lift net. This will process the movement of people and baggage in the most expeditious way. Depending on the conditions at the time, boats may be boarded at different locations but will arrive at the freighter simultaneously. The prospective immigrants will be dressed like typical tourists, and the key to success is leadership coming from within the group leaving. Extensive training and instruction will be provided for those selected to be group leaders."

As the meeting moved along, little participation came from Stellar. Max knew he had set Stellar aback, and until he left to catch his plane, he found Stellar cold and distant.

Stellar and Bram had the luxury of having separate bedrooms, and after everyone had gone, they ate sandwiches Marku had brought in and both went to bed early for their long ride back to Moreni.

Bram was awakened by his six o'clock alarm. He dressed, walked to the living room, then went to the front porch where the sun was just rising in the east radiating its luster and brilliance across the calm, wavy, blue waters of the Black Sea. *He breathed in the early fresh morning air yielding to nature's flow of invigorating renewal. This sight alone, thought Bram, was worth the effort of making the trip to this meeting.* Someone would be coming shortly to take them where they had parked their vehicle. For security, they rarely parked their car where they stayed overnight. Returning to the living room, he heard nothing coming from Stellar's bedroom. He knocked on his door. "Stellar, are you awake?"

He heard nothing, pushed the door open, and saw only a rumpled bed and suitcase on the floor. He was about to turn and leave the room when two envelopes on a pillow caught his eye. One envelope was unsealed with his name written on the front. The second envelope was sealed showing the name: Gavriella.

When he read the letter addressed to him, the scenic wonder he saw on the front porch of the rising sun was blown asunder:

Bram, my dear friend, I have had a sleepless night and

234

have wrestled with the forces at work inside me. I must make a journey from which I may not return, so please take charge of completing the project at the old Lupel mansion. It is my request no effort be made to find or contact me. If you see me again in this country, it will be the result of a battle I've lost. Please give Gavriella the letter I've written that explains my decision, and If you find it convenient, please take her some fresh fish.

Your dear friend, Stellar.

Bram's world crashed in upon him. They were best friends, bonded as brothers, a David and Jonathan. Stellar carried him wounded back to their partisan camp in the Serbian mountains during the war. Rushing through his mind was the pain his dear friend was going through. Then came a streak of anger—*it was because of that woman. She had disrupted and confused Stellar's psyche, and now there is no telling where he is or what he's doing.*

Bram packed everything belonging to Stellar in his luggage he left behind and noticed in the front room a leather-covered book with the name Max written on the inside. Not wanting to leave anything in the home that could be traced to their meeting at this site, he added it to his personal effects. It was a decision that would change his life in the months ahead.

Chapter 27

Project without Stellar

On the drive back to Moreni, Bram felt lost, dislocated, and alone. Loneliness had been much of his life's experience, the difference being his present state was from a friend's absence, unlike the loneliness created from childhood anti-Semitic vilification, fleeing at night from SS Nazi troops and the loss of family members now in unmarked graves. He and Stellar had been childhood friends, had advanced to matriculation at the University of Bucharest at the age of sixteen but forced to flee to the mountains when Germany invaded the country. Now alone without his friend, he would have to prove to himself and others, that he had the strength of a Stellar.

The resentment he held toward Gavriella was overruled by Stellar's request: he took time to purchase a good supply of fish as she requested. The drive back to the Lupel mansion gave Bram a lot of time to ruminate over actions considered viable, yet be compliant with Stellar's instructions. He might consider moving to a room at the mansion site. He was pleased the very capable Popescu was there in charge of the day-to-day operations. This meant he'd rarely have to deal with Gavriella.

Upon reaching Moreni, Bram first drove by Gavriella's place and found no one there except the housekeeper who was also the cook. She was pleased to receive the fish and

Bram quickly left for the Lupel project to relieve himself of his other burden.

The site was a beehive. Workers were carrying debris outside the home and packing it in trucks to be taken to the city dump. Gavriella was talking with landscape designers when she saw Bram coming in her direction. She stopped everything, saying to the landscape people, "We'll continue this some other time." Then turning to Bram, asked, "Welcome back....Where's Stellar?"

"He chose not to come back. When I got up this morning he was gone, and I found two letters on his pillow, one addressed to me, and one to you. I was devastated and still am. I leave with you the letter he requested me to deliver, and I'm leaving with you the letter he wrote to me. This puts a burden on all of us."

Bram saw Gavriella's countenance change to a state of shock, and without saying anything took the two letters and walked into the dense floral beauty surrounding the old house. She wanted to be alone.

A thousand thoughts were running through her mind after hearing what Stellar did. She was surprised he made this rash decision. It didn't seem to fit his nature, and his action seemed to show a certain weakness. She garnered enough strength to open the letter.

Gavriella,

My dear faithful friend and colleague, Bram, has been asked to deliver this letter to you to explain my absence. You have introduced into my life by your affirmation of faith a competitor to what I believe and have been taught. You have drawn a line between us, and for me to step over that line, I would have to deny what I am and what I believe. This is the battle now raging inside me, forcing me to take a journey from which I may never return. Bram is commissioned to assume my place and finish our assignment in this country. Whatever happens to me, I will always remember you and the beautiful person you are— inside and out. I have requested Bram that no effort be made to find or contact me.

Your friend, Stellar.

Gavriella looked away with tears coursing down her face. Her strong, stalwart spirit that had been taken to that line in the sand with Stellar was experiencing the ravages of frayed human emotions. She resisted wiping her tears from her smooth, rosy cheeks, a willful act, leaving the message that she was willing to accept the consequences of human vulnerability. It was a scene of a paradoxical enigma, a picture of nature's peaceful arms of floral beauty cradling God's image that was bruised with emotional hurt. Nature's ambient floral beauty listened as an audience of one to a prayer coming from Gravriella's lips: "Lord, help Stellar to find Moses' desert where the brazen serpent on a pole awaits him. Help him find your way, your truth, and your life."

Bram, now alone without his friend, went inside the old mansion under renovation and was amazed to find how much change had taken place in two days. He saw Popescu seated at a makeshift table away from the work area going over floor plans. The old man looked up and saw Bram.

"Where's Stellar? I need to talk to him about financial requisition issues!"

"He's not here, but I'm in a position to answer any questions you may have."

"My questions need to be addressed by both of you."

"I'm sorry to say, Stellar will not be with us on this project. I have been assigned to take over his responsibilities."

"And does Gavriella know what you're telling me."

"I'm sure she knows by now. Stellar wrote a letter telling her what I'm telling you, and I'm sure she has read it."

Both saw Gavriella coming toward them with a determined stride. "Bram, I want to talk to you about business, and I want Mr. Popescu to be with me as my friend and counselor."

"I agree that we should talk," said Bram.

"I support more than you will ever know your mission and the project you have here in this country; however, I have to be guaranteed that there are funds available to complete the project before we get further along in construction."

"I'm glad you brought this up," responded Bram. "This is what I propose. We'll fly you and Mr. Popescu to Munich where a bank account will be set up in your name in the amount of five hundred thousand dollars. You will transfer as needed the funds from your account in Germany to the local bank here in this country into an account that will be registered in both of our names. All disbursements for materials and labor will come from our account in this country. After your account in Munich is set up, we'll have a local lawyer draw up legal documents giving me fifty percent ownership of the property and business. I must be seen by the government as a businessman making an investment in this country in order to function and carry out our mission in this land. Funds not used from the account in your name in Munich will be returned after completion of the project."

"I'll have no problem getting a visa to West Germany, and since Mr. Popescu just came from there, his is still valid."

"We'll get you booked within the week," said Bram.

Chapter 28

The Brazen Serpent

When Stellar left the seacoast town near the Black Sea, he left in the middle of the night with only the clothes on his back, his wallet, and passport. Though he was born in this country, it was his passport of another country that gave him the freedom to come and go at will. By daylight, he had reached the outskirts of Bucharest after finding nighttime truck drivers who'd take payment for a lift. Words spoken by Max were still reverberating in his head. He walked through the doors of the first hotel he saw, registered, went to his room, and without undressing threw himself on the bed wanting to escape his tangled, confused world. Sleep gave temporary repose. He awakened at two in the afternoon with Max's words still pounding in his head.

Two forces were struggling inside Stellar. One had a face to it—Judaism and his Jewish cultural upbringing—the other gnawing at him was less definable though its energy gave the feeling that it had eyes in search of something lost.

Lying in bed, he stared at the blank, sterile wall holding neither picture nor décor. It was but a mirror showing where he was in life—alone, empty, and bewildered about a battle going on inside he didn't understand. He had fallen into a deep, dark pit with walls straight and high with none to cast a rope, nor a hand to lift from despair. *The depth of darkness was always measured by the strength of light and holding neither candle or torch his soul cried out all the louder, "Where was the ladder— the secret passage from darkness to light?"*

For two days, Stellar neither ate nor shaved. The water he drank came from the faucet in the bathroom sink. Frequent thoughts coming at him posed questions on the subject of mental health—was he on the verge of a breakdown? However, in his state of swirling mental quandary, cognitive skills came to his aid. He was a lawyer, and in the juridical realm, cause-and-effect was always the starting point in examining an issue. He could blame the lovely and gracious woman who came into his life as the cause of his bewilderment—the conflict between them over her faith in Yeshua, and his lack thereof—but it was deeper and more complex than that. Yes, his conflict was between him and another party but not the lady who refused to cross her drawn line. His conflict was with God.

On the third day of his self-imposed confinement, Stellar braved the short journey of a walk on the street in front of his hotel. With unshaven face, rumpled clothes, and scraggly hair he gave the appearance of homelessness. When passing a medical clinic, his eyes caught the scene of the Hippocratic Medical Oath showing a serpent on a pole. His walk came to a stop, but his world inside sped up. He remembered Gavriella's story about Moses and the brazen serpent that brought healing to those bitten on the desert floor. He stepped closer, but what came into view was a reflection of himself in the glass—the figure of a haggard-looking person whose outer appearance was showing what he was on the inside. He heard himself say, "I am on *Moses' desert bitten by a poisonous serpent from which there is no recovery.*"

After picking up sandwiches at a deli, Stellar continued his stroll back to his hotel room passing in front of glass display windows showing more visual scenes of how far he had fallen. His disheveled, frail condition left the message that he was a prisoner locked in a dark, underground, medieval cell without key or friend to help.

Weakened from lack of nutrition, Stellar found his dexterity and coordination greatly reduced, but he managed to open his hotel door and place his sandwiches on a nightstand. He took note that the housekeeper had just left leaving fresh towels, a vacuumed floor, and a neatly made bed. His eyes stayed with the bed where he saw a book the woman had forgotten. Without touching his sandwiches, he took the book hoping it to be something he could use to escape his imposed dark world. He found it to be a religious volume, an anthology of Jewish writings describing the history of the Jews and the rise of the Christian movement.

Three hours later, with sandwiches untouched, Stellar was sitting up in bed reading the book of Isaiah, justifying doing so that it was Jewish literature. He'd never read the prophets, and when he came to Isaiah fifty-three, it moved him to read it again. Then turning to the Torah, the books he was familiar with, he read from Numbers the account of Moses and the brazen serpent on the desert. By this time, it was eleven o'clock in the evening, and his sandwiches were still untouched. It was a book he couldn't put down.

Gavriella had a line drawn in the sand she wouldn't

cross over, and until this moment, he never knew that he also had a line in the sand, one taught from his youth: he was forbidden to read what was called Christian writings that came out in the first century, literature Christians called the New Testament. But there was a light coming from his reading Isaiah, a force of energy pulling him to the forbidden line. He started with Matthew and was surprised that everything was Jewish. Three hours later, he came across the account of Jesus saying in the book of John, *"Just as Moses lifted up the snake in the desert, so the Son of Man must be lifted up, that everyone who believes in him may have eternal life."*

Three compelling scenes were now gripping Stellar: Moses' raised serpent on a pole in the desert; the wounded person of Isaiah fifty-three; and the statement of Jesus casting Himself as the fulfillment of Moses' serpent on a pole.

The big man, Max, surfaced in Stellar's memory. He resented the religious verbal intrusion into his space at the time, but something was becoming clear in what he said: *He who knew no sin became sin.*

Stellar closed the book. Weary from lack of sleep, he turned off the light. Something was happening inside his confused world. It was the book he'd found on the bed that put him in this circle of truth. Strobes of light now flashed on his barren, lifeless, prison wall. He was on Moses' desert floor suffering from the venom bite of death in need of an antidote—but the cure was beyond his reach—it was on the other side of the line he'd drawn in the sand, a forbidden place to go. The ground shook underneath Stellar. Rippling through the man was the light of truth from another world, something not seen before.

The law of causality forced its way across Stellar's path. It was a principle in everyday life, and being a student of historical events that shaped the world, he remembered Julius Caesar who altered the face of Roman society. The epic point of change was when General Caesar looked across the Rubicon River with his military and made the decision to cross, knowing that once the crossing was made there would be no turning back and that by doing so, an unknown future awaited him.

Stellar was now at the crossroads of his life, his own Rubicon River crossing. By crossing over that line, he would be compelled to believe that Moses' brazen serpent was an introduction to the drama of the suffering Man found in Isaiah fifty-three, a Man whose death bore the sins of many.

Stellar's battle, unlike Caesar's, wasn't with many but with one—his Creator. Truth from the Holy Writings had brought him to this point of the water's edge. However, the cure of the Serpent's bite was across the river, and once the crossing was begun there could be no turning back.

Lying on a bed in a room of total darkness, a cold mist formed inside Stellar, giving sparkles of light and life to all he had read in the book he found on the bed. From the deep inner bowels of his soul where faith was birthed came the whispers of affirmation...*I believe...I believe that Jesus was the Jewish Messiah who became the Passover Lamb and was the antidote sin offering for those bitten by the Serpent."*

A long pause of inner quietness followed. *Stellar had made his journey across his Rubicon. Faith with knowledge had given the birth of new life to one bitten by the Serpent.* Max's words having caused distress earlier now embellished the body of truth that formed him into a new person. Lying silently in the darkened room in his state of euphoric change, Stellar continued his journey when a bright, propitious light appeared at the foot of his bed, followed by a blanket of deep, tranquil sleep.

It was three o'clock in the afternoon the next day when Stellar awoke. The light he saw the night before and everything he'd read still lingered inside. He grabbed the book he'd read the night before and read once again Isaiah fifty-three, then quickly dressed and found a taxi.

"To the telegraph office!" said Stellar to the driver. He had the need to send Max an urgent message. He would use Max's code name, and the message would read: "Little Man, thanks to you and Gavriella, I have found the Passover Lamb in Isaiah fifty-three! Don't answer, I'm out of town."

Chapter 29

Munich

Bram had managed to keep his attitude and feelings about Gavriella under control. He knew that for a successful outcome of the operation here in Romania, personal conflicts had to be kept at a minimum. He had actually come to admire her competency in business management and organizational skills.

As agreed upon, Bram made arrangements to finalize his partnership with Gavriella in the old mansion project by sending her to a bank in Munich along with Popescu. After a two-hour flight, they found Michael's driver, Luis, waiting for them. The presence of the driver left the message that Bram was in communication with the overseas coordinator. Both would stay at the guesthouse in Michael's compound.

When Michael's driver saw the old man, the two embraced. "My dear friend," said the old man, "I want you to meet a very special person: this is Gavriella."

"Please to meet you, Ma'am."

The tall lady being introduced carried a smart look of elegance. She gave a slight smile with a nod of recognition, adding, "We need to get right to the bank, Luis."

"Just don't you worry, Ma'am. I'll have you there in fifteen minutes"

Bram's men in Munich had done the necessary

paperwork in creating an account in her name. After arriving, she was directed to a side office where documents were signed and given a bank statement showing a balance agreed upon by Bram. The only security Bram's organization had was the lady's long-standing reputation of helping Jews and fifty-percent ownership of the Lupel mansion once the documents were finalized in Romania. The old man, like a father, was at her side during the entire transaction, looking out for her welfare and best interests.

When they reached their transport, the driver was standing with an open door waiting for them to board. "I just got a call from Michael. He and Max are taking both of you out to dinner tonight. He said, 'the project at Moreni would serve a vital part of the operation.' I don't know what that means but apparently, you do, and what Michael tells me stays with me."

The old man turned and faced Gavriella. "Michael generates loyalty even among his drivers—that boy is something else, and it appears he's broadening Max's responsibility in overseas operations."

"Luis, before we go to Michael's guesthouse, take us to the central headquarters of Katharina Enterprises. Gavriella needs to know some important history."

Three hours later, Luis pulled in front of a posh restaurant. Gavriella followed Popescu through the front door where two men awaited their arrival. One was tall and blond with striking blue eyes. The other had a massive frame with a glistening baldhead. Gavriella saw Popescu greet the big, burly man with a handshake, then turn and embrace the blond man.

"I want you gentlemen to meet my dear friend,

Gavriella," said Popescu. "She has invited me to assist her in the project of creating a first-class hotel that will act as a business cover so operatives can stay in the country for the mission of moving Jews to the coast."

"Your commitment to that cause is most noble," responded Max.

"We all agree with Max," asserted Michael. "This includes the administrative team at Katharina Enterprises. But let's not discuss formalities here in the lobby, we have a dining room waiting for us.

They were led to a small, private dining room. Gavriella knew this was all business and not a social event. She had resisted up to this point the urge to explore the name, Pencovich. Now everything was rushing at her. Many who survived the Holocaust in Romania made folk heroes out of those who resisted the Nazis and became legends of their time. The man leading this session of business, Michael Pencovich, was at the top of that list. Michael led the conversation.

"Those who own and administer Katharina Enterprises are dedicated to the support of the state of Israel. They believe what the prophets taught: that the Messiah will return to Jerusalem to govern the earth, and by supporting the return of Abraham's descendants to their ancient land, they are fulfilling what God has called them to do.

"All of us, except Max, carry the pain of the Holocaust where we lost families and friends to an evil genocide unknown in modern times. However, justice may be slow coming but come it does, and in your case, Gavriella, when you inherited the Lupel property, it was poetic justice. Imagine, a Jew becoming an heir of Nazi property and that property being used to help promote Zionism.

"Thank you, Mr. Popescu, for joining Gavriella in what comes naturally for you in support of Israel and her people. Gavriella is fortunate to have you helping her.

"I have asked Max to be with us tonight because the chairman has expanded his portfolio to include working with the different entities inside the country of Romania. We do not want to see the creation of a monolithic underground enterprise. What is preferred is a loosely knitted group, where if one part of the organization has a problem, the problem will not extend to others. We need many moving parts to this operation so if one entity gets into trouble, it will not bring the whole operation down,— thus we support and welcome Gavriella's partnership with those who are skilled to do what they do. The country is rife with graft and corruption, and there may be times when that will be to our advantage when money will buy silence with certain authorities and should be used only under emergency situations."

Gavriella and Max had retreated to a wallflower role while Michael and Popescu carried the conversation. It was uncharacteristic of Max, but he held a special message for the lady among the group and was preoccupied with when and how to deliver it. That would soon change.

"Michael, what's the current status of the Funar trial?" asked Popescu.

"Funar has a medical condition with severe heart damage, and the Court has imposed a suspension until he receives medical clearance. West German law doesn't permit the death penalty, so most likely when the court resumes, he will be judged guilty and spend the rest of his life in prison."

The discussion of Funar brought silence until Popescu spoke. "Funar, prior to his escape to Munich had a relationship with the Lupels, and if Gavriella feels up to it, it would be interesting to hear how she came about the Lupel mansion and Funar's influence in bringing that about. Bits and pieces have come to us about Gavriella's inheritance story of the old place, and I would like for it to be told in detail from her own lips."

Up to this point, Gavriella appeared shy and reserved. She had said nothing, and when she began to speak she demonstrated communication skills as compelling as her performance on the violin.

"To comply with Mr. Popescu's request, I will begin by reading aloud a personal letter written by the owner of the Lupel property:

Dear Gavriella,

As you now know, you are the sole heir of all my estate and I came to this decision based on several things. First, because of the person you are, and second, I had the need to expunge guilt from my conscience of unknowingly protecting someone guilty of war crimes.

I made an unwritten agreement with my nephew to take title of the property with life tenancy and signed a will giving title to a trust through which he could hide true ownership upon my demise. This was why I would not sell you the property, but things changed when a photo of a certain Colonel Funar, arrested for war *crimes, appeared on front pages of newspapers. It was like a light thrown on my history here at this old mansion. <u>I remembered seeing that colonel on this property at night on several occasions after I had occupied this place under the agreement I made with my nephew.</u>*

There are <u>secret hidden chambers in that old house,</u> put there by his father. For twenty years, I lived in that house and never saw the inside of some of them. Sometimes, one learns to compartmentalize his life, and in doing so he can choose which compartment to live in. I lived there with the memory of my sister and her son carried the memory of his father. Both he and his father were devout and committed Nazis. My nephew presently works for the communist government in the department of foreign service delivering vital information as a courier to this country's embassies in Europe. <u>He goes by the name of Teodor Popa.</u> I hope you will not see me as a bad person, and this is not intended to be a deathbed confession. Perhaps my story of turning on a family member will somehow touch people that need to hear it, people who lack the courage to stand for what is right.

Your friend, A. Lunga

The men at the dining table saw Gavriella hand the letter to Michael, saying, "As you review this letter, note the underlined portions that emphasize the war criminal being discussed. The mansion was used as a central

252

meeting site for Nazis, Colonel Funar being one of them, and that the building itself had secret hidden chambers, some of which he never explored.

"Now, I would like to address some of the issues just mentioned. When I took possession of the property, with the help of others there was found hidden in the house stolen Jewish wealth in the form of diamonds, gold rings, watches, broaches, and necklaces. Also, found hidden were files containing records of executed partisan resistors. These were files used by Nazi officers to create new identities to hide behind, war criminals who should have been put on trial. There is no way to know how many slipped into hiding and were never found or detected. What we do know is that Lupel became the respectable Mr. Teodor Popa, an employee of the communist government and that Colonel Funar managed to escape to West Germany.

"With sincere deference to Mr. Popescu, I will forever be thankful for his wisdom and help in finding and expunging from one of the secret chambers the evil spirit of Nazism cloaked with the darkness of occultism. I will leave with you photographs taken of the stolen Jewish jewelry along with photos taken of the secret room where occult practices were carried out under the portraits of Nazi leaders. The photos explain more vividly than what words can describe. It is a house of mystery waiting to be fully explored."

Gavriella paused, handed Michael an envelope containing photos, then continued discussing the Lupel property.

"It remains to be seen what we'll find in the old

253

mansion. I must credit my dear friend, who is like a father to me, for being wise in so many things. I'm not quite sure I would want to go through with the challenge in front of me if he were not at my side."

Those who saw Michael noticed a smile coming across his face upon hearing the endearing words about Mr. Popescu.

"Gavriella, the man of whom you speak is a family member. He was at my Bar Mitzvah when I was twelve-years-old." He stopped short of citing his youthful years of playing with his two sons who were later killed in the war.

"How could I be so lucky," said Gavriella. Turning to the old man, they all heard her say, "Thank you, Mr. Popescue, for being my friend and helper!"

Max couldn't contain himself. He had sat the whole time saying little. He reached into his vest pocket and took out a copy of the cable sent to him from Stellar.

"Gavriella, I'm going to make today a day of all days for you. Here's a cable sent to me two days ago by someone who means a lot to you."

Those at the table watched her silently read the telegram sent to Max:

Little Man, Thanks to you and Gavriella, I have found the Passover Lamb in Isaiah fifty-three. Don't answer, I'm out of town. Stellar

She raised her head showing no expression, then looked down again and read it the second time, folded the telegram and handed it back to Max.

"Max, thank you for what you did for Stellar. If you

gentlemen will excuse me, I'll be back shortly."

The old man looked at Max. "Since you made your telegram public, are you going to keep us in suspense, or are you going to read it?"

"Of course I'll read the telegram. It's good news for all of us."

After Max read the cable, everyone showed a reverent, somber tone. A Jewish man had come to believe that Yeshua was the Jewish Messiah, and when Gavriella returned from the ladies' room with red, swollen eyes, Michael thought intervention was necessary.

"All of us here will celebrate with Stellar his step of faith and my hope is that the next time we meet it will be in Israel with Stellar among us."

Chapter 30

The Prodigal and the Ring

After Stellar sent the telegram to Max, he returned to his hotel room and for the following five days stayed in his room reading the Jewish writings he'd found in the book on the bed. He lost interest in food and the outside world, grew thin and gaunt. He read the first thirty-nine books from *Genesis* to *Malachi*, then read the Major and Minor Prophets again. After reading the Christian first-century set of twenty-seven books, he re-read them paying special attention to the book titled, *Acts of the Apostles*.

Stellar felt like a different person, then realized he was. His experience had made him more Jewish. His people in history were a special people, a people to whom God gave oracles of truth that always pointed to Yeshua, the beginning and end of all things.

Every morning inside his hotel room Stellar awakened to a new world. *What would this new world mean to him in everyday life?* He remembered Gavriella's history, a history of rejection by her own family when she became a believer. Was this to be his fate? He remembered reading what the Messiah said of those who would follow him: "For I have come to turn a man against his father, a daughter against her mother, a daughter-in-law against her mother-in-law. A man's enemy will be those of his own household." *Was he willing to accept the same rejection? Was it providential that Gavriella had come into his life so that both could be strength for each other, or that she could be a pillar for him?*

It had been ten days since Stellar and Bram drove out of Gavriella's compound, and now he felt like a Jonah having been coughed up in a foreign land. The ground he now stood on was new and different, almost strange. Though his inner person was renewed, his outer person had not fared well: he had lost weight, his clothes were soiled, wrinkled, and in need of cleaning. He remembered reading the story of the prodigal son who arrived home at his Father's house in need of clothing and acceptance. He would visit a clothing store and start his journey to a new life with no guarantees waiting for him. Even Gavriella may not have a welcome mat.

Gavriella had returned from delivering lunch to Mr. Popescu and Bram at the Lupel construction site and was walking up her outside stairs leading to her large patio entrance when she stopped. Startled at what she saw, both hands went to her face to cover her volcanic feelings. Stellar was seated in one of the patio chairs, appearing gaunt and haggard. Showing a state of shock, she stood staring at eyes that looked strong and bright but whose frame was fragile.

She said nothing, walked over and sat next to him taking his hand in hers. "Are you alright, Stellar? You look poorly."

With a faraway look, he responded: "I'm strong in the inner man because I have met God but weak behind my thin veil of mortality. Daniel was left weakened by his exposure to another dimension and had to be strengthened by an angel to continue. That night when I confessed that Yeshua was the Messiah, I saw a miraculous light at the foot of my bed. The following days, I hardly ate but spent my time reading the sacred texts of Jewish writers.

"Gavriella, I don't know where my life is going from this point on, and I even thought that you'd forgotten about me."

Stellar looked at her hands that held his and saw she still wore her wedding band. "I've never left thinking about you, but I have a question for you, Stellar. Are you willing to accept rejection from your Jewish family and friends?"

"I have already traveled down that road. I would not have returned here if it were otherwise."

"I want you to stay here and I'll bring you something to eat with a glass of milk."

It was painful when she released his hand. The warm touch had told him someone cared. She slid away leaving him the words, "Don't go anywhere, I'll be back shortly."

In the absence of Gavriella, Stellar made note that his new world extended to heightened levels of appreciation of scenic beauty and sounds of nature. He'd been on this patio deck before, but today the chirping and singing of birds gave new luster among the rustling, bright leaves overhead.

His musings were interrupted when a tray holding a glass of milk, fruit, and toast were placed in front of him. Hands holding the tray were in visible sight. Gavriella had removed her wedding band, and now her gifted fingers for music were bare—a signal she was willing to step into his world and invite him into hers. Stellar's heart pounded.

"I bring to your attention as you have already noticed, the wedding band has been removed, something I have never done before."

"Does this allow me to ask for your hand in marriage?" asked Stellar.

"I opened that door of my life when I removed the ring."

Stellar stood to his feet, and for the first time had the freedom to walk through the door she'd opened. He pulled her into his embrace, asking, "Will you marry me, Gavriella?"

He felt her arms responding with the sound of a whisper coming from her lips to his ear, "I will marry you if you promise to love me the rest of our lives!"

Stellar buried his face on her shoulder weeping, broken over her acceptance of him into her life. She held him tight and welcomed his gentle strokes over her long-flowing, wavy dark hair.

For three hours, Stellar and Gavriella sorted out their lives. Both were born in Romania, yet Stellar carried a Yugoslavian passport. Stellar had come to this country on a secret mission with Bram under the auspices of a Zionist covert organization supported by Katharina Enterprises whose mission was to organize a stealth infrastructure to smuggle Jews to the coast for transfer to waiting freighters.

They chose to act with two options in mind. First, if Bram wanted Stellar to work with him in their mission after being told of his newfound Messianic faith, they would postpone their wedding until the Lupel mansion project was completed. The second option was if Bram chose to go it alone without Stellar, they would plan a wedding immediately. Regardless, Bram and Popescu would be told of their engagement today.

Stellar took in all the changes going on at the Lupel mansion when Gavriella pulled onto the building site. The landscaping team of workers had already put a new face on the old place. When they entered the first floor, Stellar found the entire bottom completely framed with the new floor design. Bram's architectural and engineering skills were showing even in the early stage of renovation. They saw Popescu supervising workers, but Bram was nowhere in sight. Tear-out had already begun on the second floor and workers were using the stairs as a pathway to remove the debris. Knowing Bram would need a large table away from work activity, they went to the third floor and found a room with an open door. Stellar stopped in the doorway with Gavriella behind. Bram was stationed at an improvised drafting table looking down at his work.

"Hello, my good friend," said Stellar in a quiet, subdued voice.

Bram's body language signaled his startled state. The voice he heard was like a voice from the dead. Eyes focused on building plans slowly moved toward the open door where Stellar stood. His face carried the look of unbelief. It was Stellar—but not the Stellar he had known. Not only was he frail and thin, his eyes carried a strange new look, an aura of peaceful zest not seen since the war. When he fled the coastal village in the middle of the night, he didn't believe he'd ever see him again inside this country. Then his eyes moved to the figure standing behind

Stellar, the lady who had captured Stellar's heart.

"Hello Stellar. You don't look well. Where have you been and what have you done to yourself? You told me that I'd never see you again in this country."

Stellar took Gavriella's hand, and together they walked to the middle of the room. Bram saw the emergence of Stellar's self-confident courtroom performance. "To be exact, I said, 'If you see me again in this country, it will be the result of a battle I've lost.' I'm here to tell you, I have lost the battle, a battle I'm glad someone else won. For days I read Jewish writings that we Jews call the Tanakh, as well as Jewish writings Christians designate as the New Testament. Truth came to the dead man inside me, and I was made to see that Jesus was the Jewish Messiah, the Passover Lamb of Isaiah fifty-three.

"In this country, we have two objectives in front of us: make a viable business investment and lay the groundwork for moving Jews to freighters at sea. My question to you does not address the Lupel mansion project because I'll be here with Gavriella regardless of what others wish. But my question to you is, do you want me to remain in the operation of the mission after the hotel project is completed?"

"Stellar, I wouldn't be here today had you not carried me back to our partisan camp after being wounded. We were one in those days, and we will be one from here on out."

He walked from behind his desk, embraced his old friend, saying, "I'm glad my friend came back!"

"I have a special announcement for you," said Stellar. He put his arm around Gavriella and pulled her to himself.

"Gavriella and I are engaged to be married, and the date of the wedding will be close to the time when the hotel project is completed."

"Let me be first to congratulate you," said Bram.

Then came a voice from behind, "And let me be the second to congratulate you." It was the old man Popescu standing in the doorway with a smile from ear-to-ear. "I'm glad you're back with us, Stellar. You two make a beautiful couple. The reason I came up was to talk to Gavriella and Bram about a matter of historical interest that involves this old building. However, in view of this wonderful news about a wedding, what I have to say can wait until later tonight!"

Gavriella never left anything hanging or undone. "We can walk and chew gum at the same time," said Gavriella. "We're all together at the site that demands our interest and energy, and I'm sure we can take time to hear what Mr. Popescu has to say."

"Well, that being the case, let's all go down to the first floor so I can show you what I have found."

Chapter 31

Another Mystery Room

Popescu led the group down to the area where the old fireplace was undergoing renovation.

"We all know," said the old man, "that plans for the makeover of this old mansion call for a new, larger fireplace. In the process of the tear-out, the workers noticed a section of the hearth had settled four inches, and assuming there was a major problem, the workers called me over to inspect it. I assigned them another project on the second floor and proceeded to inspect the site myself. To construct a new fireplace, I needed to know the compaction of the substrate that had settled. Using a long metal rod as a probe, I made entry at three different points and found no resistance, leaving the message that the area underneath the hearth was merely open space. I dismissed the workers for the day and went immediately to the third floor to discuss the matter with Gavriella and Bram."

Bram interrupted Popescu. "Was it wise to cause a work stoppage by sending the workers home for the day? This will delay the good progress we've made."

"Mr. Bram, I will answer that question later, but first hear me out. Gavriella has inherited a very interesting piece of history. This old mansion was built before 1850, was the only one in the area and it came with a lot of land. In those days, homes like this were built with secret passages and hiding places, so when the wrong people came around, landholders had a place to flee and hide. Those secret chambers were also used to conceal valuables as well as persons. The void space underneath the hearth floor may speak to the mystery of a secret underground passage.

"The reason I'm showing this to you is that it must be examined as a potential liability to structural soundness, and it must be done without the knowledge of the workers. We cannot afford to have conspiracies roaming about the community, especially if something untoward is found and workers see or know about it. It is in our interest that we attract no attention."

The old man looked at the three staring at him in disbelief. "With what's showing on your faces, you don't believe me!"

Popescu was sometimes a paradox to those with whom he now worked. They all knew he had little formal training but was always insightful, could even do mathematical equations as well as Bram, an engineer. Bram was first to respond.

"Mr. Popescu, please don't think I'm speaking disparagingly of you, "but what gives you the experience and knowledge in making these postulations? You certainly know more and have greater insight than I do in certain matters, but don't you think this is a little over the top?"

"Mr. Bram, why did it take an old man like me to know there was a cellar underneath the flooring behind the metal door in the basement? In this matter about the hearth, I relied on my knowledge of old buildings that were constructed for personal safety beyond the wind, rain, and cold.

"Now, my question to you is, when do you want to work on this problem—tonight, or tomorrow night? The workers must know nothing about what we've found."

Stellar spoke up. "Let's open it up and see what's down there, then act on what we find."

"Bram, you have the muscle," said the old man. "Take that large sledgehammer and hit the outside corners of the hearth."

It took one heavy swing. A large chunk of the hearth flooring fell into a cavity below. Each looked at the other saying nothing. Everyone, except the old man, was aghast. After the dust settled, Popescu took command, pulled out his flashlight, and directed the light into a six-foot dark hole.

"Up to this point, I thought we'd found all the mystery spots in this old mansion, but it looks like we have a new one to examine. Notice the tunnel beneath this flooring has walls lined with stone and appear to be in good shape. Look, there's an old collapsed ladder used at one time to enter and exit the passageway! Apparently, the tunnel leads away from the fireplace to another area where there's probably a holding section or an external escape route."

A curtain of silence hung in the atmosphere, mostly from the embarrassment of disbelief of what the old man told them. Gavriella was first to open conversation. "Do you think the Lupels knew of this tunnel?"

"No, the Lupels never knew this existed, and if you look closely, new flooring at some point was put down without removing the original, thereby covering the hatch door and concealing it until today.

Bram watched Popescu place an eight-foot ladder into

the hole. All four were standing at the mouth of the caved-in hearth when Popescu continued.

"It's best if just two of us go into the tunnel. I'll lead the way and the rest of you can delegate the other party. The margin of safety is higher with rock-lined walls, and whoever follows me must have a flashlight and avoid touching or moving anything. You can expect to find strange things, some living, and some dead, and by that, I refer to rodents. The person following me should make a mental map of distance and direction. It's very easy to get confused in total darkness. Also, don't slide your feet. That'll minimize our exposure to the dust that carries bad things that have been incubating down here without natural sunlight."

Gavriella and Stellar watched the old man descend the ladder with Bram following. Both had flashlights as they lowered themselves into a chamber that effused the smell of damp, stale air. They moved along single file, taking short steps. At a distance of ten feet from the entry, the tunnel made a ninety-degree right turn toward the outer wall. Both were looking for cracks and weak spots that would be telling points of subterranean shifting which would have a direct bearing on structural viability. Fifteen feet from the first ninety-degree turn, the tunnel made a left turn where it widened allowing what appeared to be on both sides of the tunnel stone benches. The men said nothing. There was too much to take in for dialogue. It had been over a hundred years since human feet walked this tunnel.

The old man leaned over to inspect the stone benches, found that only the top was stone and the base was built out of wood. He slid the rock slab forward uncovering the wooden framework that was now in a dry-rot state. Inside sat an old rusty metal box. The first words spoken came from the old man.

"Bram, look at what we have here."

"Looks like an old metal box with a cover," responded Bram. "Can you lift the top off?"

"No, it's frozen tight. A hundred years of storage will rust anything shut."

"Perhaps a few good whacks with that stone seat cover will do the trick," said Bram.

Bram had the strength of an Olympian weightlifter, and after several crushing blows, he asked, "Is it broken loose yet?

The old man laid his flashlight aside and with both hands managed to lift the cover from the box.

Bram dropped to his knees alongside Popescu. They couldn't believe what they had uncovered. The old, rusty metal box was full of gold bars, bright and shiny as they were the day they were put there.

"Bram, let's check under the other seats and get a count on how many boxes are down here. If you find a box, shake it to be sure it's not empty. Remember to replace the stone seat as it was found."

It had been fifteen minutes since Popescu and Bram disappeared into the mystery tunnel under the hearth, and worry was showing on Gavriella.

"I hope they're alright," said Gavriella.

Stellar looked at her. "I'll go down and give them a yell."

There was sufficient light coming from the open hearth

that Stellar was able to see to walk to the first ninety-degree turn. At that point, he could vaguely see the movement of light.

"Are you fellows alright?" yelled Stellar as heartily as he could.

Returned were soft, muffled words that sounded far away, "Yes, we're fine! We'll be out soon!"

Stellar walked over to the foot of the ladder, climbed out. "They're fine and will be out soon. It's strange though, the voice seemed to carry an upbeat sparkle in its tone."

Shortly, they heard grunting struggles of two men carrying a heavy object.

"Stellar, take the ladder out of the hearth opening," requested Popescu, "we have something to lift out."

Once the ladder was removed, the two men placed what they had brought out on the edge of the hearth opening, then climbed the replaced ladder looking like they'd been in a dust storm.

Together, they pulled the metal box to the center of the room and the old man took charge.

"First, I will now address the question Bram raised earlier. Yes, it was beneficial to cause a work stoppage by sending workers away from the site. Had they seen what we found, you would be kissing goodbye any effective operation in this country of moving Jews to Israel."

Bram lowered his head showing embarrassment in Popescu's rebuke; however, his thoughts were running wild, asking, why is this old man always right?

"I'm a bit confused with what you're saying," responded Stellar. "What's in the box that has such influence?"

268

Knowing Bram felt rebuffed, Popescu put down a bridge he could walk over and save face. "I leave with Bram the task of answering that question."

They all watched Bram open the metal box and take from it two of the items inside, handed one to Gavriella, the other to Stellar.

"These are solid gold bars, and there are five additional boxes down below in the tunnel. The knowledge of these gold-filled boxes probably went to the grave with someone over a hundred years ago.

Popescu took charge again. "As previously stated, old mansions frequently have built-in secret passages for the convenience of personal safety. Because the escape hatch was found covered up when a new floor had been installed speaks to the change of a less violent and more governed society, leaving the tunnel as a storage site for valuables with access from some external location, which we will eventually find with further examination."

Gavriella and Stellar stood holding the gold bars. *At a loss for words, their faces said it all. The old mansion had heightened the level of mystery.*

"Mr. Popescu, why were these gold bars never found?" asked the new owner of the estate.

"There could be several reasons, and therein lies the mystery. The owners of the mansion were wealthy, and only a few would have known about the tunnel. From what we know at this point, it's most likely that only the person who hid the gold had knowledge of it and didn't live to retrieve it or tell others about it. Today's find embellishes the mystery of the old place.

"There's a narrative that goes with this discovery of

gold. History shows that gold has always been a medium of exchange. Paper money is a modern invention. It wasn't uncommon for people to carry gold around with them for business transactions, just not a lot of it because of theft and robbers. While we're on the subject of the history of gold, the country of Romania is known to be one of the richest countries in Europe in gold deposits. The Roman Emperor, Trajan, in the early second century carried back to Rome from this country 165 tons of gold.

"If you saw the size of the gold bars inside that box, you would've noticed they're much smaller than what we see today. Smaller bars were easier to use in business transactions."

"You are a man of wisdom, Mr. Popescu," said Stellar. "How does it come about that you know all this?"

"Experience, my friend! Also, I remember what I read, see, and hear. Those qualities are dimming in my late years, but I do alright for myself, for which I thank God!"

They saw Gavriella return her gold bar to the metal box, and in her elegant way, she put closure on the mystery of the old mansion. "It just may be that this old mansion has yielded its last mystery by giving us a piece of its history before the rise of Nazism, the bastion of twentieth-century evil, the time when our Jewish people suffered in this land."

A long, silent pause hung in the air before Stellar spoke with his legal mind in motion. "There are several things we have to consider here. First, is the question of ownership of what has been found? If those boxes cannot be legally traced to an owner, the person who holds clear title to the property on which they were found becomes entitled to all rights and privileges therein. Gavriella, who holds clear title to this property?"

"At the present time, I alone hold clear title. However, when our partnership is finalized, you and Bram will own fifty percent of the property and business."

"What's in those boxes is not part of the real property and cannot be part of any partnership arrangement, no more than any article of movable furniture inside the mansion. Therefore, the burden rests on Gavriella to make the final decision."

"How much does each box weigh?" asked Gavriella.

"You could probably put a seventy-pound average on them," said Bram.

Gavriella's thoughts were swirling with confusion. How could this be happening to her? She had struggled to survive after her husband was killed by developing a bed and breakfast in the large home her late husband left her. Now, everything was falling her way. But Why?

She quickly calculated the value of the gold found on her inherited property. "That's about two hundred seventy thousand dollars at the present price of gold," spoke Gavriella, "and if it's within my power, I will see that half of it goes to the support of moving Jews to Israel. The other half will be kept in reserve for needs that arise among us and in the community. Helping the community will give us a good public image."

"That being the case," said Stellar, "we'll make plans to hide the gold away from this property and see that it reaches a freighter at sea."

"The sooner we do this," said Popescu, "the better I'll feel about everything. We'll take this box home with us

271

tonight, but before we leave, we'll nail a three-quarter inch sheet of plywood over the open hearth and that will provide safety for the workers and privacy of the tunnel, and it will be our responsibility to finish off the floor before we allow the workmen to resume activity in this area."

"I agree with Mr. Popescu," said Gavriella. "Let's cover the hearth, load the box, and go to dinner. The cook will have everything ready by the time we arrive."

"I agree with that," said Popescu, "providing you favor us with a religious number on your violin!"

Chapter 32

Living with Rejection

A man stood alongside the boarding ramp of a freighter docked at the port of Constanta displaying nervous tension while waiting for a passenger to arrive. The evening air was cool with a slight breeze rumpling the ship's proud flag high above the docked vessel. On the deck below, the ship's crew, having off-loaded its cargo was tying everything down so departure could get underway. From the bridge, the captain kept his eye on the waiting man at the boarding ramp. Though the man looking down may be the captain of the ship for navigation, the person waiting for the special passenger was senior to him in matters of company policy and special operations. Tonight, a special operation was underway.

A tall, thin figure emerged from the shadows dressed in dark clothing and was identified to be female by the headscarf worn to conceal the person's identity. The two talked briefly.

"I'm Bub, welcome aboard. I've been told your name is Gavriella."

"That's correct, and you're Michael's lifelong friend?"

"Yes. We've known each other since childhood."

"I have requested two extra berths for my parties. Can you confirm this has been arranged?"

"Yes, we managed to do this. Let me have your

luggage case and we'll go up and I'll show you what we have."

Gavriella followed Bub up the ramp through the maze of cargo containers to stairs leading to the berths that came with windows. He opened the door, allowed her to enter first.

"Have you been informed about the special cargo we'll be bringing on board?"

"I'm aware of it," said Bub. "All baggage will be loaded separately from passengers with one lift which will expedite everything. Your special cargo will arrive first as a separate part of the operation accompanied by reliable people.

"When the pickup happens, it'll be in international waters, and from that point, it's nonstop to Haifa, Israel, the sailing time less than two days. I have used my master key to open this berth, but I'll be back in a few minutes with keys for all three staterooms."

"Thank you for your help, Bub!"

After Bub left, Gavriella unpacked her luggage and took from her personal effects a 5 by 7 photo of Stellar, placed it on the nightstand beside her bed and proceeded to check out the rest of the room. Everything was modern, convenient, and clean.

With a knock on her door, she found that Bub had returned with keys he said he'd drop off, and before leaving he notice Stellar's picture on the nightstand.

"Is that Stellar," asked Bub.

"Do you know Stellar?"

"Yes, we've crossed paths in our work."

"He has become the light of my life. We're getting

married this week in Israel, and if you're in Israel, I extend to you a personal invitation."

"Please accept my congratulations, and if I'm still in Israel, you'll see me there."

Bub turned to leave when he heard a request from the lady he'd helped to her stateroom. "May I ask you to do a favor for me? One of the three berths I have requested is reserved for my mother and father who are supposed to be among tonight's pickups. If it were within your capacity, would you find them after they are on board and bring them to the stateroom next door? I don't want them to see me until you bring them to the room."

"I love reunions and surprises," said Bub. "I'll do my best to fulfill your request." He lowered his head, looked over the top rims of his glasses, saying with a facetious grin, "And the third stateroom is for Stellar?"

"You are perceptive, Bub."

The evening was quiet at the Constanta port. Gavriella felt the hum of the ship's diesel engines and the movement of the large ship. She turned off the lights in her berth, stepped outside to watch the bright glow of the city as the vessel moved out to sea. Her heart gave a leap thinking that when she returned to this land, she would be in a marriage union with the man in the photo she'd placed on the nightstand. *She looked at her hand decked with a large sparkling diamond engagement ring, brought it close to her eyes, saying to herself in a soft whisper, "The sparkles inside my heart are greater than what I see in the dark."*

The lights onshore grew smaller and dimmed with

distance. Gavriella returned to her darkened room, avoided turning on the lights. The right kind of darkness was a welcomed friend. It had the power to switch on other kinds of light inside the soul. It muffled the sounds of the natural world allowing truth to emerge from hidden crevices, those deep parts inside that persuaded actions of the day. The words of David came to her, "Thou desireth truth in the inward parts." If darkness served no purpose, God wouldn't have made the night. Tonight, she needed darkness for renewal for what lay in front of her—the strength to face those who gave her life but abandoned her because of her faith in Yeshua.

Rushing through her mind were the horrors of the Holocaust. Nothing could match the pain of those events. But for her, it was compounded by her family's rejection when she came to believe that Jesus was the Messiah. It was an experience of another kind of Holocaust, shunned, and forced from family as a young woman, only to be taken in by righteous Gentiles.

It was Stellar who gave her strength and courage to do what was soon to take place: confront her elderly parents with an attempt of reconciliation. Until now, all previous efforts had proven futile.

The lady who boarded the ship dressed in dark clothing left her stateroom with a flashlight in hand. The lights of Constanta no longer gave its sparkle, and after navigating the stairs, she moved across the main deck and stood next to a shipping container. She had knowledge of how everything would come together. A small speedboat would first arrive carrying Stellar, Bram, and the special cargo, followed by another boat delivering the passengers' baggage on the top deck, then taken below where immigrants would later make claim. The rest of the operation would consist of three boats carrying a total of two hundred immigrants, each wearing a life vest under the supervision of trained attendants. The whole event was scheduled to take no longer than twenty minutes. Bub would be in charge of the project onboard the ship. Trained personnel would take all immigrants arriving down below where sleeping bunks, restrooms, showers, and food would be available.

The midnight sky was clear, and a full moon was casting its reflective image across rippling waters. Nature had chosen to smile upon an event that would mark the beginning of a new life for two hundred Jewish immigrants denied exit visas. The intermittent gusts of cool breezes punctuated Gavriella's strange feelings. Two emotions from two different worlds were convulsing inside, one from the excitable joy of reuniting with Stellar, the other, from the world of hurt, having been rejected by her family because of her faith.

The large freighter cut its power to the spinning propeller bringing the ship to a quiet crawl, leaving a constant hum throughout. A flashing light was seen coming from a small boat at the distance of a quarter of a mile. The darkened, slow-drifting vessel was suddenly effused with directed lighting at the side of the ship where a loading crane was lowering its cable for a cargo net pickup. Gavriella prayed this would come off as planned. Stellar and Bram would be part of the lift from the small boat along with the cargo of six wooden crates of gold taken from the tunnel under the Lupel mansion.

The lady dressed in dark pulled her shawl down over her shoulders revealing long, wavy, dark hair. She wanted Stellar to see her and not her covering. While waiting for Stellar to appear, Gavriella remembered the old adage, *Absence made the heart grow fonder*. For six months, she and Stellar had worked closely together, sometimes apart when he was out organizing and training his people in the complexities of moving immigrants to ships at night. But those separations were nothing like what the last few days had been. Her heart pounded. Love was a beautiful creation of God, and when held in commitment, it deepened the union of marriage.

The large crane began reeling up the cargo net showing two men grasping the ropes. When it reached a hundred fifty feet above the water, the winch swung over the deck of the ship and slowly lowered its cargo. Gavriella felt a sudden weakness. The event was over. She continued to observe the professional way everything was carried out. Bub was in command directing six crewmen to carry the valuable boxed cargo to a secured area. Bram and Bub followed the crewmen. Stellar was left by himself looking about for Gavriella when she stepped out in the open.

"I'm over here, Stellar!"

As he neared, she couldn't restrain herself but ran and leaped into his open arms. Words spoken in her ear by Stellar were savored with ecstatic feelings. Their reunion would be strength for the burden that awaited her in the stateroom.

After the baggage drop, Gavriella and Stellar walked Hand-in-hand to the side rail to watch the boarding of two hundred passengers from three boats lined up and ready to deliver their human cargo. Stellar timed the first group of sixty-five. From the time the boat pulled up to the loading ramp until the arrival of the next group, it took five minutes.

"Not having to carry baggage," said Stellar, "greatly decreases the loading time."

Stellar knew Gavriella hadn't seen her mother and father and saw tension mounting. Having a bird's eye view of everything going on down below, when the second boat pulled up to the ramp, she recognized her mother and father. Stellar saw tears in her eyes. She leaned into him and felt his arm tightly around her.

Speaking in soliloquy, Stellar heard her say, "My, they have aged so." Then turning to Stellar, she added, "For me to marry you, I had to know if you were willing to go through what I've been through with the rejection of my family. For Orthodox Jews, family and Judaism are everything, but my experience with God and His truth, I found strength to accept the burden of family rejection."

Stellar wanted to be a pillar for the lady of his life. He, unlike Gavriella, had no mother, father, or sibling to reject him—they had died in the Holocaust. He did have a friend, Bram, and they were still friends. He even agreed to be his best man at his Messianic Jewish wedding. He knew he was marrying up, and the woman he would live the rest of his life with was a lady of steel.

Stellar and Gavriella were in her stateroom waiting for Bub to bring news that her mother and father had been taken to their berth.

"Do you want to do this by yourself," asked Stellar.

"Some burdens," responded Gavriella, "have to be carried alone. Those are the kind that measure character and resolve, and this is one of them."

When Bub arrived at her stateroom, Gavriella knew her mother and father were settled inside their berth. Stellar and Bub went together to the radio room to report in code form the successful transfer of two hundred immigrants and would arrive at Haifa in forty-two hours. This was the first major operation in the land of a modern Egypt, a country that refused to let God's people go, not to a desert but to a country finding its place among the nations of earth.

Gavriella knocked on the door of the stateroom she had arranged for her mother and father, waited for a response, and was about to knock again when the door opened eight inches. Gavriella, taking charge of her mission, pushed the door open without concern for privacy.

Startled and shocked, her elderly parents stood frozen like they'd seen a ghost. Religious blindness covered their faces, the kind of blindness that justifies the rejection of a daughter who had come into the faith of Yeshua. The mother's eyes showed a guarded compassionate softening, unlike the father whose cold stare looked away. History hung like a heavyweight inside the berth. Shunned and ostracized as a late teen because of her faith, she found among righteous Gentile believers others who became her mother and father. Now, she stood in the presence of those who had inflicted the worst kind of emotional abuse: disownment and rejection because of her faith. *Though Stellar offered to be at her side, she had the need to stand alone for a show of strength in what she had become through her faith in Yeshua.*

"Hello, Papa! It's good to see you, Mama! You never answered those letters I wrote you through the years. In those letters, I never asked for anything. In fact, I even sent money with them, and yes, you returned the money without a written script. I want you to know that my faith is stronger today than when you disowned me as your offspring. What you did made me a stronger person, though I carry a lot of scar tissue from it. Above everything, I want you to know that I hold nothing against you, though I bear the record of having cried many nights over your refusal to restore our relationship. The essence of God, the Father, is love, and it comes unconditional, unlike what I experienced from my father. Unconditional love would show itself by embracing me with loving open arms.

"My letters to you that were returned, over which you wrote 'deceased,' were written in tears requesting a restored relationship. Your being here in this berth tonight is because I requested it, and is not intended to be perceived as another letter requesting a relationship but has been arranged as a forum for an announcement to say that you will never hear from me, except at your invitation. I have found a mother and a father in the person I will marry this week in Israel. He is a Messianic believer, like me, and it may, or may not, please you to know he is Jewish and lost his family in the Holocaust.

"Papa, you are a man of the Scriptures. God promised Abraham and Isaac two kinds of offspring: those who would be numbered as sand and those who would be counted as stars. The sand descendants are those who can be seen and felt, those who occupy geographical boundaries. The other promised descendants were to be counted as stars. These are not earthly but heavenly. To measure and see this offspring one has to look up to the heavens. I am counted among both of these posterities. I am a Jew, counted as a member of the sand community, those who occupy geography, but I am also a member of another kingdom—Abraham's star offspring, those who possess light from another world. Papa, the ram caught in the thicket that Abraham offered as a sacrifice in place of his son Isaac on Mount Moriah was the Passover Lamb of Isaiah fifty-three. His death gave birth to Abraham's star offspring of which I belong."

The father, still poised like a lifeless marble statue, showed no emotion. His eyes, set like steel, said nothing to his daughter, and when his wife, who now had tears forming and running down her cheeks, began to move toward her daughter, he grabbed her arm showing resolute resistance, sending a physical, silent message.

The only speaker throughout the ordeal was Gavriella. In closing, she held up Stellar's photo she brought with her. "This is Stellar, the man who is now my mother and father and the person I will marry this week. I have brought a personal invitation that I give to all my friends who wish to attend. I am leaving you one, and if you choose to attend the wedding, I will consider you our friends. Goodnight Mama…goodnight Papa."

Gavriella turned, opened the closed door, then quietly left pulling the door shut. It was the face of her father's cold state of sentiency she would remember. She lingered long enough outside the stateroom to hear deep sobbing coming from her mother. Stellar's light was on in his stateroom, and she had the need for him to hold her.

His door opened, and arms gave a warm welcome to one whose emotions were frayed and spent. An hour later Gavriella found herself in her bed remembering the embraces of the one who would be her husband in a few days when a slight knock was heard at her door. *Was this Stellar? Who would be knocking at this hour?* She put on her robe, cracked the door with the safety-chain lock still attached. It was her mother.

With each holding the other, the only words heard came from the mother: "My child, my loving little girl, the one who gave me joy in life. Many a night I cried myself to sleep. My love for you has never waned, and there were times I wished myself dead rather than live without you. You will never know what being with you tonight means to me. Now I can die with peace having told you my feelings."

Broken and dispirited, Gavriella found it difficult to express herself. "Had I only known what you're telling me, life would have been different. If we could have just talked then, like now, life would've been easier. I was a widow through the years and never had a Stellar—he would've made up the difference. Mother, you and Papa are welcome to come and live in the hotel that I own in partnership with another party. It's a beautiful place, just finished, and is filled with clients from many parts of the world."

"Your father would never agree. You saw him tonight."

They both fell asleep in each other's arms, like mother and child. It was eight o'clock when Gavriella awoke and found her mother gone. She quickly bathed and dressed in something frivolously colorful to match the spirit of her lifted burden. Without an invitation from her mother, she chose not to encroach her father's space by revisiting their stateroom. She would wait until the strength of motherhood matched the resistance of her father.

Hidden in the cocoon of steel in the belly of a freighter, two hundred descendants of an ancient people were returning to the land God had promised them through Abraham. They were part of a modern exodus from a land of imprisonment, a people who would pave the way for others to follow.

Chapter 33

Arrival

I will cause them to return to the land that I gave to their
fathers, and they shall possess it. (Jer. 30:3)

Bub had everything organized on board the ship that had anything to do with new immigrants. Women and children slept in one area and the men in another. Because of the size of the dining room, breakfast, lunch, and dinner were served in three shifts to accommodate everyone. No one was allowed to go on deck for security and safety reasons. The ship was scheduled to arrive in Haifa early the next morning.

Gavriella knew Stellar would be working with Bub and Bram. When she went below and entered the area where immigrants were housed, she saw Stellar seated at a desk assisting passengers with immigration papers. Rather than interrupt him, she waved after eye contact was made giving a hand signal that she'd bring him a cup of coffee.

Her spirit was still high from the night before, and when entering the dining room, her mother was seen seated by herself, and the mission of taking Stellar a cup of coffee eluded her. In spite of her buoyancy over the release of her burden with her family last night, history swung back forcing her to remember the painful years of rejection. However, her strength of character seized the opportunity to continue what was begun last evening.

"Good morning, Mother. Where's Papa?"

Serious visible depression hung on her mother's face. "Your father and I have had grave disagreements. My being with you last night made me a different person. I told your father, 'I'm going to your wedding and then accept your offer to live with you in the land that I despise.' He was left with the message that his sunset years would be lived without me."

Gavriella sat next to her mother, placed her arm around her, saying, "Mother, you are being very strong. You have restored my faith in motherhood."

"No, my daughter, you're the one who kindled the fire of motherhood. In the time I have left on earth, I will attempt to expunge my sin by being a mother to you till the day I die."

Gavriella's newly heightened world of light and warmth in her restored relationship with her mother suddenly plummeted with a force of cold reality: her mother would be leaving her father for her. What had she done? For years, she sought what she found today, a restored relationship with a parent, but in doing so she was causing a union of marriage to break apart, a union from which she was created.

Gavriella now felt like her feet were walking over a slippery, thin layer of ice on a frozen lake and could hear the cracking of what was beneath her. Heavy remorse settled in over her psyche. How could she extricate herself from this dilemma without hurt to her mother? Then came a temporary reprieve: a familiar hand placed a cup of coffee on the table in front of her. After the hand released the cup, she held it, kissed it, then brought it to her cheek.

"Mother, I want you to meet the man I love and will marry this week."

Stellar leaned over and kissed the lady who held his hand, then turning to the mother with an extended hand, said, "It is my pleasure and honor to meet you. May I call you, Mother?"

Both mother and daughter couldn't hide the tears coursing down their cheeks. Taking Stellar's extended hand, she drew it to the front of her face, clasping it with both hands. "Yes, you may, and is it acceptable that I call you my son?"

"Yes, I prefer being called your son."

That night, mother and daughter occupied the same berth, and the father took his luggage case and moved to the heart of the ship where other male immigrants were sleeping.

Cool, coastal breezes over ancient waters that floated vessels in history swept across the deck of the freighter where two-hundred immigrants were allowed to gather to watch the sun come up over the port of Haifa. Breakfast had been served, luggage cases delivered to the ship's baggage handlers, and descendants of the ancients were viewing their new homeland. The prominent view of Mount Carmel nestled in the rising hills behind the port city stood out like a background stage prop marking the historic conflict of Elijah and the prophets of Baal. They were returning to a land brought back by the sword in preparation of the returning Messiah.

Another form of conflict was in play onboard the ship.

Inside Gavriella's stateroom, mother and daughter were bonding, and the father was left wandering across a barren desert he had created by his actions in disowning his daughter because of her faith. The decision the mother made was to stay with the father until he was settled in at the absorption center, then return to the country she just left to live with the daughter she had found. Her husband, a well-experienced, skillful goldsmith, had skills that would be in demand in his new land. Mother and daughter joined the crowd on the open deck, saw Stellar and Bram checking each passenger's immigration card as they filed down to the disembarkation ramp.

Strange quietness spread across the deck of the ship with everyone gone. Only Bram, Stellar, and Gavriella were left standing at the side rail. They watched the new immigrants down below board buses that would take them to the absorption center. The upscale, coastal business resort that acted as a front for collecting and moving Jews to the freighter at sea had proved to be a valuable asset. It required time and effort from devoted people to make it happen and with dedicated professionals organizing and directing the pickups, efficiency would only improve. Everyone knew these efforts came from the vision of the chairman of Katharina Enterprises, a person whose wealth was used to move Abraham's posterity back to their homeland in preparation for the return of the Messiah.

What had been a bustling, noisy, interactive scene on the ship's deck was now quiet and still. Gone were those who created life, the children who played and frolicked, mothers who talked proudly of their toddlers, teenagers who spoke of their dreams, and the old men who loved to speak of how things used to be, remembering their younger years better than what happened yesterday. This community had been in someone else's world, someone else's country. Now they were in their land, their country, a place where Jews could celebrate who and what they were. No longer would they be looking over their shoulders in fear of those who despised their ancestry. It was geography promised to them from the time of Abraham.

Gavriella, Stellar, and Bram continued to watch in silence those boarding buses down below. The vibrant energy that pulsated the atmosphere on the cold steel deck of the ship still had its lingering effect as the crowds boarded the buses. Gavriella's mother, now standing alongside her husband waiting to board their transport, looked up at three small figures peering down from the ship's deck, one waving a white handkerchief, to which she responded with one taken from her bag.

When the last bus pulled out, Gavriella saw two oversized vehicles with darkened windows pull up and stop. The drivers jumped out and assisted their passengers. The outline of seven human figures was seen coming in the direction of the large freighter, one appearing to be a lady dressed in a fashionable manner. Gavriella knew something important was going down, and turning to Stellar, she asked: "Who are these now coming aboard the ship?"

"They are Katharina Enterprises people and have come to Israel to evaluate the first major operation of moving Jews from Romania to their homeland. Word came over the radio last evening that they would arrive by plane early today. We're scheduled to meet in the dining room at nine o'clock this morning for a conference."

"Look," said Gavriella, "there's Popescu, Max, and Michael. I knew Popescu would be here for our wedding. He was supposed to fly out to Munich, then on to Israel but not today!"

"The company plane picked him up early this morning in Bucharest," said Stellar. "He has become the Gentile face we need in his country, and because of his leadership, Max and Michael wanted him in this meeting."

They observed the group of seven nearing the embarkation ramp, causing Bram to ask what others were thinking. "Who is the lady among them?"

"That we will soon find out," responded Stellar.

Stellar and Bram left for the operational assessment meeting and Gavriella made her way to her stateroom to work on her wedding plans. No sooner had she entered her stateroom that she heard someone at her door. It was Bub.

"Madam, your presence is requested at a meeting now being conducted in the dining room down below. The chairman of Katharina Enterprises himself requested that I bring you."

What a change of events in her life! Everything was coming fast and furious. She had been a quiet, unseen sleeper providing information to covert Zionists within the country. Now, she was being brought into the inner circle— all because of her upcoming marriage to Stellar.

"Bub, why would they want me to be present in this meeting?"

"Because you're one of the spokes in the wheel that strengthens the efforts of moving Jews from Romania to Israel. I don't want to speak for others, but you did ask me a question. It goes without saying, you do have a reputation of helping your people."

With the scheduled private meeting of key operatives responsible for moving Jews from the repressive country of Romania to Israel, ship personnel had been cleared from the dining room area. Even the cooks were removed after preparing a buffet of coffee, pastries, and fruit. It was a meeting that demanded confidentiality.

Now deep inside the ship, Gavriella and Bub made their way alongside a row of large shipping containers made into bunkhouses. Each container accommodated eighteen sleeping passengers, all resembling the tight quarters found on board a naval ship. Everything was steel, the substance of strength but resisted the absorption of sound. A pin could be heard if dropped, and what usually went unnoticed and unheard, the swishing and shuffling of feet were amplified throughout the cavern of metal. Sound waves were rejected leaving reverberating, unpleasant echoes. *Gavriella couldn't escape the image coming at her. The heart of the ship she was walking through was a picture of her father: someone made of steel but couldn't absorb her into his life because of her faith in Jesus, and when in his presence, she was but an empty, meaningless echo.*

Bub knocked on the door of the dining room where everyone had already gathered. It swung open wide. Gavriella didn't recognize the man standing in front of her with tall physical features sporting a thick head of blond hair and eyes that carried the look of wisdom beyond his years.

"Welcome, Gavriella! I'm Hans Isler. Please come in and meet our team." Bub took his place with the others in the room.

Though Gavriella hadn't met the man welcoming her, when she heard the name Isler, she found it hard to believe that the young gentleman holding the door open and speaking to her was the chairman of Katharina Enterprises, one of the wealthiest men in Europe, yet was acting in a gracious servile manner.

The measurable traits that always followed Gavriella were her ability to think fast on her feet and give a quick assessment to nuances lurking behind the scenes. Being greeted by the chairman who had opened the door confirmed his reputation of humility and servitude. Her eyes fell across the room again. There were eleven people in the room counting the chairman. She had met them all except four: two women and two males.

"Let's go over and I'll introduce our team."

They'd all been served coffee or tea and were seated around two large tables pushed together. The chairman took charge.

"I'd like everyone to meet the lady who has joined us," said the chairman.

To her surprise, the chairman did something uncharacteristic of someone in his position: he moved around the table introducing each one giving a brief description of their role in Prince Henry operations. The informal setting created a family atmosphere, and she paid special attention when he introduced the four people she hadn't met.

"Gavriella, I want you to meet Sheena, my wife, the

love of my life, a lady who helped me find the way back to my Father's house. She was part of the crew on board this operation serving as a doctor in the medical room checking out the children. Next to my wife is Sonje, my adopted sister, the one who taught me most everything I know about business and investment, and who carries the responsibility of keeping the company's bottom line in the black. You've already met Michael, my uncle, who stole the heart of Sonje. Next to Michael is Moshe, Michael's lifetime friend who serves as our mobile operative. He flew in today with us for this special meeting.

"Last, but not least, is Marku, the capable one who guided everything at the luxurious resort on the Black Sea to its completion which is now being patronized by vacationing Europeans. He manages everything at the site including the adjunct deep-sea fishing venture connected with the resort which serves a double purpose—one to make a profit in the daytime with the tourism industry—the other, to be called upon in the dark of night to deliver immigrants to waiting vessels."

After the chairman gave deference to those he introduced around the table, he addressed the group. "The lady who has joined us at my request is a special person. Some bear the reputation of valor and gallantry in the light of day; others carry that honor in the silence of the night and go unnoticed. Gavriella's record is of the latter. Her quiet reserve goes unnoticed in the clamor and noise of the day but carries the reputation of having helped Jews to her own endangerment. She has always been a reliable source of information to Zionists and will continue to do so in a greater way by the management of her upscale, remodeled hotel, which allows Stellar and Bram to remain in the country with business visas, two professional men who are on loan to us from their underground Zionist organization."

Pointing to the vacant chair next to Stellar, the chairman said, "Please grace our team by joining our company here at the table." The chairman sat yielding the meeting to Michael. He stood up alongside his wife leaving an imposing physical image.

"It is an honor to congratulate Gavriella and Stellar on their marriage engagement. This is a special week for them and an exceptional event for us who will attend. Stellar and Gavriella are Messianic believers and hold the belief that their mission is to assist Jews in returning to Israel in preparation of the coming Messiah."

Michael then moved to the purpose of the meeting. "A lot of effort has been made for everyone to meet together here in Israel, but the chairman deemed it necessary. Up to this point, Prince Henry operations included all Soviet contiguous Black Sea countries, Romania being one of them. However, this week's pickup was exclusively Romanian, and its success shows the effectiveness of the front operation of the Constanta Resort center. The unsung heroes are those working the fields away from the glamour of the resort itself. Pickups will continue throughout the Black Sea, but because of our solid infrastructure and organization inside Romania, our greater efforts will be in that country."

After three hours of discussion and deliberation, a loud knock was heard at the closed dining-room door. Again, the chairman demonstrated servitude. He arose from where he sat, walked toward the dining-room door. "This is our lunch on wheels," he said, "delivered to us by a catering agency onshore, and I believe we have the choice of three items on the menu," He proceeded to open the door and push one of the several carts over to the dining table near the engaged couple.

"We will honor this special couple the best way we can by serving them first," said the chairman. "Also, I would like to announce that everyone around this table has a place reserved at a special seaside resort we always use when in Israel. When we're through today, a shuttle will be waiting to take everyone to the site."

While the chairman was speaking, no one noticed the vice chairlady writing on her notepad, and when the chairman sat, she folded the sheet of paper writing on its surface the name of the person who would read it, then passed it over to Gavriella. The note read:

It is in the interest of Katharina Enterprises to buy up gold for special kinds of investments, gold that cannot be tracked to its origin. You will be paid one-third more than what the international market value is, and if you choose this option, we will take possession of it as of today and will deposit in your account in Munich an agreed amount. This will prove to be a benefit for both parties.

After reading the note, Gavriella wrote a response passing it back to the lady seated by Michael. The vice chairlady glanced at what was written, looked at Gavriella, smiled, and showed a *thumbs-up*.

Hans Isler, the young mastermind of Prince Henry operations, had seen the birth of his dream. Two hundred immigrants had been delivered from a repressive country to the shores of their ancestors, and for Hans Isler, it was a personal triumph that demanded a week of quasi-hiatus. His team would spend a week at his favorite beachside resort evaluating operational systems with the climax of the special event of a Jewish wedding.

Chapter 34

Life from Dry Bones

Nearby the coastal villa where Prince Henry operatives were booked, the blue waters of the Mediterranean lapped at the bare feet of Hans and Sheena Isler as they strolled hand-in-hand along the water's edge, leaving footprints in the sand. The evening salt breeze ruffling Sheena's long, wavy hair reminded her husband of previous encounters at this beach site when her loveliness became part of the scenic landscape. They had taken this walk many times before, but today Hans would find it had special meaning.

He stopped. Still holding his wife's soft, delicate hand, he looked down the coastline where breaking waves fell on grains of sand that numbered Abraham's descendants. His ruminating thoughts were sober, yet celebratory. This week was an epic time of his life. He had seen a boatload of Romanian Holocaust survivors delivered to the new nation of Israel, the land from whence their ancestors were taken. With eyes fastened on tumbling waves and foaming water moving across the sandy beach, he saw a message beyond the picture of nature's performance. He stopped, looked at Sheena, saying, "Nature's voice sometimes speaks to us in strange ways. I see a hidden oracle of truth here at the water's edge. As far as our eyes can see down the coastline, there are no human footprints embedded on grains of sand, but looking back where we have strode, one can measure and count our steps. However, with the coming tide, our footprints will be gone tomorrow like the ancients of history who carried sword and shield. Gone are the warriors and conquerors who invaded this land, defeated by time immemorial, but the grains of sand their feet walked over still lie on the shoreline as they did at the beginning. God chose to compare Abraham's descendants to that of sand on the seashore in numbers and endurance."

Sheena saw Hans' eyes move from looking at their feet in the sand to the open sea whose deep blue waters carried Holocaust survivors back to their ancestral land. She looked admiringly at the man she loved.

"Hans, you have left big footprints where you've walked. You were a modern Moses plucked from the fires of the Holocaust as an infant by the wealthy wife of a Nazi general, but unlike Pharaoh's daughter who found Moses in the bulrushes and given a life in the culture and learning of the elite, your adoptive mother, though wealthy, shaped you with simple living in preparation for what you are now doing. You took the wealth she left you and created complex systems of moving Abraham's descendants to their homeland. First, they came from Soviet lands refusing to let them go, then came the largest ever this week from Romania, the country of your birth, the land where your family is buried in unmarked graves.

"It was your insight, vision, and skills that brought together the right people to form a loyal family unit to fulfill your mission. You were a good, compassionate medical doctor before inheriting your adoptive mother's wealth, but now a doctor of healing of a different order for a different cause. What you touch in life is made better, whether it be business, operational systems, or a person. And I must say, I am one of those you have touched and made better."

"If that be the case about you and me," said Hans, "let's get the order of events correct. You were the first to leave fingerprints on a prodigal. I had lost my way, and without your touch, I would have never found the path back to my Father's home."

The long shadows of Hans and Sheena dimmed with the sunset now fading through earth's prism, leaving a radiant, orange glow on the horizon. Twilight was serenading the two with one carrying a special announcement for the other.

"Hans, I have waited for this hour under nature's idyllic sunset with sounds of ocean waves to whisper a special message in your ear. Hold me in your arms as you held me when you asked for my hand in marriage."

"That will be my pleasure, and I'll do more than that— my lips pressed against yours will remind us that we have been made one, and it will seal our event here on the beach."

Wrapped in her husband's arms, she heard him say, "Now, what about the whisper you promised?"

Moving her lips close to his ear, he heard soft-spoken words that shook his world.

"Doctor Hans, I am pleased and proud to announce that I am expecting our first baby."

Hans froze saying nothing. Arms around his wife tightened and Sheena welcomed another impassioned kiss in celebration of the news of his expected firstborn.

Gavriella had taken a large suite at the villa resort so those working with her in finalizing her wedding plans could come-and-go at will. Her first call was to her mother at the resettlement center, leaving her phone number and an invitation to visit. Stellar had selected a room nearby and made himself available when called upon. A recommended Messianic Rabbi had agreed to perform the small Jewish wedding ceremony in the villa's large conference center.

The mornings at the villa were taken up with business sessions, and for the rest of the day, everyone was free to do what they wished. It was on the third day after Gavriella arrived at the villa she received a call from the office.

"Ms. Gavriella, there's a party here who wishes to see you. Upon your approval, I'll send them to your room."

"And who is the person requesting to see me?"

"Would you hold please and I'll get that information."

This was a strange event, thought Gavriella. Who would be coming here to see me? Her concerns ended when the office came back online.

"The lady tells me she's your mother!"

"By all means, give directions to my room!"

Gavriella felt a strange rush of emotional history flow through the part of her life that carried deep scars. She had reunited with her mother onboard the ship, invited her into her home, but history was surging itself with the flood of energy hidden beneath the scars of rejection. A light of truth came to her spirit—forgiveness was a dynamic instant event, but the healing of hurt was a process, a long journey across turbulent waters. She was now on board that boat riding the wave of the process—she wished for Stellar's presence, but he was away shopping for items needed for the wedding. If only she had known earlier of her mother's arrival, she could've requested Stellar's accompaniment.

There was a knock on the door. Expecting her mother, she found Stellar standing with an armload of packages. She pulled him inside, saying, "Thank goodness you've arrived just in time."

"Just in time for what?" said Stellar, putting what he carried on the table.

A knock on the door brought an answer to his question. "This is my mother. She has come to visit me upon my invitation, and I'm now finding it difficult to look at the emotional scars hidden deep inside me. The euphoria of reuniting with my mother on the ship has evaporated and history is now rushing at me, and I'm discovering a profound truth: forgiveness is the denial of one's right for retribution, is instant, and never given in stages. However, forgiveness doesn't erase memory, and recovery from emotional injury requires the healing balm of Father Time."

Stellar took her hand. "We'll travel that road together. Let's go and open the door and let Father Time begin the healing process."

Both were shocked to find in front of them a distraught mother whose face carried the look of fear and confusion. Without embracing her daughter, she seized Gavriella's arm leaving the message that tragedy had come her way.

"Something has happened to your father to cause him to ask me to bring him to see you! He is not inside the building but outside in the taxi that brought us here. He didn't want to come in unless you agreed for him to do so."

Stellar and Gavriella looked at each other. The blanket of a strange world settled over a daughter who had been excluded as a family member because of her faith in Yeshua. She had survived that state of exclusion and gained strength from it. Though she and her mother had a restored relationship, it was difficult to believe her father was requesting a meeting with her after his adamant rejection a few days before. A strange new world was forcing itself into her reality. *Why was this happening with such urgency? Showing up on his daughter's doorstep after years of unanswered letters and rejection didn't match who he was. Perhaps he was facing a terminal illness and had the need to confess the rejection of his daughter.*

"Is Papa ill?" asked Gavriella

"Your father is not ill physically but has undergone some very strange things. Do you object if I bring him in to see you?"

"No, of course not," responded Gavriella. "We'll wait for you to bring him."

Gavriella's inner world continued to swirl with questions. Everything was transitioning in front of her for which she had no answers. Her life carried the history of struggle, and only recently did her fortunes change with the inheritance of the old mansion and what came with it. These dramatic events, compounded by her planned marriage to the man she loved, and the request of her father to meet with her was almost too much to take in.

The door to her suite was left open, and the two walked back to the sitting room and stood facing the front door. Stellar saw Gavriella's frame of strength and courage stiffen for the unknown that awaited her. She felt his hand take hers, a silent touch that carried the message of support.

Flooding Gavriella's inner space was the temptation to exploit her position of control in what was unfolding: a father who had abandoned his daughter was now making a journey across a wasteland of his own making. The tables were turned. The human element that makes a man vulnerable to the vanity of power and control had painted a picture inside Gavriella. Today, she was in a position of strength, and it was within her power to exact justice for her treatment of rejection. Being forced to choose between her rights and forgiving the offender, she chose to follow the example of the Passover Lamb when He uttered the words, "Father, forgive them for they know not what they do." Only the offended had the power to forgive. Without sword or spear, grace from another world gave her cause to be a victor, not over the offender but over the offended.

To survive rejection, she had locked the door to those memories beneath the scars she carried. Now, with the key of forgiveness, she would open that door so memory could be free, free like birds released from cages, and though weakened in confinement, she would use the strength of forgiveness and await the outcome of her brave act.

Rushing through her were the memories when her father was loving, kind, protective, and even nurturing, the times he held her hand on walks, being read to at bedtime and pulled about in a wagon. It was beyond her understanding how a father with these qualities could choose to banish his daughter from his life.

The locked crucible of memory that Gavriella had forced open flung her back to earlier years of pain blurring her present state of mind. Confusion gripped her when the figure of a man entered the open doorway of her suite looking unkempt, nervous, and distraught—it was her father appearing as she had never seen him. Her mother stood behind him showing support in what he was about. Compassion assuaged her pain of rejection.

"Is that you, Gavriella?"

"Yes, Papa, this is Gavriella!"

"May I come in?"

"Certainly, please do."

He and his wife stepped into the room. Using hands that designed and shaped beautiful, ornate jewelry, he slowly closed the door. His face carried pallor that spoke of fear and trepidation. Stellar, who now stood behind Gavriella, saw everything as high drama. The scene could've been a stage production, but this event was in real time with frayed emotions and real characters.

Avoiding eye contact, the father shuffled his feet with eyes showing a message of intent, his wife following. When reaching where his daughter stood, he stopped, raised his head, and for the first time looked directly into her eyes, eyes he used to call beautiful but were now a two-edged sword cutting at his heart. A face showing a stone-fixed image with tears welling in age-sunken sockets suddenly yielded to the compelling energy of his mission. Kneeling in front of her, he clasped her feet with hands that held her as a child. Broken in spirit, the elderly father sobbed and wept uncontrollably. Gavriella was reaching down to show comfort by placing her hand on her father's shoulder, when Stellar, knowing the father had the need to finish the journey he'd started, intercepted the action, whispering softly, "He needs to complete his mission first."

Without looking up, the father struggled with words in the effort to describe his feelings, remorse, and failure as a father.

"I am not worthy to be here for what I have done to you. Please forgive me, my daughter. The wounds and hurt I have inflicted on you because of your Messianic beliefs will haunt me until I die. Even God will find it difficult to forgive me."

Still on his knees with an aging face showing a hollow, empty void, he looked up at his daughter. "Something happened to me last night after going to bed. I don't know if it were a vision or a dream, but a man in white came and took me to Ezekiel's valley of dry bones. He showed me what Ezekiel saw in his vision, a vision of scattered, dry bones that came together and formed what was a great army of people. But none had life in them. I saw people I knew. I saw myself among them like it was an out-of-the-body experience. We were all dead. The man in white showing me this vision, said, 'Look at the person coming to life near you.' It was someone who had come to life and was helping others find life by reading the book of Isaiah."

Gavriella and Stellar were awestruck. The father's story moved both to a state of silent catatonia. Still on his knees with eyes set on his daughter, he struggled with words. "Gavriella, my wonderful daughter, you were that person in the valley of dry bones who came to life and was helping others find the life you had. My own daughter who was given life, I discarded and rejected but am here to ask you and God to forgive me so I can be instructed in finding the life you have."

Gavriella fell to her knees and embraced her father.

"Papa, what you saw in your vision were Abraham's descendants coming back to life in their own land after centuries of being dead, dead as a people, dead as a nation, all in preparation for the return of the One who will rule the world from Jerusalem. For you to possess the life that Stellar and I have, you must believe that Jesus is the Messiah and was the Passover Lamb of Isaiah fifty-three."

Cool, Idyllic, coastal breezes invigorated the evening air where Hans Isler's special team gathered for their evening dining session. Attendants at the villa had rolled back the large glass doors in the ocean-side private dining room giving those seated around the candlelit table a full view of ancient, sparkling, moonlit waters, accompanied by the sounds of breaking waves in the distance. Included among Hans' regular family team were two additional guests: Gavriella's mother and father. Both would stay with their daughter in her two-bedroom suite.

For Hans Isler, it was an evening for a special announcement. Before the epicurean gourmet menus were distributed by the waiters, Hans took the floor.

"Three years ago when I was a doctor finishing my internship and had inherited my adoptive mother's wealth, had someone told me I would be in charge of a global mission of bringing Jewish Diaspora from lands of repression to the new nation of Israel, I wouldn't have believed it. I am glad to say that Katharina Enterprises has done this with your help. What we have seen accomplished is the result of your efforts and commitment to the belief in Yeshua's Messianic rule on earth.

"It is my great pleasure tonight to welcome Gavriella's mother and father, Mr. and Mrs. Fisher. They were among the two hundred immigrants on board the ship that arrived in port this week."

Gavriella and Stellar sat together with her mother and father. The stressed, downcast images they earlier displayed when arriving at the villa had vanished with a restored relationship with their daughter and introduction to Yeshua, the historical Messiah of this land. After hearing what the chairman said, Gavriella looked around the table and saw a group of people committed to the mission of returning Jews to their homeland. *How appropriate if her father were able to give his vision of Ezekiel's valley of dry bones to this group. He was a living voice of prophetic fulfillment, and it would serve to inspire others here tonight.*

Hans continued. "How fitting it is that Mr. and Mrs. Fisher are here in Israel and will be able to attend their daughter's wedding, an event we all anticipate."

Everyone at the dining table saw the chairman move behind his wife, place his hands on her shoulders. "My wife has given me the permission to make a special announcement. With great pride, my beautiful wife is going to make us parents of our first-born child."

Loud applause registered from everyone present. Hans leaned over and kissed his wife. Michael stood up, saying, "Let's drink a toast to this wonderful, joyous event."

Sitting next to Michael was a man who took up the space of two people. Max, the chief of security for Katharina Enterprises, looked his best with a pinstripe suit and starched shirt. This was his persona. However, his known trait of being a heavy sweater was showing itself. Beads of perspiration highlighted his glistening baldhead being wiped down from time-to-time. Though everyone who worked for him used the sobriquet "The Sweater" behind his back, tonight he had a reason for displaying his hyperhidrosis—he had a special announcement to make and was waiting for the right moment.

Still standing behind his wife when Michael sat, Hans continued his address to the group. "We have a very important member in our group that I depend on when special operations are in play. He was at my side in the early formation of what came to be called our Prince Henry operation. Max was with my late adoptive mother doing much of her bidding while she was prepping me to fill her shoes, and as events would have it, he has a very special announcement to make among his friends tonight."

Everyone saw the big man slowly stand. His size was an imposing figure that had a personality that matched his girth: rough on the outside, exhibiting no-nonsense, and sergeant-like speech. He carried the image of an unbending army officer, known to be a creator of protocols, and those who worked under him would say, "He'd die by them." But those who knew him well saw his other side—a gentle giant with a little boy inside.

It wasn't easy for Max to talk about personal matters. People knew him to be capable of conversing on most subjects, respected his knowledge, and was the go-to person when big operations were in play; but people knew little of his personal life, and that was the way he wanted it. However, something was going on that required social interaction and the opportune time had come to act on it.

Standing in the presence of colleagues and friends, the humble little boy in him was showing as he pulled from his pocket a large handkerchief and wiped down his moist-ridden, slick, baldhead.

"As some of you might know," said Max, "I am a very private person, but in recent months I moved out of that safe zone and met a very special person who has accepted my proposal of marriage. Birdie, Michael's secretary, is that special person and will have the responsibility of planning this event, and you can be sure each of you will receive an invitation. Also, I would like to add that Michael has agreed to be my best man."

Everyone applauded Max, and before Hans could continue, Bram stood to give a signal to the chairman that he had something to say. Known for his valiant service in the partisan resistance army in the mountains of Serbia during the war, respect was shown by everyone's silence. Though coffee and tea filled cups around the table, neither was touched. The chairman noticed he had placed something on the table.

"What I have to say is directed to Max. I'm new to this unique band of people gathered here tonight. Most of us are Jews, some of which have survived the Holocaust, but all of us have the goal of helping God's chosen people regain their homeland. After settling in the country of Romania for intensive operations of moving Jews to smuggling points for pickups at sea, I attended and participated in a strategy meeting where I met Max. I was the last person to leave the secluded secret meeting site and went throughout the house to be sure nothing was left behind. I found one item, a leather-bound book with Max's name written in it. Half of the book contained ancient writings with which I was familiar. Christians call it the Old Testament, Jews use the term Tanakh.

"Forgive me, Max, for not returning it to you, but I started reading the book and couldn't put it down. I'm returning it today after buying my own. My life has been changed because of this book. Other factors came my way to support the influence of the change in my life. Combined with the Tanakh was a group of Jewish writings called by Christians, the New Testament. Truth took on life when I saw a Jewish lady helping those who rejected her because of her faith."

Bram looked at Gavriella and Stellar seated together. "Thank you, Gavriella, for being what you are for your people. Most people who experience rejection because of their faith are forced to be absorbed by those outside their community. But you fought against the tide. You chose to help your people who rejected you, and now you have my good friend, Stellar, to stand by your side."

The chairman saw evidence that was akin to a metaphoric birth happening that had transcendent meaning. Being a medical doctor, he allowed the birthing process to continue under natural conditions. He took a seat next to his wife knowing there were more labor pains on the way.

Everyone turned in the direction of Gavriella, now pushing her chair back to stand. The chairman had read reports of this tall, svelte, articulate lady who went out of her way to help her people in a land of repression, and with her father and mother at her side, he knew something insightful was on its way.

"Bram spoke of a Sacred Book that changed his life," said Gavriella. "I must confirm that my life was also changed in much the same way when I was young, and that persuasive, powerful change is with me to this day. Because of the undertaking, the chairman has made in resettling Jews in Israel, of which my mother and father are beneficiaries, I have asked my father to share his recent dramatic experience that fits into the chairman's mission to the people of this land."

Every eye in the room saw the elderly father place the palms of his hands flat on the dining table and slowly push his aged frame to an erect, standing position. Looking at no one, his head hung downward, eyes bent on flattened hands. Those seated in the room could hear nature's tumbling ocean waves underneath the gravelly, baritone voice that commenced a story that would bring tears to the eyes of the listeners.

"I'm an orthodox Jew and unworthy to stand here tonight alongside my beautiful daughter. Had I conducted my life with my family as skillfully as I used my hands in plying my trade, I would not have inflicted the pain and loss of years with my daughter."

In plain view, Gavriella placed her hand over one of her father's, then looked up at him showing a daughter's smile. It wasn't the touch on her father's hand that gave rumblings in the minds of several observers at the table, it was that distinct smile that carried a hidden message. Seated around the table were some who had survived the death camps and still possessed mysterious insights about the meaning of physical gestures. Brutality and tragedies in the camps sharpened one's ability to understand the deeper meaning of the most subtle expression: the twitch, a look, the clenching of a jaw, or the shape of lips when forming words. *Today, they saw more than just a smile from a daughter—it was a message that carried a history of pain.*

The father lifted his head, found the courage to force his eyes at those now leaning forward to hear every word coming from his strong, melodious voice, a voice that didn't match his furrowed, senescent-looking frame. The sounds of distant beachside crashing waves faded into the background as he spoke.

"The other night I went to bed reflecting on where I was in my old age. I had lived my life in a repressive country that brutalized my people and was now on the shores of my ancestors without satisfaction because my daughter was dead to me having become a Christian convert, and now after arriving in Israel, my wife of many years was leaving me to live with her.

"It was the darkest time of my life. In the middle of the night, I was awakened and saw standing at the foot of my bed a man dressed in white. Everything was aglow with penetrating whiteness. Another world not measured by time had invaded my space leaving me lifeless, shaking with fear. A swirling cloud enclosed both of us, and I was transported to the lifeless scene of a great valley filled with dry, dismembered human bones. It was a picture of Ezekiel's vision he described in his writings. As I watched, I saw what the Prophet saw: bones coming together and human flesh forming on sun-bleached skeletons, and they were all dead without a sign of life. Faces of friends and people I knew in life stared at me with the look of a corpse, and I was one of the dead. We all had two things in common: we were Jews and were lifeless. It was a nightmare of horror that gripped me with unbearable fear. Then, in the midst of the graveyard of death, I saw a person who had come to life and was reading the book of Isaiah to others nearby, and those who heard the reading came to life and stood up on their feet. When that person who was bringing life to others turned and looked at me, I saw that it was my daughter, Gavriella, the one I rejected because of her faith in Yeshua."

Those in the room saw a frail father pause in his speech. He looked down at his hands with palms flat on the table, one still covered by his daughter's hand. The scene of his daughter's hand over his gave courage to continue.

"The words from the book that Gavriella read were bringing those around her back to life. But I had rejected her and her message and was part of the mass company of the dead. There is no feeling like the sense of being dead, detached from the body, yet possessing a vibrant consciousness.

"Then a terrifying thing happened. The light that filled my room at my bedside dimmed leaving me in cold darkness. For the rest of the night, I shook with fear asking God for help in finding the life my daughter had.

"It was the next day Gavriella accepted my request to visit her where I found forgiveness from God and from my daughter whom I abandoned because of her Messianic faith.

"Upon hearing my account of being visited by the man in white, my daughter left me with the words: 'Papa, what you saw in your vision were Abraham's descendants coming back to life in their own land after centuries of being dead, dead as a people, dead as a nation, all in preparation for the return of the Messiah who will rule the world from Jerusalem.'"

The standing elderly father lowered his eyes toward his daughter's hand that covered his, then looked up into empty space with cheeks showing glistening tears. The room went silent and still. As if frozen in time, those seated around the table were motionless. Neither hand, finger, or eye twitched in the closing drama of a father showing remorse. With his face looking upward, human emotions around the table hung onto every word in his closing statement: "I thank God for those who took my daughter in when I rejected her, and now in her forgiveness, she has accepted me, an unworthy father."

The old man sat. Everyone saw Gavriella put her arm around her father's slumping shoulders. The somber quiet now hovering over the room demanded a sealed chamber of private bonding between father and daughter. Nature was generous: coming from the beachside were the sounds of crashing waves, creating a momentary curtain between father and daughter and the audience now awestruck with suspended silence. Strong men and women, people of valor who had seen war, death, and tragedy sat with tears. Without speech to fill the void, images of truth unfurled in the minds of Abraham's descendants seated about the room. They had been among the dead in

Ezekiel's valley of dry bones but had come to life by the power of the message of Yeshua.

Hans Isler felt emotional energy moving about the room. Some present at the table had friends and family who knew rejection because of their faith. The chairman was slow getting to his feet, but everyone present could see what was written on his face.

"Friends, what we've experienced tonight is only the beginning of what is to come. After Stellar and Gavriella's wedding tomorrow, an event that carries a mystery of transcendent truth, we will all return to our mission and calling, some to a desk, some to a ship, others to obscurity in a land of tears." Those near Gavriella saw her mother pass a written note to her daughter. She read the note showing pleasure, then placed it in front of her father sitting next to her. It read: *In view of our restored relationship, I will be staying with your Papa in Israel and will wait for your visits from time-to-time.*

Chapter 35

The Wedding

Hans Isler sat alongside his wife admiring the changed look of the villa's conference room. It was known for festive, non-religious events, but today was different. Everything was festive but entirely religious. The room had been transformed into a pristine Jewish wedding sanctuary, the centerpiece being the colorful, flower-laden Chuppah, the bridal canopy. Tradition had always influenced Jewish life, and the marriage canopy reaching back to early tent-dwelling days in the desert was part of the marriage ceremony. The religious formal rite would include the bride's long walk down the aisle, the father of the espoused at her side. Under the canopy, the ceremony would commence with the bride circling the groom seven times for the seven days of creation and rest, all showing the groom being the center of her life.

While the seven-piece orchestra played for the attending wedding guests, Hans Isler, a man of known wealth, looked at the cadre of people seated around him, people he had brought together and made into a family unit to carry out the mission of moving Jews to their homeland, people whose lives were scarred by the memories of the death camps. Having arranged his team of key operatives to spend a week at the villa with the climax being this wedding event, was all part of his design to bond together those involved in Prince Henry operations.

The company plane was waiting at the Tel Aviv airport to carry Popescue and Marku back to Bucharest and others on to the corporate office in Munich. Bram, Moshe, and Bub would board a company freighter, return to their respective mission stations, followed by Gavriella and Stellar after their Mediterranean cruise.

Hans' eyes were drawn to his wife now showing signs of pregnancy, then remembered before the break of dawn today he had held and kissed her before rising to take his early walk on the nearby beach. It was the time when stars overhead were yielding to the rising sun that would give luster to a soft, orange, iridescent glow across the horizon. He remembered slipping his shoes off at the water's edge, then welcoming the caressing sand beneath his feet and the overhead twinkling stars, both sending a message of biblical truth: that God promised Abraham his seed would be as numerous as the sand on the seashore and the stars of the heavens. Ancient seamen, who sailed the oceans, whether departing or arriving, were always greeted by sand on the seashore, and when the Mariners needed direction, nighttime overhead stars led the way. It was these visuals common to man, the sand and overhead stars, that God used to tell the story of Abraham's prolific posterity. Loud voices of truth billowed inside. He was a Jew walking on a beach in Israel, numbered as one of the grains of sand under his feet and counted as one of the stars overhead. *He was always a Jew, always a grain of sand on a far-strewn beach. Now he was a star in the heavens by the birth from the Light of another world.*

The orchestra's sudden change in its upbeat tempo

inside the wedding chapel pulled Hans back into his world in real time. The marriage ceremony had begun. A Messianic Rabbi was now beginning his walk down the aisle, followed by the groom and his best man. Once stationed in and around the bridal canopy, two bridesmaids entered, followed by the bride escorted by her father showing tears in his eyes. Those present who knew the history of father and bride understood the message of his tears: he was unworthy to be at his daughter's side for having rejected her and her faith. It was a living picture of the wounded made strong by the power of forgiveness, a picture the Psalmist described as going from strength to strength, all serving to carry the weak.

The wedding vows were brief, and Hans felt a delicate, soft hand clasp his. Then came a quiet whisper. "Do you remember our wedding vows, Hans?"

"Every day," responded the man in control of a global enterprise, and with a soft, quiet voice, added, "Look at Sonje wiping her eyes. She's probably asking Michael the same question."

Flashing strobes of history faded in and out of Hans, memories of being saved as an infant out of the Holocaust by two angels: one clothed in white from above, the other with mortal motherhood who became his adoptive mother and the force behind what he became. Hans took from his pocket an envelope that had Gavriella and Stellar's names written on its front, checked the contents showing wedding gift tickets for a Mediterranean cruise with a sizable amount of cash.

Pronouncement of the newly married couple as husband and wife brought resounding sounds from the orchestra's upbeat rhythmic wedding march, the bride, and bridegroom leading the way where guests would extend congratulatory expressions. Enthusiasm and the orchestra's performance muffled the sounds of a helicopter landing on the villa's helipad—part of the gift package in their travel to the waiting cruise ship.

Watching the newlyweds board their flight, Hans heard his wife say, "They're leaving for their honeymoon just like we did—aboard a helicopter."

"I arranged this so you and I could feel what others felt when they watched our departure on the day of our wedding."

Hans and Sheena were part of the enthusiastic crowd waving congratulatory goodbyes as Bride and Bridegroom looked down at their friends. Hans felt a tug on his arm from his wife, now showing a need of reassurance, "My dear, do you remember that I told you before we were married that 'I wanted three daughters?'"

Looking down at his wife with his blond hair being swished about with swirling gusts of wind from overhead propellers, he saw a face beaming with pregnancy pride.

"I'll never forget." The drama of a long pause ensued, and then came the words, "I'm well on my way with my first girl!"

Hans' world came to a stop. The sound of the departing helicopter went unheard, even the crowd around him went unnoticed. "You didn't tell me you had a sonogram."

"You didn't ask, and besides, I thought the news would be more appropriate after the wedding event. You don't mind girls, do you?"

"I'll welcome all the girls you give me because they will be just like their mother."

"You're a doll, Doctor Isler!"

"And you are my Queen, Doctor Sheena!"

On a private balcony onboard a Mediterranean cruise ship, an artist could be seen mixing his paints to match the ink-blue tinge coming from a sea that floated ancient Roman ships, all serving as background for his subject sitting in repose. The artist's challenge was not in duplicating colors in nature but rather a consummate expression of what was felt in his heart—his love for his beautiful subject—his new bride of three days. Gentle breezes that moved ships of history now swathed the open balcony ruffling the subject's long, dark, wavy hair, covering and uncovering eyes that matched the sky's deep cerulean blue, eyes that spoke silent utterances to the man now giving life to her on canvas. Emotions gave way to conversation.

"My dearest subject, Gavriella, the portrait I'm painting of you will show what your eyes are telling me. Eyes carry secret messages, and if an artist can open that door and put it on canvas, it will give life to his subject."

"What do you see in my eyes?" asked Gavriella.

"Let me tell you first what I don't see: gone are your pain of loneliness and the hurt you carried from your family's rejection."

Gavriella reached for his hand. "Both of those are absent because you came into my life. Now tell me what you see in my eyes."

Stellar placed his face in front of his new bride. "Your beautiful eyes tell me that you are God's gift to me, the lady who gave me the message of Yeshua, the Passover Lamb. I was one of the dead in Ezekiel's valley of bones and it was your message that gave me life, and now you belong to me."

Stellar was about to kiss his subject when someone rang the doorbell of their suite.

"Did you order room service?" asked Stellar.

"No, but since you mentioned it, I suggest that we do. That will give us more time for you to finish your painting."

"First, let's see who's at the door."

Stellar went into the stateroom suite to answer the doorbell, and Gavriella stood, walked to the edge of the balcony to watch the rhythmic movement of the ship sliding over scenic swirling waters down below. The sound of her name brought interruption.

"Gavriella, come!

Stellar was holding a telegram in his hands. "We've received a telegram from Michael Pencovich, Overseas Coordinator for Katharina Enterprises and it's written in code form. Come and sit by me and I'll translate it."

Because the telegram was in code, Gavriella knew it contained significant information. She watched her husband with pen in hand decipher the message. It read:

Congratulations to two beautiful people on their wedding cruise, an experience you will remember forever! We are fortunate to have you as our new team members whose mission is to move Abraham's people back to Israel. One week after your cruise ship returns to Haifa, Israel, you will board a freighter that will drop you off at the port of Constanta where you will resume your work of moving Jews under the cover of darkness to their new homeland in preparation for the return of Yeshua, Who will rule the world.

Neither spoke. Gavriella watched Stellar take the deciphered message, place it in the sink, and put a match to it.

"Shall we resume the painting or my description of your beautiful eyes?" asked Stellar.

"In view that you give me a choice, I prefer the artist resuming the latter."

He will assemble the scattered people of Judah from the four quarters of the earth...He will strike the earth with the rod of his mouth. With the breath of his lips he will slay the wicked...the wolf will live with the lamb...the leopard will lie down with the goat, the calf and the lion and the yearling together; and a little child shall lead them...for the earth will be full of the knowledge of the Lord as the waters cover the sea. (Isa. 11: 6, 9, 12 NIV)